PRAISE FOR ANNA SALTER'S PREVIOUS MICHAEL STONE THRILLERS

FAULT LINES

"An excellent novel. . . . A breathless, action-packed finale. . . . Anna Salter provides another compelling look at the criminal mind."

—*Chattanooga Times* (TN)

"Steadily gripping in its psychology. . . . There are shocks here, and each plot twist turns on a kink in an insanely brilliant mind."

—*Kirkus Reviews*

"The smart and vulnerable Dr. Stone may be Salter's alter ego, but the radiantly evil Alex B. Willy is her most impressive achievement in this strong story."

—Amazon.com

"A fast-paced novel with lots of little twists and turns and surprises. A quick, fun, hard-to-put-down read."

—*The Pilot* (Southern Pines, NC)

"Offer[s] a more realistic side to forensic psychology than many recent thrillers."

—*Publishers Weekly*

SHINY WATER

"The best first novel I have ever read. Anna Salter takes us into the disturbing world of forensic psychologist Michael Stone with just the right amount of wit and humanity. Don't miss this memorable debut."

—Anne Perry, author of *The Twisted Root*

"Forget about your demolition experts and your air-traffic controllers; Michael Stone, the stressed-out heroine of Anna Salter's jolting debut mystery, *Shiny Water*, has the real job from hell. A forensic psychologist at a Vermont hospital, Michael carries a caseload that would make the angels weep.... [An] interestingly abrasive protagonist, whose own testy personality gives her a sharp perspective on her difficult patients and a dangerous edge when she testifies on their behalf in court ... [where] a misapplication of justice ... turns Michael into a tiger for the truth.... [Salter] handles this touchy material with integrity, tugging on our hearts even as she ties our nerves in knots."

—*The New York Times Book Review*

"A terrific tale with plenty of twists and turns and an almost lethal twist of the tail."

—*The Toronto Star*

"A suspenseful novel that really delivers! Salter has done what few first-time novelists are capable of: draw from personal experience to create both utterly believable characters and a truly gripping story."

—Janet Evanovich, author of *High Five*

"Exceptionally captivating ... frighteningly realistic."

—Roy Hazelwood, former special agent, FBI Behavioral Unit

"Forensic psychologist Salter has graced her protagonist with a compelling and likable voice in the tradition of Patricia Cornwell."

—*Library Journal*

"Salter weaves a tight, compelling chain of consequence."

—*Ms.* magazine

"Harrowing. . . . Briskly paced."

—*The Florida Times-Union*

"Stunning. . . . *Shiny Water* is a war-zone dispatch from a battle-scarred veteran, ringing with power and truth."

—Andrew Vachss

"A tough, quirky narrator carries this engrossing debut. . . . [Salter's] skillful pacing, a gift for sketching minor characters, and a clear passion about the fate of abused children add texture to an admirably suspenseful tale with a genuinely surprising conclusion."

—*Publishers Weekly*

"Entertaining. . . . Salter, herself a psychologist, really could quit her day job."

—*Mademoiselle*

"Salter delivers a suspenseful psychological thriller."

—Christine McGuire, author of *Until We Meet Again*

Books by Anna Salter

Shiny Water
Fault Lines
White Lies

Published by POCKET BOOKS

WHITE LIES

ANNA SALTER

POCKET BOOKS

New York   London   Toronto   Sydney   Singapore

An *Original* Publication of POCKET BOOKS

 POCKET BOOKS, a division of Simon & Schuster Inc.
1230 Avenue of the Americas, New York, NY 10020

Copyright © 2000 by Dr. Anna Salter

ISBN: 0-671-02351-9

First Pocket Books printing May 2000

10 9 8 7 6 5 4 3 2 1

POCKET and colophon are registered trademarks of Simon & Schuster Inc.

Cover art by Tom Hallman

Printed in the U.S.A.

For my sister Linda,
"Who lit the spark, long ago"

ACKNOWLEDGEMENTS

Authors write in a web of people who support them, who make it possible for them to write, and who make their writing better. In my case, like so many others, writing is hardly a solo sport. I would like first of all to thank my nanny, Minna Alanko, who gives my children such exquisite care and thereby offers me the peace of mind I need to write. I would like to thank my children, Jazzy and Blake, who make my home vibrant with all their sweet colors and provide the life force needed to keep on truckin'.

It seems over the years my friends just matter more and more. I would like to thank Regina Yando, my mentor at Harvard and my friend, for her support of me and my writing through the last two decades. My friend Ardis Olson is kind enough to check my books for medical accuracy—not to mention her friendship is a joy. I would like to thank my childhood friend Jennie Jeffries for coming back into my life, Dalene Washburn, Suzanne Brooks, Lynn Copen, and Linda Cope for staying close. Writing exists within the context of a life, and these folks make mine better.

The originator of statement analysis, Avinoam Sapir, has been kind enough to allow me to use his material on deception, and I am appreciative. His is a brilliant contribution to the field of deception detection. In addition, I am lucky to have some good friends in the polygraph community. Donnie Dutton from the Department of Defense Polygraph Institute has reviewed and strengthened the material on the polygraph and has been generous with his advice and counsel over the years. Thanks also to the pathologist Mark Witeck for his generous advice about poisons.

I am very lucky to have Sandi Gelles-Cole to edit my books. She does a fine job. Helen Rees is not only such a fine agent but a unique and gifted friend. Linda Marrow, my editor at Pocket Books, provides humor and perspective and belief in Michael Stone, and I am grateful.

Finally, to my friend Rick Holden, polygrapher and interrogator extraordinaire, I can only reverse the old Texas saying "Big hat, no cattle." Rick is a little bit larger than life but he's the real thing: big hat, lots of cattle.

I

You gotta wonder why they shoot spies. Soldiers rape, pillage, burn and shoot everybody in sight. They'll run a tank over your house with you in it. Spies, on the other hand, obey traffic lights, don't jaywalk, and mostly take pictures of military installations, or whatever. There's something weird about this. If the Japanese had caught the bombers of Hiroshima and Nagasaki they would have been required to read them their rights as prisoners of war and make sure they got the right amount of mail from the Red Cross—although they may not have been in the mood—but those are the rules. If they'd caught a spy taking pictures of the rubble, they could have shot him on the spot.

I dragged my obsessing little mind out of the netherland, where it lives a good deal of the time, and back to the business at hand. I was sitting in my office waiting for a man whose name I didn't know with a problem I didn't know anything about. It wasn't par for the course but it wasn't completely unusual, either, given what kind of psychologist I am. I assess and treat perpetrators and victims of various kinds of violence. Given that, it wasn't like everybody just fesses up over the phone. Whether you were the victim or perp, it was a rare person who wanted to talk about it over the phone to a complete stranger.

But usually, I knew the person's name or at least something and this time I knew nothing at all. My mysterious caller had identified himself only as Reggie. When I told him I couldn't assess or treat him without knowing who he was, he said he'd prefer to give me his name when he came in.

I didn't recognize the voice but, given his secretiveness, I assumed I'd know the name or the face, which wouldn't surprise me. Given a world where a Nobel Prize winner was caught molesting boys, where a university president was taped making obscene phone calls, where one judge was found molesting another's child at a judges' conference on sexual abuse, given all that, it would be hard to imagine a famous name that would surprise me.

I looked him over carefully when he showed up, but his face, at any rate, didn't ring any bells. He was a well-dressed man with a beard, in his early forties, tall and distinguished looking with short, dark hair. He wore horn-rimmed glasses, an expensive suit and a Rolex watch. The watch and suit spoke to more than money. Half the surgeons I knew wore jeans and small, cheap digitals—one I knew roller-skated to work—and God knows they made enough money. So I had in front of me one of those conspicuous consumption types who wanted the world to know how successful he was.

He walked from the waiting room into my office and immediately went over to the wall where my credentials hung. I watched curiously. There was nothing wrong with my credentials—my Ph.D. hadn't come in the mail, I was licensed to practice in the state—but few people bothered to examine them. People who had concerns usually checked me out before they came.

And ten to one he had, too. So why was he making this elaborate ritual of reading the fine print on every commendation and award on that wall? I said nothing and waited. Whatever hand he was playing, I'd let him play it.

"Harvard," he said. "Not a bad school. I did my undergraduate work there. Didn't take many psychology courses but I did take Larry Kohlberg's. Did you, by any chance?"

I smiled and said, "I'm sure we have a lot in common, but I have the feeling your time is very valuable and I wouldn't want to waste it. Do you have any concerns about my credentials? I'd be happy to answer any questions you have."

"Oh no," he said, walking over to sit down across from me. "I'm at Boston Harbor View Hospital and you were suggested to me by the hospital. I'm afraid my lawyer has checked you out quite thoroughly."

"Boston Harbor View? That's a bit of a drive." As in three hours. I let the question hang.

"I'm sure it's worth it," he replied smoothly, then he laughed, "Besides, to tell the truth, my mother lives in the area and it's a good chance for me to visit."

"Then what can I do for you?" I said. "For starters, what's your name?"

"Reginald Larsen," he said, watching me for a reaction, "but call me Reggie."

I glanced at the credentials on the wall, where the Reginald Larsen Teaching Award was hung.

"Are you any relation . . . ?"

"I'm his son."

"Really," I said, surprised. Reginald Larsen was a former chairman of Pediatrics at Jefferson University where I worked. He was the first originator of the Teaching Award that I had won several years ago and which was named after him. I had been based in Psychiatry, but because I worked in child abuse, I had also been on the faculty of Pediatrics. It wouldn't have mattered where I was. Everybody in the medical center knew Reginald Larsen.

He was a legend in Pediatrics. He had been gone over a decade and he was still talked about. Dr. Larsen had a kind of extraordinary warmth, especially with patients, and he was visionary about the department, always seeing the future, always building for it—unlike any chairman since him. I still heard faculty say, "If Reginald were here . . . Reginald would never have . . . I wonder what Reginald would think . . ." as though the decade since he had died of a heart attack was only a couple of months.

I was silent for a moment trying to think if this made my seeing his son a conflict of interest. Would I be influenced by the fact that he was Reginald Larsen's son?

Maybe. I hadn't known him that long or that well but the memory was still vivid in my mind.

"I don't know if I can see you," I said. "I knew your father and his influence is still felt in the medical center. I'd be happy to hear what the problem is, though, and refer you if I can't see you myself."

"I certainly hope you don't turn me down," he said with a touch of bitterness in his voice. "There doesn't seem to be anybody on the East Coast who didn't know my father, especially in Boston, where he spent decades. Driving to Vermont is bad enough. I hope I don't have to commute to the West Coast to get an evaluation."

"I'll have to think about it," I said. "Why don't you tell me what the problem is?"

He sighed and paused, seeming to have trouble getting started. "I'm an anesthesiologist," he said finally, "at Boston Harbor View. I've been there over twenty years. Before that I was in Fort Wayne . . . I did my training in Texas. It was about as far as I could get from my father's influence," he said. His laugh had a strange sour sound to it. Larsen had dropped his voice a notch when he said "Fort Wayne" and he had let the words trail off slightly as though he were sorry he had mentioned it. I made a mental note about that. I didn't know what Fort Wayne had to do with the current problem, but maybe something.

I put on my Ericksonian hat. Milton Erickson was as famous in professional psychological circles as Freud. He was a genius at—among other things—microanalysis of tiny body language changes in his interviews with clients. He listened for the catch in the voice, looked for the raised eyebrow. He watched on what words the person blinked, looked for changes in respiration patterns and when they occurred. And from all that he could tell what really mattered to people and what was just fluff.

"In any case," Reggie went on, his voice rallying, "things have gone very well professionally. A few years ago I started a line of research on adverse reactions to anesthetics." His voice picked up energy and his respiration deepened. He was in safe territory now. "To make a long story short, I devised a test that will tell whether someone is likely to have a life-threatening adverse reaction to a major anesthetic that's used in about eighty-three percent of all operations.

"The test works like a skin test that's commonly used with allergies. Thus far, ninety-two percent of the people who had adverse reactions to the anesthetic have an adverse reaction to the skin test. We're double-checking the data now, but it looks like we can dramatically reduce allergic reactions to the drug during surgery by testing prior to it.

"I don't have to tell you the advantage of finding out *before* you're in the middle of a major operation whether or not the patient is going to have a reaction to the anesthetic. If we knew that, there's another family of drugs we could switch to. They're trickier to use so they're nobody's first choice, but very few people have an adverse reaction to both."

There was an undercurrent of excitement in Reginald's voice even though he seemed to be trying to mask it. Maybe he loved his work. Then again, maybe he just had some kind of patent on the test.

Whatever his motivation, I was as impressed by his achievement as he wanted me to be. If this was true, the man in front of me was about to become exceedingly famous in medical circles, and maybe beyond.

Unfortunately for him, being famous would also increase the chances everybody from Fort Wayne to Siberia would find out what his problem was. Famous people—even people just famous in their own fields—had a whole lot of trouble keeping their secrets to themselves.

"That's incredible," I said quite honestly. "If it works, it would be a major contribution."

"Yes," he said, "yes, it would." He looked off for a moment. What, I wondered, was going through his mind? Did he want to be on the cover of *Time* or did he just want Dad to say he was good enough?

"But it's not why you're here," I said gently. He had found safe ground and, left to his own devices, he'd probably stay on it.

"No," he said, and for a moment his face fell. The contrast between his Nobel Prize fantasy and the reality of whatever brought him to my office was probably pretty big.

"I . . . the hospital referred me . . . I mean . . ." His voice trailed off.

"Okay," I said patiently, "why?"

"Why what?"

"Why did the hospital refer you?"

"Because . . . well . . . the truth is . . . I don't know. I mean, I think I know but I'm not sure."

"Excuse me?"

He shifted uncomfortably in his seat. "They won't tell me what the charges are. All I know is that I am being accused of some kind of sexual impropriety with somebody."

"A patient?"

"They won't even tell me that. They say it could be with a patient or with staff . . . but I think it's with a patient."

"Why do you think that?"

"Because it's true." He looked straight at me and for the first time I saw his father in him. I sat back and almost smiled. The smile was totally inappropriate for what he was saying but I was remembering the first time I learned his father was a man to be taken seriously.

It was over fifteen years ago and I was new in Psychiatry and bitterly discouraged. In one of my first days in the department I had sat through a case conference where a man who shot and killed his wife in front of their children was described, not as a murderer, but as an accessory to suicide.

It was "suicide-by-proxy," the clinician had said, because the wife had dressed up and told her husband she was going out to party with other men. The clinicians in the room seemed to think her actions made the whole thing a kind of suicide. I had pointed out that they were only hearing one side of the story—the other side being dead—and what did they expect a convicted murderer to say, that he killed her for the fun of it? My comments were about as welcome as toxic waste.

I was so depressed by the whole thing that for the next few days I thought seriously about quitting and doing anything else—selling hot dogs for a living looked good—when there was a bad incident in the Intensive Care Nursery. A premature infant narrowly escaped dying when a nurse left an IV valve open at the wrong time. The line had flooded her tiny body with potassium and it had thrown her into cardiac arrest. It had taken an all-out code to save her.

The case was staffed at the Pediatric M&M, the

Mortality and Morbidity conference where medicine tries to learn from its mistakes. The issue came up of what to tell the parents.

People were just warming up with a lot of bullshit about how telling the parents a nurse had nearly killed their child would destroy their trust in the child's caretakers. I couldn't believe they were going to get away with lying to the parents to protect their own tails and, worse, justifying it. I was mentally getting out my application for a hot dog vendor's license when Reginald said, "I don't think we need to spend our time on this. It's obvious what we're going to tell the parents."

No one spoke. It wasn't obvious to anyone else, not even me, what he meant. I'm sure Reginald read the silence but he didn't make anyone admit they didn't know, he just said matter-of-factly, "We'll tell them someone made an error and left the valve open."

Again, no one spoke. Finally, the person from Risk Management said, "Ah, Reginald, I appreciate that but, uh, the question is, why would we tell them that? There are . . ."

"Because it's true," Reginald had said and looked straight at him in much the same way his son was looking at me now. Probably I was in the field right now because I heard at least one person say, "Because it's true."

I turned my mind back to this Reggie Larsen. "So tell me about it," I said, but I knew at that moment I shouldn't take this case. This Reggie was riding on his father's coattails with me. I was predisposed to like him, Rolex watch and all, and that was very bad.

This Reggie might be a carbon copy of his father and, then again, he might not. Some apples fell close to the tree and some fell in the next county.

"I had an affair with a patient," he said, sighing, "but it was years ago. I don't have any idea why it's coming up now. And I don't know why they won't tell me what the charges are. They're acting like she's afraid of me. But what can I do? Sue her for telling the truth?

"Look, I'm not proud of it. The truth is she had a fibrosarcoma, a tumor attached to the back of the abdominal wall. They got it but she had a lot of pain, afterward, that just wouldn't remit. She was referred to me for pain management. I've thought a lot since then about whether she really wanted to get involved with me or whether she was afraid to alienate the person who was managing this rather significant amount of pain."

Good question, but there was another one as well: how much would somebody with acute, chronic abdominal pain feel like having sex with *anybody*? "So what happened?" I asked.

"Nothing," he said. "It was right after I was divorced and—I know it's no excuse—but I was terribly depressed and she was just a very nice lady. When I came to my senses, I stopped it. We really didn't have that much in common, anyway. That's about it."

"What happened to the pain?"

"Oh, that. It eventually got better. She's doing well—at least she was the last time I saw her."

"Which was when?"

He paused and thought for a moment. "A couple of years ago, I think. She was moving and she came in for a last checkup. She had had some minor flare-ups, but nothing significant."

"What was that meeting like? Was she angry with you?"

"No, not at all. She seemed fine. The affair seemed light-years ago. She was remarrying—she was divorced, too—and she was moving to where her fiancé lived."

"So, why do you think this is about her?"

"Because there's nothing else it could be about," he said simply. "There isn't anything else."

I was writing notes as we spoke and I took a moment longer to write so I could think about it. He was quite believable. Actually, he was totally believable. But then, so were a lot of people who were lying through their teeth. I hated the fact that I had seen enough, heard enough, that I no longer believed anything without corroboration. It was a sad business, but true, that doing my job well meant being suspicious of everything that breathed.

And there was one minor thing, Larsen's body language was subtly wrong. His hands, which gestured freely when he was talking about his work, had stopped moving the moment he started talking about the affair. This was not a good sign. Research showed that people who normally used their hands when they spoke tended not to when they were lying—probably because they were concentrating so much on what they were saying.

And there was one other thing. Not huge, but

there. He wasn't reacting physically to anything he said, not even when he was talking about having an affair with a woman who was dependent on him for pain control. And I knew that when anesthesiologists talked about a "significant" amount of pain, they weren't kidding.

And he should have been reacting physically. If it was true that he had done something he had worried about ever since, the pitch should have changed in his voice, even just slightly. His pupils should have contracted when talking about worrisome things. His respiration should have been slightly faster, but it hadn't been. Something. The fact was, he was showing no signs that he was feeling any emotion at all when he was talking about emotional things.

So maybe he didn't really believe there was anything wrong with having an affair with a patient who was depending on him. Or maybe he was just naturally calm and out of touch with his feelings. Or then again, maybe he was making the whole thing up. All put together, I couldn't rule out the possibility that Reginald Larsen's son was lying to my face.

"Why are you here?" I said to Reggie. "What are you looking for from me?"

"The hospital has put me on leave," he said. "They are insisting on an evaluation before I return to work. I want to get it done as soon as possible. The longer I'm out the more the cover story about 'personal reasons' is wearing thin. I'm going to be ruined if this gets out, even if the charges are proven false. And the timing couldn't be worse. Word is getting out about the anesthesia test and

I'm getting calls and e-mail from all over the country. Hell, they won't even let me use my office."

That was odd, very odd indeed. Medicine wasn't like business. People weren't routinely locked out of their offices while they were being investigated. They weren't even locked out of their offices when they were fired. "Are they prepared to tell me what this is all about?" I asked.

"Why?" he said, surprised. "Do you have to talk to them? Can't you just evaluate me? I think that's what they want."

"No," I said, "I can't. Let me tell you a little about what this process involves so you can decide whether you want to go through it or not. I won't evaluate you unless I have the details of every charge against you. I have to know what the problem is supposed to be.

"Second, an evaluation in a situation like this is tricky. There is no interview technique and no psychological test that will say *absolutely* whether someone is a sex offender or not. If you're being accused of raping a patient in an elevator, for example"— Reggie paled slightly—"no matter what technique I use I can't say for certain whether you did that particular act or not. Ultimately, guilt and innocence of a specific crime is a question for the courts." At the mention of court, his color paled a little more.

"But the more I learn about what kind of sexual problems you have and how honest you are about them, the more I can figure out what you need in terms of treatment—if you need treatment—and what you need in terms of a work setting where you'd be unlikely to reoffend.

"To do that kind of an evaluation, I need to compare what you tell me with what the complainants tell me. That way I learn something not just about your problems but about how honest you are about facing them."

"But the complainants could be lying," Reggie sputtered.

"They could," I replied calmly, "but so could you. That's part of what I have to sort out. Maybe not to the same level of proof needed for a court of law, but with enough certainty to figure out whether you need treatment, what that treatment would be, and whether you can do the same kind of work in the same setting again."

"Just for the record," Reggie said, "I object to your talking as though I'm some kind of sex offender. I don't want to whitewash the affair with the patient, but it wasn't exactly like raping somebody in an elevator."

"The point is," I said coolly, "I don't know whether you're a sex offender or you're not. You may be an innocent man or you may have molested every child in the pediatric ward. I don't know. That's one of the reasons I have to know what the charges are, so I know at least what you are accused of being."

"But I told you . . ."

"You told me you didn't know, you were guessing what the charges were. Even if you told me you knew for sure, I'd still get it from them. You have to understand, a lot of people who are accused of sexual improprieties don't tell the truth. No offense, but I don't have a clue whether you are being truthful or not."

"Well," Reginald said, sighing and sitting back, "if that's what you need—"

"I haven't finished," I said. "That's just the beginning. After I get the complaints, you will need to write down every deviant sexual act you have ever committed. It's called a 'deviant sexual autobiography.' I'm not interested in consensual sexual experiences with other adults. I want to know about child molestation, rape, exhibitionism, voyeurism, etcetera. Anything to do with children, with violence, or with violating other people's boundaries."

"Jesus Christ," he said, and I noticed I was seeing the shallow respiration, the contracted pupils, the raised pitch that told me he was finally emotionally involved in the conversation. "Now you're saying I'm a child molester. I have never in my life even *looked* at a child sexually."

"Then it won't be a problem for you," I said calmly. "Sex offense evaluations are standardized these days. We ask about every possible type of deviation. I won't bore you with the research unless you want me to, but the bottom line is that a whole lot of sex offenders have multiple deviancies."

"But I don't," he said angrily, "and I told you. I'm not a sex offender."

"Good," I said, "there's nothing wrong with a short deviant autobiography. There's nothing wrong with a blank piece of paper."

He looked relieved and his breathing started to recover.

"But remember, you'll have to take a polygraph on whatever you write."

"What?" he said. "That's crazy. Polygraphs aren't admissible in court."

"This isn't court," I said flatly. "This is an evaluation and we get to use whatever tools we feel are appropriate.

"But just for your information," I added, "they're admissible one way or the other in thirty-eight states, but that's beside the point—for now." There was no way around it. Doing an evaluation of an alleged perpetrator meant selling fear. You had to be some kind of fear merchant with perps to get anywhere. The saving grace of the whole process was that people who were innocent were a whole lot less afraid than people who were guilty—which was as it should be.

"But they're not accurate," he said.

"Well, actually, that's not true either. With the right examiner the new computerized polygraphs are reporting about ninety percent accuracy rates in detecting innocence and far higher than that, ninety-six to ninety-eight percent, in detecting guilt, at least according to the Department of Defense Polygraph Institute and Johns Hopkins University. In any case, they've been better for decades than people are at telling who's lying."

"I'll have to think about it," he said. His ardor for an eval seemed to have cooled considerably at mention of a polygraph.

"You should," I said. "It's a very involved process and I'd advise you to think about it and to run it by your lawyer. I have to think about it also, because of the connection with your father whom I respected very much. Why don't you give me a call next week?"

"Next week is too long," he said quickly. "I'll decide by tomorrow. I have to get this evaluation done right away or it's not going to matter what the outcome is. The rumor mill will kill me."

"Run it by your lawyer first," I said. Fair was fair. People faced with sex offense charges didn't always think straight. I didn't mind pressuring people from here to Shinola if they had someone to represent them, but I felt like I was taking advantage of desperate people if they didn't.

We set up a time he would call me and he got up to leave. At the door, he paused and turned back around. "My mother knows you," he said. "She said my father always had confidence in you. He said you were the best thing that ever happened to Psychiatry. She said if it was my father's career, you'd be the one he'd choose. She said to say hello."

He left before I could respond. Afterward my chest felt tight and the weight of the world descended. A decade of fighting in Psychiatry had left me immune to attack, but strangely vulnerable to trust. I wanted nothing more than to give something back in exchange for all that faith.

And why not believe Reginald Larsen, Jr.? He'd sounded good and he'd looked good—sincere as hell. But the nagging in my head wouldn't go away. The things that Reggie didn't have conscious control over—pupil dilation, changes in voice pitch and respiration—hadn't been there when they should have been.

And there was something else: the small business of what he denied and what he left out. People lie more often by omission than commission. If you don't force people to lie, most of the time they just leave out what they did, they don't openly deny it. I had raised rape, child molestation, voyeurism, exhibitionism, a whole host of nasty hobbies. The only one he had waxed indignant about was child molestation.

Maybe he just thought it was worse than all the rest. Or maybe it was the only one he wasn't guilty of. And what would Mrs. Reginald Larsen, Sr., whom I remembered very well, think of that?

2

I was between clients and still thinking about Reginald Larsen when the phone rang, startling me. "Michael," Marv said, with relief in his voice. "I wondered if I could consult you on a case—perhaps this evening?" Marv had been, until recently, my favorite psychiatrist in the department, my favorite psychiatrist in the whole world, for that matter. Things were rocky between us right now, but not enough for me to turn down a request for help.

"This evening?" I said, wondering what the rush was. When Marv didn't take it back, I just said, "Sure, that's fine."

"Good. It's just . . . if you wouldn't mind, we'll just talk about it then?"

"Not at all," I said. "Why don't I come over to your place after work?"

"Oh, I'm happy to drive out," Marv said. "I'm the one seeking assistance." Marv lived in a townhouse a few blocks from Psychiatry and I lived out in the country.

"Well, to tell you the truth, it's your art works. They're growing on me."

"Well, then," Marv's voice warmed up. "In that case, come on over. I have a new wood carving from Bali. Frightfully detailed piece of work. Exquisite."

"I finish at six," I said.

The truth was I knew less than nothing about art. I didn't even know what I liked. But I loved to watch the light in people's faces when they talked about things they loved, especially when I didn't understand them at all. Then the mystery of why one person loved cooking and another loved working on diesel engines was right in front of you. Marv's paintings weren't growing on me; Marv's love of them was.

Besides, we needed something to distract us. I'd never been good at repairing torn friendships. Usually, I just dropped people if things didn't work out. All right, so I knew it wasn't the mature thing to do. I knew it was silly and juvenile and all of that. I wouldn't advise any client of mine to do things that way. Yadda, yadda, yadda.

The problem was I hated long, serious, dreadful conversations and working-things-out. I remember once seeing an old tombstone that read, "God knows I tried." But how much did "trying" really help? Some people talked about relationships like they were cars you could bang around, add a part here, sand the rust out there. But I didn't buy it. Things were more elusive than that: there was a magic in relationships that couldn't be reclaimed once the trust was gone.

Marv made a very bad call once. He gave up some private information about me to get a client off his back. It didn't help that he hadn't realized what he'd done. We had come within an inch of just nodding to each other in the halls. I don't know why I didn't drift away. Once upon a time I would have. Maybe I was growing up or maybe I was wearing down. It's always hard to tell the difference.

Marv was wearing his purple slippers when he came to the door. Sometimes I thought he searched as hard for ugly colors to wear as he did for gorgeous colors to hang on his walls. It was one of those strange things I'd never known how to raise with him. What could I say? "Marv, you dress like a dork. It's not that I care. It's just that I don't get it. How can you care so much about the colors on your walls and never notice what's on your body? Don't you own a mirror?"

I was known for being direct but that seemed a little abrupt, even to me. So I never said it which meant, of course, I thought it every time I saw him.

The man in front of me was short, pot-bellied, and partially bald. Supposedly, the East Germans used to look at children's body types and train them in the activities their body types fitted best. Marv would had been signed up for psychoanalytic training by age five. Somehow he'd found his own way there.

"Come in, come in," he said, and his affection washed over me like a warm tide. Maybe that had a little something to do with why I hadn't just moved to the nodding-in-the-halls stage.

"Oh, Marv," I said walking over to the nearest wall,

"you've changed things around." As long as I'd known him Marv had kept his paintings in the same places in his house.

"A new start," he said, and looked away. "Come see my new acquisition."

I followed him to his study where an intricately carved chess set stood in solitary splendor on his desk. A new start? Did that have anything to do with me and the disastrous case we'd both been involved in, or were Marv's relationships with his paintings as complex as those other people had with people? Who knew?

The chess set was exquisite. Even I could tell that, but I learned more by watching Marv look at it than I did by looking at it myself. It didn't seem a bad way to live—a new lover whenever you could afford one.

"A chess set?" I said. "I never thought of them as works of art, but this one could change my mind."

"Oh, yes," he replied, picking up one of the pieces and handing it to me to inspect. "Take a look at the detail on the face. Extraordinary, don't you think? There's actually a long tradition of artists making chess sets. Goes back centuries. They were frequent presents to monarchs. And, of course, some monarchs commissioned them. I used to collect them at one point."

I "oohed" and "ahhed" over the figure like I knew what I was talking about and then reluctantly put it down. There was something captivating about the tiny warlike figures that made me want to get down on eye level with the board and imagine a war going on. He handed me the different pieces and seemed almost kid-like as he did it. We could have been two ten-year-olds discussing action figures, the glee in his voice was so clear. Eventually we pulled ourselves away and went to the study to talk.

"Do you play?" I asked, settling down in a particularly comfortable, overstuffed chair.

"Chess?" Marv said. "Well, a little. Or I used to. A long time ago. I haven't for years. Iced tea?"

"Sure," I said. Iced tea is mother's milk to Southerners like me. Mostly, there are two kinds of Southerners: the iced tea kind and the Jack Daniel's kind. I am the iced tea kind but I have plenty of relatives who favor Jack Daniel's. Enough to keep me drinking iced tea.

When he came back with the tea I asked, "Why'd you quit?"

"Chess?" he asked. Jesus, Marv, I thought. What else are we discussing? "It's a long story," he said, and busied himself serving the tea. It seemed clear he wasn't inclined to tell it.

"All right," I said. "Tell me about the consult."

"Well, I have a client," Marv said. He looked at me. Marv read me far better than most. He sighed and cut to the chase. "The rush is that she has recovered memories of her father sexually abusing her and she wants to confront him."

"Uh, Marv, that's a very tricky business. That is nothing to rush into. There are only about a million ways that can go wrong." I settled back in my chair. I wasn't going to see my precious A-frame in the country anytime soon. "Why don't you start at the beginning."

"Her name is Jody," Marv said. "She is a twenty-seven-year-old young woman. She was born in . . ."

"Uh, maybe not that much at the beginning," I interrupted. I knew Marv. He would know what her mother ate when she was pregnant.

Marv paused as he tried to figure out where to start. "She came in about six weeks ago," he said finally. "I'm her third therapist. She has a history of depression and anxiety attacks. She has been intermittently symptomatic since high school and she was hospitalized for a suicide attempt in her junior year. She began college at a small university near Manchester—her family lives there—but dropped out after one semester because of depression. That time, too, she was hospitalized.

"That second hospitalization was at Jefferson. When she was released she decided not to return to the Manchester area but worked here as a waitress for a year. She entered Jefferson U this fall, but, again, has gotten rather seriously depressed.

"She sought therapy for the depression, but very quickly the emphasis has shifted. She has become increasingly distressed over some recurrent dreams that began this fall. The dreams have been of a man looming over her while she sleeps. She feels very tiny and he seems enormous. She wakes up convinced there is a man in her room and she is always struggling for air. It feels, she says, like there is a heavy weight on her chest.

"Then two weeks ago, she was driving to work when she reports having little flashes of memory break through. The pictures resembled dreams except for the fact that she wasn't sleeping. They became so intense she had to pull over. She says she remembered a man coming into her room and looming over her, just as she saw in the dreams. She says he raped her and she realized in the car that day that the man was her father, although she couldn't see his face. She got out of the car and started throwing up."

"How does she know it's her father if she couldn't see his face?"

"She can't answer that. She just says she knows."

"Any hypnosis?" I asked.

"None," Marv said.

"Sodium amytal?"

Marv shook his head again.

"I know you don't use guided imagery or memory recovery techniques, but what about the previous therapists?"

Marv shook his head again. "I know them. She has seen two psychiatrists in the Manchester area. They are both very active in the Psychoanalytic Society and they still believe the women who reported sexual abuse to Freud were hysterical. It's not clear to them that sexual abuse of children in this culture even exists, at least not in any appreciable numbers."

"No evidence of any sort that anyone could have suggested the memories of abuse to her?"

"None," Marv said. "She doesn't even have any friends who talked to her about being sexually abused themselves. Her previous therapists certainly weren't looking for it. And neither," he said dryly, "was I. I was considering whether her depression had to do with some sort of crisis over independence. It always seemed to occur at transition points out of the family. Abuse was never a consideration."

"It should have been," I said bluntly, "on your differential diagnosis. Depression and anxiety disorders of all sorts are elevated in abuse survivors."

"But why at transition points?" Marv said. "Why always when she was moving out of the family?"

"Who knows?" I said. "Why when they're forty or fifty or sixty? Nobody knows yet why these things come up when they do."

"Today," Marv said, "Jody came in and said she wanted to invite her father to the next session. She wants to confront him about the abuse."

"Marv," I said, "this is totally and completely premature. This is a very bad idea. What does she think he's going to say?"

"I don't know, but she seems adamant," Marv said. "I managed to put her off for a session or two but I think she's going to insist."

"Don't do it, Marv. Read my lips. Don't do this. She has barely gotten the memories, or whatever they are, back. She doesn't even know if they're real or not. Ten to one she has a fantasy that she will confront her father and he will fall on his knees and say, 'Oh baby, I'm so sorry. I've worried about this for twenty years. How can I ever make it up to you?' Ten to one she wants him to validate the memories for her.

"Not to mention she thinks her mother is going to whack him on the head with her pocketbook and say, 'You louse, how could you hurt my poor baby?'

"This is not going to happen, Marv. What is going to happen is that the father is going to say, 'What? I'm a respected businessman. How could you say those things about me?' And the mother is going to say, 'You know your father loves you. How could you say those things about him?' And she gets exiled from the family, who then join the Association for Falsely Accused Families—

I'm sure you've heard of AFAF—and then call the newspapers or vice versa: maybe they call the newspapers first. Her parents will end up on the AFAF speaker circuit and your client will end up in an inpatient unit. And you will end up getting sued. I can't say this strongly enough. Don't do it."

Marv was silent. "I'm not sure I'm going to have a choice," he said finally. "She says she's going to do it with or without me. If what you say is true, then without a therapist, or someone in the room to support her, she'll be devastated."

"You're not getting this, Marv," I said. "The backlash against child sexual abuse is in full swing. First of all, if you're in the room, you're going to get blamed for this. The moment you're in the room, all the dynamics switch. Dad doesn't say, 'How could you say this about me?,' he turns to you and says, 'How could you brainwash my poor daughter into saying this about me? My poor daughter is a victim, all right, not of incest, but of *therapist abuse.*'

"He's not going to care whether you used hypnosis or not. He's not going to care whether you used memory recovery techniques. He's not going to care if she's had the memories since she was five. He's not going to care if the memories are totally accurate. His reaction will be worse if they *are* accurate. Once you're in the room, you're scapegoat of the day. You're part of the 'incest machine,' which is supposedly making huge sums of money convincing perfectly well-adjusted young people they were victims of sexual abuse.

"We are talking lawsuits here—against you, her

too, probably. We are talking ethics complaints. We are talking the hassle of your life. We are talking *court*, Marv. *Court.*" Marv was well and truly phobic about going to court. He once said the only reason he didn't prefer hell to court was he couldn't tell the difference.

"But," Marv said evenly, "can you honestly tell me that she'd be better confronting her father alone? Or are you just saying that I should stay out of it to protect myself, and simply abandon my client?"

Now it was my turn to be silent.

3

On the way home I fretted and worried. Maybe Marv was right. Maybe I had spent so much time in court I'd started thinking like a lawyer. It was a sobering thought.

Protecting your ass wasn't supposed to be the only goal in my profession. I was supposed to be thinking about what the client needed, not just about the best way to avoid getting sued. But what the client needed, I was pretty sure, was not a disastrous meeting with her family. The point wasn't just that Marv shouldn't be there, the point was no one should be there, at least not this early.

I swung into the driveway outside my tiny A-frame and was surprised to see Adam's car pulled off to the side. Oh, shit. I'd told my favorite police chief, who doubled as my sometime lover, I'd meet him for dinner. Guilt flooded through me. That was the problem with the world. Those of us whose worst crime was to forget a thank you note lived with enough guilt to keep a horse from getting up in the morning. The other half—those folks who mugged little old ladies for a living—were never sure what the word meant. If God had distributed the thing a little more evenly, She would have gotten a whole lot better product.

I didn't see Adam anywhere and my house was locked. I hurriedly unlocked it and walked in. "Adam," I called, although I was pretty sure nobody, but nobody, could get into my house without a key. Adam had helped me to be sure of that. There was no answer and I walked through the house and unlocked the door to the deck. He must have walked around the side.

I immediately spied a man's shirt on the deck and a few feet farther a pair of pants. Ummm. My evening was looking up. The trail of discarded clothing continued and led around the corner of the deck. There, tucked away in an L-shaped alcove made by the house on one side and the garage on another, was my beloved hot tub, situated so you could see the moon and stars through overhanging pine trees.

"There's a nude man in my hot tub," I said, walking up.

"Better call the police," Adam replied.

"Oh, the police never come when you need them," I said, leaning over to kiss him.

"Wanna bet?" Adam said, and grabbing my shirt, he pulled me into the hot tub.

"Adam, Jesus Christ," I sputtered, at the unexpected dunking. He wrapped his arms around me, wet clothes, wet everything. "I'm dressed, you clown," I said stupidly.

"Want to lodge a complaint?" he asked, nuzzling my shoulder.

"Yes," I said. "You got my clothes wet. I still have my *shoes* on." Adam had caught me off guard and I was fumbling to catch up. I didn't feel as gruff as I was trying to sound. Actually, I didn't feel gruff at all. The man in front of me seemed so close in the moonlight and so alive that I wanted to hide my face in his shoulder so he wouldn't see it. My face felt more naked than his body.

"You're right," he said. Jesus Christ, that testosterone-soaked voice in the moonlight was doing just what he wanted it to do. I could feel parts of me come alive I hadn't even noticed all day. "You shouldn't be wearing wet clothes," he said, starting to unbutton my blouse.

"My, you're frisky this evening." I laughed but I didn't push his fingers away.

He unbuttoned my shirt slowly and then slipped it off over my shoulders. He reached around and undid my bra and slowly slipped that off too. He'd stopped laughing and pulled me away from him far enough to look at me in the moonlight. The mood turned sweet and serious, which always made me nervous. I liked the laughter more. I felt—well—exposed, without it.

"You're beautiful," he said simply, and touched my long, curly blond hair.

"Well," I said, "well . . ." and my voice trailed off.

Adam didn't say anything. He just took his hand and ran it gently down my cheek and down the curve of my neck. He slowed down when he reached my breast and slowly ran his hand around it, then cupped it gently. I closed my eyes and caught my breath.

"Adam," I said. "I want to run a case by you."

"Not now," he said.

"It's really important."

"Not now," he said, firmly.

The truth was, I didn't have a case to run by him but I could have come up with one. It was just that Adam, more than any lover I had ever had, had a way of making sex, well, personal.

Somehow, it scared the bejesus out of me. Half the women in the world complained that they wanted a more intimate lover. All I wanted was a good man who kept a little distance. It was bad enough Adam was single. Worse, he just wasn't settling for sports-sex. Heck of a thing.

Don't worry, I thought as his hand slowly slipped underwater. It'll never last.

Tennessee Williams was right. You do wake up smiling. I reached over absent-mindedly and patted an empty pillow. Adam was off early. Well, it was Friday morning and a workday. Still, I found to my annoyance I missed him, which, of course, was the problem with men. They were as addictive as peanuts although, I reminded myself, thank God, they were still not as addictive as thoroughbreds. I had never gotten over my adolescent horse thing and, in my opinion, there were thoroughbreds, and then there were a lot of other animals—including people.

As a species, men weren't even close to thoroughbreds and still, women sniveled over them. I hated the whole female cultural obsession with them. I hated the romance books and the endless magazines over how to catch him and how to keep him and how to get him back. I hated the notion of spending *years* of your life in a beauty parlor and I wouldn't paint my nails if God offered to cut out all elevator music in exchange.

But even if you were philosophically opposed to spending your life mooning over a group of people who were responsible for ninety percent of the world's crime and a hundred percent of the world's wars, half of whom didn't pay child support—even so, there was still the problem of living with estrogen.

Estrogen was an underrated drug. It ought to be a controlled substance. After all, it made some women delusional. There were seemingly sane, competent women out there living with totally irresponsible and even violent dorks and no question, estrogen had something to do with that.

Worse, estrogen caused brain fever and even chocolate couldn't do that. The best chocolate known to womankind never fostered the fantasy it would make you thin, but given a sexy enough guy, a whole lot of women developed the fantasy he would never do it again, whatever it was. He wouldn't sleep with their best friend, conk them over the head with a two-by-four, or sell drugs out of their living room. After all, he was turning over a new leaf. Sure he was, and one side of a leaf looks pretty much like the other side.

On the other hand, the problem with bitching about estrogen was that there were times like last night. Adam should have been a pianist with hands like that. And the outline of his shoulders against the skylight over my bed . . . well, it was almost as good as flying over a four-foot jump on a horse that moved like silk. Which is to say, it was pretty damn good.

I slipped out of bed and picked up my bathrobe, a luxurious terry-cloth affair a friend of mine had given me. It was a wound-licking kind of robe, and, unfortunately, I had many times used it just that way. But it wasn't bad for opening up and wrapping around your lover on a bright summer morning either. I wandered downstairs for coffee and then out onto the deck. There was some part of me that was hoping Adam was sitting outside in the sunlight drinking his coffee and waiting for me to wrap both of us up nude inside all that terry cloth.

He wasn't on the deck. The night was over and now he was off catching criminals. I looked at my hand. I had the phone in it of all things. What was I thinking of—calling him? For Christ's sake, I'd spent the night with him. I hardly needed to call him at six-thirty in the morning. What was it you did in AA when you were tempted to drink? Call a buddy? I raised the phone and dialed.

4

Carlotta's kitchen was a bright white with blond wood counters and high ceilings. In the middle of the room was a kitchen table made from a four-inch-thick slab of redwood. The redwood owned the room. You couldn't be in that room without looking at it or sitting at it or stroking it. Absent-mindedly, I fingered the free-form edges of the table.

"Carlotta," I said. "I almost called Adam this morning."

"So?" she said. My oldest friend was sitting across from me in a turquoise silk robe that probably cost more than my car. Worse, she was wearing matching earrings. Earrings at seven o'clock in the morning. But for once I wasn't hassling her about her obsession with all things feminine.

"Well, it was stupid. He spent the night. He'd just left."

"So?"

"So, I didn't need to call him." Somehow I had the feeling I wasn't getting my point across.

Carlotta was silent for a moment. "This is a crime, right?" she said testily. Maybe seven was too early for Carlotta. All right, so I knew seven was too early for Carlotta.

I sighed. "I didn't have anything to say," I said. "I just wanted to talk to him. . . ." My voice trailed off.

"Michael," she said. "You're a piece of work. You could have a deranged killer in your house and you wouldn't call me. You *did* have a deranged killer in your house and you didn't call me." Carlotta could hold a grudge over *nothing*. "But you want to call a man you've spent the night with and whom you genuinely care about and you think it's an emergency?"

"So?" I said, defiantly.

"So," she said, "deal with it," and she picked up her coffee and went back to bed.

By nine A.M. I was starting my seminar on child abuse for the psychiatric residents and quietly fretting about Marv: "He doesn't know what he's doing," the off-key soprano sang in the back of my mind. "He's going to get his ass kicked."

I closed the door and turned to the group. There was time and then there was Department of Psychiatry time. The first thing medical schools must teach docs in training is to keep people waiting. Unless you played Attila the Hun, nobody showed up for *any* seminar on time. But I was impatient with stragglers and everybody knew it, so all but one of the first-year class of psychiatric residents were sitting at the round table when I shut the door.

Every other service called their first-year folks "interns," but Psychiatry, always feeling one down because they weren't "real docs," elevated theirs to "residents" right away. It didn't change the fact that up until a few weeks ago, these kids had been sitting in classes taking notes. The only time they had seen a patient was peering over somebody's shoulder.

It was our first meeting for the year. July is the month that the new interns and residents arrive and the old ones move up or graduate. Since the first-year interns do most of the work on any medical service, July and August are bad months to get sick: the interns never know what they're doing and they're usually too scared to admit it and ask a nurse.

The truth is, the only time to get a disease where you don't *have* to die but you *could*, is in the late spring. That's the point where the first-year residents are as knowledgeable as they are going to get. By July 1, they're gone and a new set of totally blank ones begins.

I started to go around the room and ask the residents how much experience they had had with child abuse and what they knew. It was usually a depressing exercise. They generally knew zilch but were loath to admit it.

"Nothing," the first one, a good-looking kid named Dexter, surprised me by saying. "This is our first rotation and they put us on the inpatient ward. So we know less than any staff in the whole building and we're responsible for the sickest patients. I have a woman on my service who's cutting her vagina, for Christ's sake. Does anybody want to tell me why a nonpsychotic woman would cut up her vagina?"

He was my kind of guy. What I'd call an honest man and my esteemed chairman would call a dedicated troublemaker. I looked around the room. Nobody was answering him but nobody was disagreeing, either.

Reginald Larsen wasn't out of my mind for long. There were two messages from him when I got back to my office. Not content just to leave a message at my private practice number, he had tracked me down at Psychiatry and had called twice within an hour. I called him back.

"Michael," he said warmly. He could have been talking to his best friend.

"Dr. Larsen," I responded evenly. I was bound and determined to stay objective about this.

"I've decided to go ahead with the evaluation. How soon can we get started?"

I was surprised. I had pretty much written Larsen off. After all, once I said "sexually deviant autobiography" and "polygraph" in the same sentence, most voluntary, alleged-sex-offender clients did a quiet shuffle sideways to a therapist who believed in trust. I tried to cover my surprise. "Have you spoken with your attorney?"

"I've put in a call to her but she's in court today. I left her a message. I'm definitely going through with it."

"You really need to talk to your attorney first.

You need to understand what the ramifications are."

"I understand what the ramifications are," he said testily. "If I don't get an evaluation pronto, I'll lose my job."

"Dr. Larsen," I said exasperated, "are you under the impression that you can pull your release if this evaluation doesn't come out the way you want? That you can suppress it?" He was too confident and it worried me.

"I won't need to, but, of course, I can. Are you telling me I can't?"

"Yes and no. You can pull the release and tell me I can't give the eval to the hospital. However, if this matter ever goes before the state licensing board for any reason, they can demand that you release all evals or surrender your license."

"I'm not sure that would hold up—"

"I'm sorry but I am. Believe me, once you get started on this, it's not so easy to back out if you don't like the results. You need to talk to your attorney and then call me." I hung up.

Why was he making this so difficult? I had thought about the session and decided he was hiding something, maybe not much but something, and I had more than enough loyalty to his parents to make sure he read the rule book before he asked me to open any of his closets.

"Marv," I said, plopping down on a chair in his office, "I had the first meeting of my seminar today. What the hell is happening to Psychiatry? Where are all those stuffed shirts we used to get—those pipe-smoking twenty-five-year-olds with elbow patches on their blazers who wouldn't admit they knew jack shit. These guys act like real people. Something's broken down in the system. Toby must be having apoplexy."

Marv laughed. "No doubt," Marv said. "Which will at least deflect our honorable chairman from you for a week or two."

"Not on your life," I answered. "He'll decide I'm behind it." Marv laughed again, even though we both knew it was true. Part of the problem with being the unofficial gadfly of the department was that I got credit for all sorts of things I only wish I'd done.

"Anyway, I've got a question. In confidence, of course. In total confidence." Marv raised his eyebrows. It was understood that everything we said to each other about clients was in confidence. "The question won't make sense without the name," I said in explanation. Usually, we deleted names when discussing cases.

"Would you see Reginald Larsen's son for an evaluation if it was more than 'I'm-just-miserable-with-my-life' stuff, if it was something maybe illegal or at least potentially career-ending?"

"No," he said quickly, far too quickly.

"Why not?" I asked, surprised.

"Because his parents talked to me about him years ago," he said. "Many years ago. And that's all I can say, Michael, that's really all."

I looked at him steadily. "They were worried about him?" Marv didn't reply. "Worried about what?" I tried one last time. "How worried?" But I knew better. Marv wasn't going to budge no matter how much I wanted to know. And, in truth, I didn't have any right to ask him.

"All right," I said. "Just one thing. Are you saying you wouldn't see him if it were *you* because his parents talked to you years ago or are you saying you wouldn't see him if you were me?"

"I would not see him if I were you." Silence fell.

"Okay," I said slowly. I'd just have to think about it. "On other fronts, how are you with this confrontation meeting we talked about last night?"

"As a matter of fact," Marv replied, "I had a call waiting from Jody when I got in this morning. She wants to bring her parents to the next session and confront her father then."

"Uh, what did you say?"

"I agreed."

We were both silent. I had a very bad feeling in my stomach about this whole thing. This was not going to work. It was premature and put everybody at risk.

I tried to think of how to tell Marv he was being a complete nit without saying he was being a complete nit. My poor little brain just wasn't wired that way. When I didn't reply, he went on, "She gave me an ultimatum. She said it was something she had to do. Her first plan was to go to her parents' house and confront her father right away. Really, the best I could do was to ask her to wait until our next session, which is on Friday. She was going to confront him with or without me."

"Marv," I said finally, "if someone was going to

shoot themselves, you wouldn't just invite them to do it in your office because somehow that would make it better."

He bristled. "I don't think that kind of hyperbole is helpful."

"It's not hyperbole," I said and I heard my voice rising. "Don't you read a goddamn thing about the backlash?" I exploded. "People are being crucified for what you're about to do. They are losing their licenses for confronting alleged perps in their office. Not to mention clients are losing their minds. She's going to crucify herself no matter what you do. You don't have to get up on the cross with her. You need to be stopping this, not colluding with it."

"Michael," he said and his face started turning red. "I can't stop it and I won't abandon a client. You know as well as I do that whatever happens, this will be easier on her with support than without it."

"All right, all right," I said, getting up. "It's none of my business, anyway. You're going to do what you're going to do. What can I say if you want to self-destruct?" I turned to leave. I got as far as the door and stopped. "All right," I said again, trying to calm down. I just stood there for a minute rocking from one foot to the other. Maybe I wasn't just ticked about Jody. Maybe I was also a little ticked that he wouldn't tell me about Reginald Larsen, which wasn't fair of me at all. I turned around. "Okay," I said, "I want to be there."

"Michael," he said dryly, "I don't want to offend you but that is the last—"

"Marv," I said with my voice finally under control, "I'm not talking about being in the room, although I can get a grip on myself when I need to." Marv should have known that from watching me in court.

"I'm talking about being behind a one-way mirror—with permission from everybody, of course. You need to have a witness taking notes or you need to tape it, and I'll bet you any amount of money Dad won't let you tape."

"Why do I need a witness?"

"Because," I said, with a reasonable attempt at patience, "you wouldn't believe some of the claims that are made about what goes on in these sessions. You're taking a bigger risk if it's just your client and her therapist. At least I'm an outside member of the department who isn't involved in the case. The least I can do is testify for you when you get sued," I added dryly.

"But doesn't being there put you at risk of getting sued too? If Jody and I are going to climb up on our respective crosses," he said, "you don't have to climb up there with us."

"Well," I replied, sourly, "first of all, I tend to work with the kind of people who don't think about suing you, they think about shooting you, so this is actually an improvement for me. But second, you're going to do it with or without me and I can't just abandon you, even though you're being a total nit." I turned to leave. We both knew I had just validated his decision. After all, if I wouldn't leave him twisting in the wind how could I blame him for not leaving Jody?

* * *

At four P.M. the phone rang and I answered to find Reginald Larsen on the line again. "I've talked to my attorney," he said quickly before I had a chance to say anything, "and I want to set up a time to meet. I've already started working on my sexual autobiography. Is there any special way you want me to do this?"

I looked at my watch. Oh boy, I had met him barely twenty-four hours ago and he had called how many times? Some righteous pressure was coming down on him from somewhere.

"You have a choice," I said. "I have a form you can use or you could write it out in your own words. If you to wait until I see you I can give you the—"

He interrupted, "There's no point in waiting. I'll just do what I can and then we can go over it."

"Remember," I added, "this is inappropriate or deviant sex. I don't care about consensual sex with other adults outside the hospital setting. But, whether you consider it inappropriate or not, I want every sexual contact of any sort with any staff member, employee or patient of the hospital or any sex act that took place in or on the grounds of the hospital with anybody. If you could even *see* the hospital from where you were, I want to know about it. I also want every kind of violent sex anywhere as well as, of course, any kind of sexual contact with children anywhere. Okay?"

"I told you before . . . never mind," he said, "I understand."

"I need to fax you a release to sign to let me talk to the hospital. I want to do that soon, before we get too far into this process."

"I've already taken care of the paperwork," he said. "I have release of information forms here. I'll just fill one out and fax it to you."

Given his hurry I wasn't surprised when he said, "I can do this in the next couple of days. How about meeting on Thursday?"

"Thursday's fine," I said. "Eleven o'clock?"

"Sure," he said, "and Michael," he dropped his voice until it became softer and warmer, "thank you for seeing me so quickly."

"No problem," I said, ignoring the tone. Was this the problem? Reggie's the name; seduction's the game?

So Thursday it was. The week ought to be interesting. Reggie Larsen's son was fessing up to God knows what on Thursday. Marv was presiding over an emotional bloodbath on Friday. By the end of the week life would be different for a whole bunch of people and, most likely, a whole lot worse.

5

By Thursday I was having second thoughts about whether getting involved with Reginald Larsen was a good idea. In fact, I was wondering how I had slipped past the "I'll just listen and refer you" stage into setting up an appointment for an eval without even making a decision I was going to do it. Somehow in the flurry of phone calls, I had set up the appointment and now, with Reginald Larsen sitting in my waiting room and a three-hour drive behind him, I didn't have the heart to say, "Whoa, I'm still thinking about this."

He was over an hour early which, given the number of phone calls he'd made to me in a single day, didn't surprise me. I was free but I didn't take him into my office. I knew if I did, then he'd come even earlier the next time and be ticked if I didn't take him in, even if I was with another client. There were times when even I knew it was better to color within the lines.

At the appointed hour, he bounded into my office and put down a shiny, very expensive leather briefcase—one of those Neiman Marcus specials: $599 on sale for a limited time only. I looked at it. How did a man with a leather bag like that have a father who carried a forty-year-old doctor's bag with dents dating back to the days when he made house calls.

But why did I wonder? I knew from experience that the Reginald Seniors of the world tended to produce children who carried the same bag or the complete opposite. It wasn't so hard being like your parents or 180 degrees the other way. What was hard was not being one way or the other.

"How are you?" I said formally.

"Well, thank you," he replied as he sat down and reached into his briefcase. He pulled out a set of papers all neatly typed and fastened with a large clip. "I did my homework," he said.

I looked at the papers. There were a lot of them. So much for the nothing-much-to-say-single-sheet-will-do-it bit.

I was surprised and I wasn't. I knew people lied about sex all the time but there was still some part of me that wanted to yell "What? Four days ago you sat there with a straight face and told me there was nothing to this and now you come up with fifty pages of *'nothing'*?"

I didn't say it. "All instances of deviant sexual behavior?" I asked calmly. Any hint of surprise at the volume he had produced would shut him down. Too much surprise and he'd grab the papers, stuff them into his briefcase and run.

"All," he said proudly. "It feels good to get it all out. I had an epiphany when I was doing this. I realized that this is the first time I have told the truth, the whole truth and nothing but the truth since I was eleven years old. Really. Eleven. I have had to lie and hide my entire life. It feels wonderful to get it all out. It feels like a new beginning."

It always amazed me. He was totally unapologetic about having lied through his teeth.

"Now," he went on, "it's in your hands. Be gentle with me." He laughed as he said it and handed the papers over. For a moment as I reached forward to take them his eyes caught mine. They were intensely blue. He held my eyes for a moment and gave me one of those soul-searching looks that could mean anything you wanted it to.

I broke his gaze and looked down at the pages in my hand. Boy, and to think this was the first pass. There were probably more than fifty pages in the bunch—fifty computer-generated, single-spaced typed pages. But maybe I was misjudging him. Maybe he got the instructions wrong. No matter what I said, half the people who did this put down their consensual sexual contacts. And he struck me as the type who would want to tell me just how successful he was with women.

Then again, maybe he was just being obsessive. Who was it who wrote fifty pages describing a penis once? Proust? D. H. Lawrence? Someone with too much time on their hands, that's for sure.

I looked through the papers and my heart sank. It didn't look to me like he had the wrong idea. I leafed through the first few pages slowly. He'd started peeping at age twelve. Some other kids had gone with him a couple of times creeping around the neighborhood looking into their neighbors' windows, but the others had quickly tired of it. He had gotten obsessed by it. He would go to bed early, then sneak out the window in his room. He had climbed trees and hung out on rooftops. He spent so much time wandering around town late at night looking for lighted windows that he started falling asleep in school. And that was all before he turned twelve. It looked like an Olympic bobsled run down-hill from there. Somehow I couldn't help thinking of his dad. Did he have a clue where his son was all those late nights he spent in the hospital?

I looked up at Reggie. Why was this man beam-ing? With forty-nine pages to go, there was very likely enough stuff in here to make it clear he couldn't practice medicine again, not if his deviant behavior had ever involved the hospital. He didn't get it. He thought if he fessed up—no matter what he'd done—I'd tell him he was a good boy and all was forgiven. Sort of the George Washington–cherry tree theory of sex offending.

I'd seen it before. Some folks felt entitled to sweep their "mistakes" out with the trash like they were ashes they'd dropped and not people they had mauled. It was nothing at all for someone who had murdered a ninety-year-old with a chainsaw to say, "I wish it hadn't happened but there's nothing I can do about it now. Hey, it's over and I have to move on with my own life, you know." Half the criminals I knew had no clue why they were being punished for something that was over and done with and they couldn't change now anyway.

"Let's go over this," I said carefully. "Page by page."

"Why?" he said, surprised. "It's all there. Just read it."

"It's not all here," I said with conviction. "It's never all here. It's a good beginning but I think when you search your memory, you'll find there are more incidents with more people. I think you'll find there's more to these incidents than you first put down. There's always more. What you've given me is just the tip of the iceberg. I've been doing this work for fifteen years and it's always the tip of the iceberg. Ninety percent of the deviant stuff you've fantasized about, masturbated to, thought about and *done* isn't in this paper."

It was a tack I always took, no matter what an offender brought back the first time. No sex offender, ever, *not ever,* tells the truth, the whole truth and nothing but the truth the first time through. I had never once been wrong about this and I knew with the kind of dead certainty Mama had about everything I never would be.

His face fell and he looked like he was pouting. I ignored the pouting and bent over the papers. I skipped to the part where I saw the first clear evidence of deception and began to read more slowly.

I started my residency at Forth Worth. After a while I drilled a hole between my office and the examining room where the female patients undressed so I could watch them. Finished my residency. Went into the army. Did that so I could do some traveling before I settled down.

My first actual involvement with a patient occurred in the army. A corporal's wife came in to see me for a physical. I had just finished looking at her ears when she opens her gown and asks me if she needs breast reduction surgery. She has these large, gorgeous breasts. I told her truthfully I thought her breasts were lovely. She smiles and well, things go on from there. I know it wasn't right but at the time I wasn't sure who seduced whom! She was in her late thirties and I was maybe 26 and still wet behind the ears.

I stopped reading. How could anybody lie that much in two simple paragraphs? Jesus. And there were forty-plus pages to go. Later, after he'd gone, I'd do a full analysis of his statement using SCAN, a technique for analyzing deception in statements developed by Allen Goldstein, a former member of the Israeli Mossad I had studied under. But even without a full analysis, I could eyeball a statement like this, which just reeked of deception, and have enough to shake him up.

I looked at the first paragraph. He had told me where he started his residency, not where he finished it. "Started" was one of those red flag words. People didn't say, "I started my residency." They said, "I did my residency," unless something interrupted it.

I looked for confirmation. You could go on one sign

of deception but it was a bad idea. You were on much more solid ground with two or more.

Confirmation wasn't far away. "*So* I could watch them . . . *so* I could do some traveling." "So" was a because-type word. Reggie was explaining things. I didn't ask him to tell me *why* he did what he did. I just asked him to tell me *what* he did. When people started explaining themselves, especially twice within a line or two, there was usually a sensitive issue in those lines.

I looked to see what was between those two "so's." In between those two "so's" were two sentences with missing prepositions, "Finished my residency. Went into the army." Two short, choppy sentences with no prepositions written by a man who was nothing if not fluid and articulate. He hadn't said that *he* finished his residency and went into the army; he left the pronoun "I" out of both sentences.

"No commitment," I could just hear Goldstein say, the genius behind the SCAN system. "If he is not committed to what he says, *you* should not be either."

"Where did you finish your residency?" I asked.

Reggie looked nonplussed. "Finish my residency?" he said. "Why do you ask? I said—"

"You said where you started your residency. You didn't say where you finished it."

"But surely that's ob—" he said.

"Really," I said. "Reggie, I don't want to play games with you. Before you answer, remember that residency programs keep records. Where did you finish your residency? Was it in Fort Worth or not?"

There was a pause. "Well, actually, no. I mean, I didn't think it was important, but actually, I did transfer."

"To where?"

"Well, I think my first year in the army was actually my last year of residency. Maybe I didn't make that clear."

"Not exactly," I said. "Strike one."

"That's not fair," Reggie protested. "You're nit-picking about things that have nothing to do with my alleged problems."

Alleged, no less. Now he had alleged problems. Fifty pages of "alleged" problems. It gave a whole new meaning to the word "alleged."

"If it has nothing to do with your problem," I replied, "then why did you lie about it?"

"I didn't," Reggie said.

I didn't answer. Technically, he was right. He hadn't lied. He had left something out, which is exactly what most liars did. The human tendency when concealing information is to dodge and weave, to imply something without ever stating it. For some crazy reason, it was a whole lot harder to lie outright than to leave things out. Mostly, you had to push people and pin them down before they actually lied to you.

But not Reggie. Because in the next paragraph about the corporal's wife, Reggie had lied to me outright. The damn thing was almost total fabrication. Reggie had betrayed himself by switching into the present tense, which is exactly what people did who were making things up. Things from memory were repeated in the past tense because the person was pulling from a real memory of events that were in the past.

"My best guess is, there was a woman, maybe a corporal's wife, and you did look into her ears, but all the rest about her flashing her breasts at you and asking about breast reduction surgery—in your dreams, maybe. You did tell her how beautiful you thought her breasts were, which, if you were looking into her ears and doing a physical, was not the most professional thing a doctor could say.

"But it wasn't the first incident, Reggie, because you got kicked out of your residency in Fort Wayne for something, and no doubt, it was something to do with this. The only reason a bright and ambitious young resident would go into the service is if no other residency would take him, the army being the medical equivalent of Siberia.

"And you didn't get bounced for anything as simple as killing a patient because that's on medicine's 'to forgive' list, unless you made a habit of it or used an ax or something. So there are only a few options. Either you couldn't make a decision, which would, indeed, get you kicked out, or, most likely, it was drugs or sex and it must have been pretty bad. By the *last* year of residency, nobody, and I mean *nobody*, ever gets thrown out."

Reggie looked stunned. "And, Reggie," I went on. "You have no idea what I'm saving you. I know this much"—I held my thumb and index finger up with a quarter inch between them—"about deception compared to the polygraph person I'm sending you

to. I personally wouldn't lie to John Davis and I
wouldn't advise you to."

Reggie had turned pale and I noted again that he
did react physically when he was upset. Which made
it all the more important to note when he should be
reacting physically and wasn't.

"What was the name of the corporal's wife?" I said.

"How would I remember that?" he said.

"You would," I said, "if she was the first patient
you ever molested, and you wouldn't if she was
maybe the twentieth. So you tell me, do you remember her name or not?"

"I feel like I need an attorney," he said weakly.

"I told you that from the beginning," I replied. "I'll
keep these," I said, putting his papers into a folder.
"You've got it on computer. Go back and do it right.

"Now let's start getting serious about this, Dr.
Larsen. I'm not going to go through the dental ex-
traction method of getting the truth out of you. I
don't care whose son you are. I am not going to
spend seventy-seven sessions trying to pull every lie
out of you with pliers. If you keep lying to me, I'm
simply going to send you for a polygraph, let you fail
the hell out of it, and then write up a report that
says you are not to be believed about anything. And
I'd have to recommend, of course, that you should
never practice medicine again."

"What?" he said. "You can't do that. How can you
say that? Nobody would believe that."

I folded my hands over the papers and said
calmly, "Yes, they would. What I have in this autobiography alone is enough to back up that recom-

mendation. Now, I'm not saying you should never practice medicine again because I don't know that at this point. It depends on a lot of things, how honest you are, how much you cooperate with treatment, what kinds of gains you make in treatment and what kind of monitoring can be set up. But if I don't get the whole picture, there's no *possibility* of setting up effective treatment and then I will recommend you never practice again. I don't mind erring on the side of patient safety.

"And if you pull your release of information and suppress this eval the hospital is surely going to want to know why. So this is like one of those car rental gates where you can drive forward but you can't drive back or you'll shred your tires. Too late to back out now."

"I think you're misjudging me," Reggie said, pulling himself up and rallying his dignity. "I didn't say anything about backing out. I always finish what I start."

I filed that last comment. His voice changed when he said it and it had an ominous ring, although I didn't know why.

"Next week, same time, same place, better homework. And don't forget to fill in the 'after a while.'"

"After a while?" Reggie asked.

"Second sentence," I said. "Missing time. What happened in the 'after a while.'"

Reggie sat without moving. "Next week? I can't do that. I told the hospital the eval would be finished this week."

"Why?" I asked, surprised. "What's the rush?"

"I need to get this over with," he said sullenly, which wasn't any answer at all.

"Time for me to check in," I said. Clearly, there was something Reggie wasn't telling me. "Whom do I call?"

"Margaret Jones," he said, "Medical Director and Orthopedic Surgeon." I had never heard of Dr. Jones, but the way he said it made me think I should have.

"What's she like?" I asked.

"I think I'll just let you find that out." And for the first time since I met him, there was something like humor in his voice.

After Reggie left I picked up the phone. I needed to talk to Margaret Jones anyway, but Reggie had made me curious.

I thought about her as I dialed. Women surgeons were still rare as hen's teeth and particularly rare in a super macho field like orthopedics. One thing I could be pretty sure of: she was a damn good surgeon. To get into surgery, a woman had to be so good the male surgeons would overlook the fact she was female. Between an equally qualified male and female candidate, there was no doubt in my mind who got chosen. The surgeons were all male. They knew male residents. They were comfortable with them. They had trained them for decades. They went with what they knew.

There was no affirmative action in surgery. There wasn't a whole lot of fairness in surgery. It was basically a cross between a guild and a Green Beret unit. Plus, unbelievably, Margaret Jones had made it to

Medical Director, which meant her colleagues respected her, whether they liked her or not.

"Could I have Dr. Margaret Jones's office?"

The transfer was instant and the phone was answered crisply. "Dr. Jones's office," the voice said. I wouldn't exactly describe the voice as welcoming but Dr. Jones's office probably fielded hundreds of calls in the course of a day and most of them were people who wanted to talk to the Medical Director more than the Medical Director wanted to talk to them. A lot of her secretary's job would be fending them off.

"This is Dr. Michael Stone calling. I would like to speak to Dr. Jones about—"

"Oh, just a moment, Dr. Stone. Dr. Jones is expecting your call."

Excuse me. Reggie's problem has enough priority that the secretary has been told in advance to put me through?

A second voice came on the phone almost instantly. "Dr. Jones is in surgery." I started to leave my number when the voice added, "If you'll just wait a moment, she gave instructions she was to be interrupted if you called."

What? What? They were pulling her out of surgery to talk to me? I was stunned. *Nothing* ever interrupted surgery. *Nobody* ever interrupted it. The president could have called and they would not have pulled her out of surgery to talk to him. I got a knot in my stomach. What had Reggie done?

I swallowed hard. I found myself thinking of some poor schlemiel lying there with his hip socket out while another one was sitting there waiting to go in. Surely they wouldn't pull her out of surgery. You didn't keep people under anesthesia any longer than you had to. Not a second longer.

Calm down, I told myself. She's got some ace resident who picks up the scalpel—never mind the scalpel, this was orthopedics, the chain saw—as smoothly as she lays it down. Surgery? They were pulling her out of surgery?

I waited maybe five minutes and then a voice came on. "This is Dr. Jones," she said. Her voice was clear and strong and the pace was quick. I had to remember my medical etiquette. To the point. No wasted bullshit about the weather.

"This is Dr. Stone," I said promptly. "I assume Dr. Larsen has given you permission to talk to me? I have a release I can fax you if you need it."

"That won't be necessary. He signed one here."

"What can you tell me?" I said. "What's his problem?"

"We were hoping you'd tell us that," she said, wryly, sounding slightly annoyed.

I was instantly defensive. "Maybe I can," I replied, "in the end. But I usually get the symptoms before I make a diagnosis."

There was a pause. We were squaring off against each other and I, for one, didn't know why. I wondered if she was thinking the same thing.

"Three reports have come in in the last year," she said, finally. "All from patients complaining of him groping them while they were groggy from surgery."

"Three?" I said surprised. "In the last year? How long has he been suspended?"

It probably wasn't the most tactful question.

"A couple of months," she said finally, and I could hear the annoyance coming back. It could be the hospital had some liability for not acting sooner. If they had acted after the first one, maybe the other two wouldn't have happened.

No wonder she had hesitated to tell me. I didn't respond and she went on. "When the first report came in we weren't sure what to make of it. The patient was groggy. She had been under anesthesia for seven hours. She was surfacing. Sometimes people see white rabbits under those circumstances."

"And the next two?"

"They came in almost on top of each other. When the second came in we called a meeting of the ethics committee. The third came in literally as the ethics committee was meeting."

"Any reports before then?" How could he possibly have operated so long without getting caught and then get caught three times in one year? It didn't make sense.

"None on record," she said carefully.

"What does that mean?"

"It means that if reports weren't founded they were destroyed. I have no idea of if there were reports my predecessor dismissed." There was clearly a message in that or she wouldn't have mentioned it, but I couldn't think of any subtle way to ask about her opinion of her predecessor.

"So you don't know if there were other reports."

"That's right."

"Anything else I should know?"

She paused. As the pause went on, I realized there was clearly something else but she was deciding whether to say it or not. I waited.

"We had one report from a staff member but she insisted on confidentiality," she said finally. "I am not at liberty to release it."

"Would it change anything if I got it or is it more of the same?"

"It is not more of the same," she replied.

"This puts me in a bind," I responded. "You know about a symptom you won't tell me about."

"Can't tell you about," she said. "I have no release."

"Can you tell me anything about the *nature* of the charge?"

"No, I can't," she said, and I heard the finality in her voice. It was what Mama called "the word with the bark on it." I never knew where that saying came from but I knew what it meant.

There was no point in pushing it. "Then do me this favor," I said. "Call the person and give them my name and number. Maybe she'll decide to talk to me on her own. Or his own," I added.

"All right," she said, "I'll do that."

All through the conversation I had been wondering why Reggie said he'd let me find out what Margaret Jones was like, as though she was some sort of difficult person. I wasn't really finding her difficult. But maybe that was because I recognized "the word with the bark on it" when I heard it. I had a feeling that someone who liked to wheedle and connive and thought "no" meant "maybe" might find her difficult.

"One more thing," I said bluntly. "Is there really a question of him getting his job back or have you already made up your mind? It strikes me that three reports are a lot and I would think there is liability involved if you let him back and he goes on to do it again."

"There is considerable liability," she responded, sighing, "either way. This could involve depriving an anesthesiologist of his livelihood, which, the attorneys tell me, is not something the courts take lightly. Not to mention Dr. Larsen is a particularly gifted physician and it would be an extraordinary waste." She sounded genuinely torn.

And why wouldn't she be, I realized. Legally the hospital was in a bind no matter what they did. They were bound to get sued if they fired him. The witnesses were groggy from surgery. Who knows if they would even say on the stand that they were *sure* it was him? Plus, he really was a talented man, about to make the discovery of the decade, and the hospital would be decimating his career.

One thing was for sure. If Reggie was worried his bosses would act without my report, he was barking up the wrong tree. They'd wait for the report and hope to put the whole thing off on me. They'd love to have someone make a recommendation that got them even halfway off the hook.

"All right," I said. "Anything you need to know from me at this point?"

"We'd like to know your procedures in doing evaluations of this sort."

"I'll write up a brief description and fax it to you. It'll save time."

"When will you be done?"

"A few weeks," I responded. "However long it takes to arrange a polygraph."

"A polygraph?" she said, surprised.

"Standard procedure," I said. "People who commit deviant sex acts tend to lie about it. Knowing they have to take a polygraph helps keep the lying down to a dull roar."

"I'll be very interested in what you find out."

"I'm afraid," I said, "you'd be very interested in what I already know."

It was a heads-up warning about which way this was going to go. I don't know why I told her but I did. I had a release but I didn't usually give any feedback until I had finished the eval. Maybe I felt some distant kinship with this blunt woman who was playing ball with people who had six inches and maybe fifty pounds on her and holding her own under the boards. Or maybe I just had some kind of admiration for a woman who could rummage around in other people's bodies with a chain saw and do something constructive. I knew offenders who had rummaged around in other people's bodies with a chain saw but they sure hadn't done anything constructive.

6

Friday morning found me fiddling nervously with the audio controls in the observation booth connected to the interview room where Marv sat with Jody and her parents. I hated being behind glass. I couldn't do anything if something went wrong and Marv or Jody needed help, and worse, I was behind glass and totally dependent on the audio system, which, I knew from long experience, had a sadistic streak.

Say what they want, machines like you or they don't and few machines took to me. When my ex-husband—who had a decent mechanical gene running around in his DNA—went out of town, I could count on one or more machines lying down and dying.

The sound popped on suddenly. Maybe it would work for the whole session, maybe it wouldn't. If Jody's father confessed, of course, it would stop on a dime.

I sat down. Marv was sitting with his back to me, at my request. I had asked to see Jody's parents and he had arranged it so they were sitting squarely across from me.

Her father was a wiry man in his late forties and his nervous energy seemed to dominate the room. He was playing anxiously with some keys and he kept glancing at the mirror. Maybe he was wishing he hadn't allowed an observer but, if so, he didn't say it.

Jody's mother, Mary Jo, was a placid-looking, over-weight woman about the same age as her husband. If Jody's father seemed edgy, her mother seemed unnaturally still. Nothing in her face or body moved. She was looking at Jody but I was almost sure her attention was on the man at her side.

Jody was tiny and thin, so thin I wondered if she had gone a few rounds with anorexia in her time. She didn't look like she fit with either of the people in front of her. I suddenly wished I had met her before this morning. The mealy-mouthed, don't-beat-me look she had—was she carrying that with her, day in and day out? Or was she doing what everybody does—regressing to age ten when dealing with their parents. If she was, it was pretty clear it hadn't been a good age ten.

Jody kept looking at the keys her father held. She would look at them, then glance away, then look back at them again. Son-of-a-bitch, I thought. He's doing something with those keys. Did Marv know that? He didn't seem to. He wasn't paying any attention to them at all and neither was Jody's mother. The keys, whatever they meant, were solely between Jody and her father.

Marv was speaking gently, explaining that Jody had requested the meeting because she had some things to talk about with her parents. The meeting was not his idea, he said firmly. He was only there to support Jody in saying whatever she wished to say.

It was a reasonable beginning. If the father was an offender, the first thing he'd likely do was try to take away any sense of power from Jody. Offenders didn't even allow the child the dignity of making her own accusations. He'd claim she'd been brainwashed, led. She was a puppet, putty in a Machiavellian therapist's hands. I didn't mind it being said when it was true—and sometimes it was—but real life didn't work like that. It seemed it was said loudest when it wasn't true.

Jody's dad, Sam, interrupted before Marv even finished his opening spiel. "What I want to know," he said, "is what's going on here." He turned to Jody. "You've got something to say to me, you've had twenty years to say it."

I nearly fell off the seat. Jesus Christ, he was aggressive and what he said was almost an indirect admission. It was the last thing I had expected.

"Dad," Jody began. "I just want—"

"You just want . . . You want this and you want that. Why is it always what you want? Don't you ever think what your mother and I want? Don't you think we deserve a little peace in our old age? Sure we made mistakes. Who doesn't? Who the hell has a perfect childhood? I sure as hell didn't. But you don't care about that, do you?"

I stopped breathing. We were thirty seconds into the session and the man's level of aggression was off the chart and rising. He was livid. Either he'd been working himself up, worrying about this meeting, or maybe he was one of these drop-a-dish-and-I-go-into-an-instant-rage types. Then again, maybe he was faking it to control her.

Whatever it was, the meeting wouldn't work. I wished I could see Marv's face. Call it off, Marv, I thought. Call it off. He knows what's coming and he's going to go wild with it.

"Dad, please don't—"

"Dad, please don't," Jody's father mimicked her in a whiny voice. "Please don't what. I've had it up to here with your whining. All you ever do is whine. All you've ever *done* is whine. You've been nothing but trouble since the day you were born." His words seemed to knock the wind out of Jody.

I stood up, although there was nothing I could do. He was emotionally beating the shit out of this kid and all I could do was watch.

"Mr. Carlson," Marv had finally got his voice back. "Mr. Carlson. You seem extremely upset and thus far no one—"

Sam Carlson looked at Marv for the first time. "How stupid do you think I am? I know what's going on here. She's going to blame us for the mess she's made of her life. You work all your life to send your kid to college and what does she do? She lies in bed all day and pulls the covers over her head and suddenly it's your fault. Do I lie in bed all day? No, I don't have that luxury, do I? I have to make a living for these shits who suck me dry."

Oh, Jesus. I glanced at Jody's mother but her face was totally impassive, only the lines in it seemed to deepen. Jody started to cry. Marv desperately tried to regain control.

"Mr. Carlson," he began, but Carlson interrupted again.

"Let's cut out the bullshit." He turned to Jody. "Say it," he said. "Whatever this is, say it now or don't you ever start up on this again. Never. Say it or keep your mouth shut for good."

I thought she'd fold. She seemed to. She slumped down in the chair, crying even harder. But then she looked up through the tears and almost whispered, "You did it, Dad. You know you did."

Carlson stood up. "I didn't do anything to you. All I ever did was treat you like a princess and what do I get for it?"

Jody curled up in the chair, almost in a fetal position. Marv held his hands up to try to calm everyone down but it was futile. This train was just picking up speed.

Jody's father opened his mouth again to speak when suddenly, Jody sat up straight and screamed at him, so loud all of us jumped. "You fucked me. You know you did. You *fucked* me every goddamn day. You *fucked* me when Mom went shopping. You *fucked* me on Saturday mornings when you took me for a ride. You *fucked* me and kept fucking me. I was in first grade, for Christ's sake." She was crying hard and gasping for air to speak but she didn't stop. "You fucked me on my birthday. You sneaked in my room at night. You fucked me every time my mother turned her back. You did it. You know you did."

The force of her outburst caused all of us to recoil, all except Carlson. He took a step forward until he was almost standing over her. Jody put her hands over her head as though to ward off a blow. Marv got up and tried to step between Sam and Jody. "Mr. Carlson, this has gone—"

Carlson stepped around Marv as though he wasn't there and held the keys up in Jody's face. "I never abused you," he shouted. "How can you say I abused you?" He shook the keys in Jody's face. She looked at them and hid her head. She stopped speaking. Marv got between them this time. "Stop," he said more forcefully. "This isn't helping anyone."

Her father stepped back then and said in a lower tone, but one that still had enough venom in it to poison a couple of cities, "I never hurt you. I never did anything to hurt you. I don't have to take this shit." He turned and headed for the door.

Throughout all of this, Jody's mother said nothing. Now she slowly got up and followed him.

"Mommy," Jody said, and I closed my eyes against the sound in her voice. I guess her mother closed her ears because when I opened my eyes again, both parents were gone.

I sat in the booth for a few minutes after they left, just trying to calm down. Son-of-a-bitch. I'd just watched a beating, and neither Marv nor I had been able to do a goddamn thing about it.

But who could have seen it coming? All I thought was that he'd deny the abuse and leave Jody feeling crazy and her mother not knowing whom to believe, maybe even leave Marv and I wondering whom to believe.

But that was the problem with these cases. You just didn't know what you were dealing with until you got an alleged perp in the room. Sometimes they weren't a perp at all. And even when they were, most of them were slick and good at covering up. They generally had no trouble pulling an outraged "how-can-you-say-that-about-your-dear-sweet-dad-this-therapist-has-been-brainwashing-you" routine that would have left everybody—even the victim—wondering how they could possibly be guilty. But there was another kind of perp out there: a violent, threatening, out-of-control type guy and every once in a while he showed up just when you least expected him.

Marv was sitting across from a sobbing Jody and looking for all the world like he wanted to put his arms around her and let her cry on his shoulder. I'd had that impulse before too and had sat there helplessly like he did now, knowing that touching a client would create a lot more problems than it would solve. He didn't move but he didn't pretend that words would help either. He just sat with her while she cried.

I left the observation booth and knocked gently on the door. Ordinarily, I would never have interrupted a session, but I had met Jody before we all went in for the session and, of course, she knew I had been observing. I thought I'd better check in so she knew I was leaving.

I poked my head in the door. "I'm so sorry, Jody," I said gently. She didn't even look up. "I'll catch up with you later, Marv," I said. I saw the question in his eyes. "No," I replied. "I didn't. I really didn't." And it was true. I had expected something

sneakier and more subtle from Sam Carlson, but
not the aggressive outburst that we got. Sneaky
might be somewhere in Carlson's arsenal, but sub-
tlety was surely not.

Marv sat slumped in the leather chair in my office. He'd spent over an hour just trying to get Jody
calmed down enough that she could function. He
looked bewildered.

"He beats her," I said.

"Who?"

"Mom. He beats her. She won't cross him."

"Are you sure?" Marv didn't really seem to care. It
was just one small part of a completely overwhelm-
ing mess.

"She's not going to help. Not now, not ever.
How's Jody?"

Marv didn't say anything. He just closed his eyes.
"I don't know," he said finally. I didn't speak either. I
didn't know what else to say. "She's on the verge of
decompensation, I think," he said finally. "I'll call
her tonight."

If she makes it that far, I thought. She'll most
likely fall apart and end up in the hospital before he
has a chance to call. The phone rang. I picked it up.
"He's here," I said. I listened to my secretary for a
moment, then handed the phone to Marv. "It's
Melissa. Jody's brother wants to talk to you. He's
pretty insistent." Marv took the phone more or less
like you would a live cobra.

"Of course," he said, with absolutely no conviction in his voice. "Put him on." I suppose he

thought he had to but he sure didn't sound like he much wanted to.

"This is Dr. Gliesen," he said. The voice at the other end started in immediately. It was so loud Marv literally held the phone from his ear. The voice sounded so eerily like Jody's dad that I wondered for a moment if it was really he, faking it.

"How dare you?" the voice began. "My mother called me crying. My father's health is fragile. How dare you let my crazy sister upset him like that? Do you know what this has done to my mother? What gave you the right to meddle in our family like that?"

Marv interrupted him. "Mr. Carlson," he said. "I don't have any permission from Jody Carlson to discuss this situation with you. I'm afraid without that—"

"Well, you listen to me, you goddamn quack. You will never get my parents in your office again without me being there. You tell my goddamn lunatic sister this is the last time she's going to put our family through hell. Her and her stupid, crazy accusations. She's been nothing but trouble since the day she was born."

Marv looked up at me then. It wasn't Jody's father but it might as well have been. He had bought Dad's spiel hook, line and sinker. What a joy it must have been for Jody growing up in that house. There was Dad and then there was Dad Junior and then there was that pale, numbed-out shell of a mother dutifully shuffling behind.

"I'm sorry you're upset, Mr. Carlson, but there's nothing I can do to help you," Marv said. The phone was slammed down on the other end so loud even I could hear it. I wish he'd stayed on the line. He had already told us more than we knew and I had the feeling that with a little prompting he would have told us even more. Ten to one he knew something about the keys. But it was definitely not the time to discuss all that with Marv.

"She'll decompensate," I said to Marv. "I guarantee it. Maybe she'll make it to tonight but she won't make it through it. She doesn't just have Dad's voice in her head. She has her brother's too, not to mention her mother's silence, which no doubt speaks loudest of all.

"I think this is going to be bad, Marv. She's told before. And we don't even know what happened. But you can bet it wasn't good. It may even be one of the reasons she's lost memory. You'd better call the inpatient unit and see what they've got open and who's on."

"How do you know she's told before?" Marv said absent-mindedly. He was still too shell-shocked to think clearly.

"Her brother just told us," I replied. "This was the 'last time'—not the first time, the last time—she's going to disrupt the family with her 'crazy accusations.' She's 'always been trouble.' Not to mention, he's furious but he's not surprised.

"Look," I said. "All we're getting now is what Jody got all along. Reality is whatever everybody agrees on. They all told her it wasn't happening. And the price of mentioning it was rage from everybody except Mom. Mom just flat abandoned her. I would definitely get an inpatient bed ready. She's not just

going to relive the abuse. She's going to relive all
the shit that happened whenever she tried to tell
somebody about it."

I don't think he believed me. But then he hadn't
seen a whole lot of these cases and, unfortunately, I
had. And what I'd finally got through my head was
that the abuse itself wasn't the only problem, maybe
not even the biggest. It wasn't just violence to the
child's body that was destructive. It was violence to
the child's reality. It was like living with a Nazi who
everybody else thought was Mr. Rogers.

Marv made no moves to pick up the phone. He
just sat there looking one step short of comatose.
What was going on with him? Surely he had dealt with
crazy patients and crazy families before. I reached
across him and picked up the phone. All right, so I'm
pushy, but he didn't look like he could order a pizza
much less an inpatient bed. I thought briefly of asking for two beds—one for Jody and one for him—but
people tell me I don't pick the right times to be
funny. This could be, I thought, what they mean.

I called the operator. "This is Dr. Stone. Who's on
in Psychiatry tonight?"

"Dr. Dexter," the voice said instantly. It was Rich,
my favorite operator. I'd never seen the man—the
operators worked somewhere in a windowless room
buried deep in the hospital—but he was better than
anyone else I dealt with at finding whoever I needed
to find.

"Back-up?" I said.

"Dr. Johnson is on this month."

Oh, Jesus. Dexter had seemed like a sensible kid

in my seminar that morning, but Johnson, the faculty member supervising him, was a major polypharmacy guy. He loaded people with so many meds they didn't know where they were. The trick would be to work with Paul to get Jody situated if she came in so we could leave Johnson out of it.

"Would you page Dr. Dexter?" I asked. "Have him call my office at his convenience." That was the only fair way to do it. The emergency folks stayed busy and paging him out of who knows what—a suicidal twelve-year-old maybe—to talk about a might, maybe, could-be, wouldn't endear me to him.

"What's your schedule?" I said to Marv after I hung up.

"Well," Marv said, "that's going to be the difficulty. I've got clients all day until nine o'clock. I've been thinking about whom I could shift. Frankly, it won't be easy to shift anyone. My schedule is the same tomorrow. Anybody I canceled would have to wait until next week and none of them are really doing all that well."

I glanced at Marv curiously. Why were none of them doing that well? Marv was as good a therapist as I had ever known. He shouldn't have a line-up that long of people who were *all* doing badly.

All of a sudden I was annoyed. I was in one of those situations where I was in the backseat, someone else was driving, he gets us lost and I end up getting stuck. I glanced at Marv thinking, I could take a hike on this. It's not my problem. Marv would get through it somehow and so would Jody—one way or another. In any case, what she was going through now wasn't any worse than what she'd gone through before. I had already done more than I had to. I had hung in for a goddamn emotional blood-bath, for Christ's sake. I had no obligation to stay.

I sighed. "Brief Paul," I said, "and tell him to call me if she comes in. I'll back him up. You go see your patients."

Marv looked up. "This really isn't your problem," he said. "You don't have to do that."

"I deal with this stuff all the time," I said. "Plus, I'm just trying to get you indebted. Wait until payback."

Marv looked doubtful for a moment. I could see him thinking he might be better off seeing Jody himself. I laughed. "Scoot," I said. "I've got work to do. I'll transfer Paul when he calls."

"Thanks," he said finally, with more emotion in his voice than I wanted to hear. He got up to leave and I looked after him for a long moment. He was an eight-cylinder engine, firing maybe two. Hell, on a good day he was a therapeutic Ferrari, only now he was put-tering along like one of the old Volkswagen Beetles.

I turned back around to work and realized something was bugging me. I had lied, sort of. Not to Marv. To myself. I wasn't doing this just to help Jody or even Marv. I was partly doing this because I wanted another round or two with Sam Carlson. These guys always had that crazy effect on me. Any-body sane wanted to run and hide. I just wanted to go under the boards with them and let a few el-bows fly.

It was that piece of Mama in me. Mama once went into a shed after a cotton-mouth water moccasin. That wouldn't have been so bad except the shed was a tiny little thing built just to house a hot water tank. There was barely enough room to stand between the tank and the wall. The snake was wrapped around the tank and it was dark in there. Mama had taken her trusty little hatchet and slipped sideways into that shed and I had no doubts whatsoever who was coming out alive.

It was not so clear I was going to do that well against the Sam Carlsons of the world. My habit of hassling them had gotten me strangled once and stalked once and almost kneecapped once. But I still couldn't help walking into that shed. Hell of a legacy. Why did I get that and not my sweet papa's affection for oblivion in a bottle?

But what was I worrying about? The Sam Carlsons of the world went after people they had power over: the depressed and heartbroken women they found or made—the children those women became too damaged to protect. They never played a game on level ground. What would save my ass was not any skill on my part. I just wasn't young enough or small enough or ill enough for him to take me on.

7

She came in because of the cutting. Probably she wouldn't have if she hadn't gone a little too deep, a little too far. But the blood was bad enough to scare her and when she got her head clear from whatever trancelike thing the cutting does to people, she slipped in the blood and that sobered her up. So she came in to the ER to get stitched up.

Before she arrived I had read her chart cover to cover so I knew she cut. She had had only one suicide attempt we knew about but a previous medical exam had revealed a series of scars on her arms and torso. From that I knew she was a self-mutilator, one of those folks who had discovered that carving on their bodies brought a short but precious peace.

Who knew why? Because it called up endorphins from deep inside the brain—which is to say cutters got an internal shot of something like morphine. Maybe it was because cutting fed the self-hate; it made them feel like they were getting the punishment they thought they deserved. Or maybe it was just hypnotic. Cutters always cut slowly and carefully and they usually said they didn't feel a thing at the time.

Whatever it was, it was addictive as hell. Once folks started, they often carved up their bodies like a kid's desk at school.

I hated cutting. I wanted to stomp on those goddamn razors. I wanted to tell people to cut out that shit, no pun intended. I wanted to yell at them, "What? You haven't been beat on enough already? You've got to get in on the act too?"

It was a big problem for me when the offender and the victim were in the same body. I just couldn't empathize with someone who was cutting on a live body, even if the cutter was the cuttee. My head knew that if people were in enough pain, they'd reach for whatever meds were handy—endorphins being nothing to sneeze at. But my head was never going to win this one. I had an internal revulsion to people slicing themselves up like turkeys.

So when Jody showed up with her arms shredded, I got that frosty thing I get when I'm supposed to feel warm and empathic and I am royally pissed instead.

"It doesn't matter," she said when she saw me looking at her. It was early, eight o'clock at night and Marv was still seeing patients so Paul had called me as soon as the ER had called him. I had just slipped into the room and was watching the ER doc stitch her up. I hadn't even said hello yet.

"Sure it matters," I said. I had an edge in my voice

but it wasn't too bad. The hopelessness in her voice had undercut a whole lot of my anger.

"It doesn't matter to me. It doesn't matter to him. Why the hell should it matter to you?" The words could have sounded angry but they just sounded tired. She tried to turn her body toward the wall but the ER doc asked her to hold still, so she just turned her head instead.

"When did you start?" I asked softly. There was no answer. "Can you tell me," I said again gently, "when you started?"

It was an important question, not because the answer would help either of us all that much but because *whether* she would answer would tell me if she'd talk to me or not. And that would tell me whether she wanted any help or—for tonight at least—she had moved beyond my reach.

She still said nothing. And then I had a flash. I had no idea where it came from or whether it was true, but I didn't have a lot to lose since she wasn't talking to me anyway. "It started over the keys, didn't it? It started when the keys did."

Her whole body went rigid. She turned her head back toward me slowly. She didn't speak. She just looked at me. Her pupils dilated and then retreated to the size of pinpricks. The change was so pronounced the doc stitching up her arm glanced up at her and then me. No one spoke.

He went quickly back to his stitching. "I'm almost finished," he said. Light-years passed. Jody made no attempt to turn away again and no attempt to speak. The doc put in the last stitch, then gathered up his things and hurriedly left.

Jody sat up slowly on the examining table. She was trembling slightly. "How did you know?" she asked. "Dr. Gliesen doesn't know. Nobody knows."

"Because your father shook them in your face," I answered honestly. "I saw it." Now it was my turn to hold my breath. What had I stumbled into? When things like this got opened up, people could get a whole lot better or they could get a whole lot worse. I only wished I knew what in the world we were talking about. But I really didn't want to admit that or Jody would clam up.

"So how old were you?" I said softly. It was the only thing I could think of to ask.

"Sixteen," she said, and when she said that, it all slid into place. I got it. I knew what the keys were and why he shook them. And I also knew why Jody was so ashamed of it.

I let out a sigh. No wonder this poor child was in the shape she was in. She didn't see herself as a victim. She saw herself as a collaborator, maybe even a perp. Sam Carlson, I thought, didn't look like the kind of guy who was smooth enough and cunning enough to entrap victims. He acted like straight violence and intimidation were his game. Wrong again. Sam had figured out that piece too.

"People can get used to anything," I said. "And they take control of anything they can, because being powerless is so awful. Lots of kids do what you did. Lots."

Jody didn't speak. She just looked at me like I was a stranger who had walked in on her while she was dressing. And I had intruded. No question about it. I had opened a door and walked into the one room in her house she didn't want anybody in. I hadn't been invited and she wanted me out. But I wasn't leaving. I was in the room where the cutting started and the only room in the house where it could stop.

"Don't tell," she said and her voice sounded like a five-year-old's. It was so soft I could hardly hear her.

"Who don't you want me to tell?" I asked, pulling up a chair. All of a sudden I had realized I was standing over this tiny young woman sitting on the examining table. Better for me to be the one who's being looked down to.

She didn't seem to notice the change, at least not consciously. She stayed silent and just stared at me and I wondered for a moment if she was still in the room at all. Would she dissociate, go away, and I'd find myself talking to a shell? But finally she answered, "Dr. Gliesen."

"One of us has to tell him," I replied. "He can't help you if he doesn't know what the problem is. It's like going to a doctor with a broken arm and saying your foot hurts."

She looked at me and closed her eyes. Any way you look at it, she'd had a real bad day. "Not tonight," she said. She was bargaining—just like she had when she was sixteen—and for the same thing: whatever time away from trouble she could get. But this time she didn't have to pay when she brought the car keys back.

It was an easy bargain for me to take. Tomorrow

was an eye blink away, at least from where I sat. "All right," I said, "not tonight."

I saw the relief in her eyes. Tomorrow did not look an eye blink away to her. She was living from one second to the next and tomorrow was somewhere out there in infinity—light-years of pain away. I knew what she was thinking. With any luck, tomorrow might not come at all.

8

I could have driven home. I did it every night. But somehow I drove by Adam's house and, well, it *was* late and home was miles away. Probably he wouldn't mind me crashing there.

When he opened the door his eyes lit up and I felt a surge of relief. When I realized I was relieved he was glad to see me I was so damned annoyed at myself I almost turned on my heel and left. I hesitated, then said, "This whole thing is getting out of hand."

"What's getting out of hand?" Adam asked. He was barefoot and wearing jeans and he did look good.

"This," I said. "What am I doing on your doorstep?"

"Is there some problem?" he laughed. "What? Is this politically incorrect or something?"

"You feel like company?"

"Depends," he said, folding his arms. "How grumpy are you?"

"I'm out of here," I said, turning to go, but Adam got in front of me, still laughing.

"Just kidding," he said, putting his hands on my shoulders and walking backward in front of me. Jesus, he's fast when he wants to be, I thought. How'd he get past me that quick and then I remembered how slow he could be when he wanted to. That too. Very slow. Fast got him in front of me quick enough to stop me but it was slow that turned me around and got me back inside.

It was four in the morning when the phone rang. Adam picked it up sleepily and then handed it over. "Michael," the voice said, "this is Ruth, in Pediatrics. We've got a problem with a kid who fell off the back of a pick-up truck."

"Ruth," I said slowly, sitting up and trying to get oriented. Ruth was the chief resident in Pediatrics and one of my favorites. She knew what she was doing and didn't call unless it was important.

I shook my head trying to clear it. I had been in some seriously deep state of unconsciousness, some place too deep for dreams where the body went about the nighttime task of restoring chemicals here and there, setting the table for morning. It was a place from which the body did not like to be disturbed and mine was bitching loud and clear. "How'd you find me?" I wasn't even home for Christ's sake; I was at Adam's.

There was a pause. "Michael, wake up." Ruth was

right. Both Adam and I were single. The fact that we spent time together wasn't exactly a secret and, even if it had been, Jefferson may be a big tertiary care hospital but it was still in a very small town.

"Wait a minute. Am I on call? I'm not on call."

"I know," she said. "Just listen, Michael. This twelve-year-old fell off the back of a pick-up truck when it hit another car. He's got a frontal lobe injury and he's disoriented. He socked a nurse and broke her orbital bone. We've got him in restraints."

"Restraints?" I said, completely alert now. "You've got a *kid* in restraints? Did you phone the on-call in Psychiatry?"

"Sure, he's the one who came up with restraints. We couldn't snow him because of the head injury. We need to monitor his level of consciousness. The on-call guy stayed a total of maybe twenty minutes."

I sighed. The Psychiatric Residency Program was an adult program. They provided so little pediatric training it was a joke. Since there wasn't a child psychiatry program, the adult-trained aren't-kids-just-short-people residents were the ones who got sent over for consults to the pediatric unit.

"Where are his parents?"

"Hurt in the accident, one of them bad."

"All right," I said, facing the unavoidable. "I'll be right in."

Jefferson Hospital was not very busy at 4:30 in the morning. Rural Vermont wasn't Boston and anyone who wanted experience with gunshot wounds had to trek up to Boston City for an elective. But on the other hand, we knew a whole lot about kids riding in the back of pick-up trucks and kids riding three-wheelers without helmets.

I took the stairs two at a time and stopped at the nurses' station. The charts were stacked vertically in a large lazy-Susan on the counter but I hadn't even asked the child's name so I couldn't find him by looking at them.

"Pick-up truck injury," I said. "Twelve-year-old." The night-shift unit secretary looked up. "Michael," she said. "Good thing you're here. We've got Rocky Balboa in Room Eleven. He's all yours."

I just nodded and swung the lazy-Susan around until I saw the chart for Room 11. Curtis Todd. I grabbed it and headed for the doctors' room to read it. "Don't get too close," she called after me. "We've had enough excitement for one night." She sounded pissed and I knew why. It scared the bejesus out of everybody when someone attacked a staff member. And when people got scared, they got mad.

"Hey, Michael," she said.

I stopped and turned around. "We're short-staffed," she said. "There isn't anybody to help you."

"What a surprise," I replied. She just shrugged. Being short-staffed had become a way of life since managed care.

The doctors' room was empty and I sat down to read the chart. The neurosurgeons had already been by and the kid had already had his CAT scan. The CAT scan looked pretty good and Neuro thought he just had a severe concussion. Still, he was pretty confused and they had him hooked up to monitoring in the observation room attached to the ward.

The social workers had tried to reach someone from the family but no one was home. That wasn't much of a surprise, since both parents were in the hospital. They were looking for relatives.

I heard him before I got there. He was yelling something I couldn't quite make out but the sound of fear in his voice turned my stomach. I braced myself when I rounded the corner to his room but it didn't help.

Morning was slanting in the window through the half-open blinds and the stripes the new sunlight made on the bed looked like bars on a cell. Well, they might. Curtis Todd was tied down by straps which were fastened to each wrist and ankle and attached to the bed, creating a cell smaller than any prisoner ever had. He was fighting the straps and yelling, but something wasn't working right in his head and the words weren't coherent. Every few minutes he'd stop, breathing hard. Then he'd start up again.

There was something sickening about making a human being that helpless. It looked like torture and it felt like torture and to someone confused with a head injury, it must be even worse. Just seeing somebody in restraints bothered everybody who saw it.

Why was this child alone? Why hadn't someone come up with some relatives, some friends? Why was this confused, frightened child left here screaming by himself, tied down in these straps?

I knew why the staff wasn't there. They didn't have the manpower, given they had sicker kids all around him. They'd compromised by putting him on monitors, which would make sure he didn't get into real trouble without anyone knowing. Trying to calm him down wasn't something anybody had time for.

But it was more than that. Ten to one, it was also the fact that no one knew what to do. Everybody knew complicated stuff to do with space-age machinery and complex blends of toxic chemicals that you could use in place of jet fuel, but nobody knew simple stuff to do with dealing with a confused twelve-year-old tied up and scared out of his fucking mind.

He more or less saw me standing in the door—which is to say his eyes stopped moving for a second when they got to me but he didn't really seem to focus. It wasn't clear how much sense he was making of anything. I came in, moving slowly, staying completely within his line of sight. People in an acute confusional state can't make sense of things. They lose where they are and who anybody is and half the time they think you're trying to attack them when you're trying to help. I slowly pulled up a chair and sat down. I got as close as I could get without being in reach of his limited movement.

I waited until he stopped yelling again and then I said, "You're in a hospital. You fell off a pick-up truck. No one's going to hurt you." He didn't look at me but the pause lasted longer. He kept breathing hard and I noticed he had started blinking rapidly. "You're in a hospital," I said again. "You're tied to the bed to keep you from hurting yourself or someone else. You need to calm down so we can get you untied."

He started to yell again, as though reminding him of the restraints upset him. I waited. After a few minutes he paused and I said again, "You're in a hospital. You fell off a pick-up truck. You've hurt your head but you're going to be okay. Your name is Curtis Todd." He knew that, most likely. People almost never became so confused they didn't know their name, but I thought saying it might help orient him.

I held my breath. I could calm him down, anybody could, if his head was getting clear enough to grasp what I was saying and hold on to it. But if the acute confusional state he was in wasn't clearing, then I could be lying about getting him untied. He didn't have to understand very much, but he did have to understand a few things and hold on to them to make it out of restraints.

This time the pause was longer still and he turned his head toward me for a few seconds. "Michael," I said, while he was looking at me. "My name is Michael." He turned his head back to the ceiling and tried to say something. It sounded less angry and more plaintive and I thought I saw tears in his eyes, but I still couldn't make out the words.

"You fell off a pick-up truck," I said again. "This is a hospital. People are trying to help you. I can't understand you. You hurt your head and your words aren't clear." He looked back at me and I felt encouraged. I couldn't say his eyes were clear for long but there seemed to be moments when he was focusing.

"This is a hospital," I said again, as I would several hundred times in the next few hours. "You fell off a pick-up truck. Curtis, listen to me. We have a rule here. You can't hit anyone. It's a rule." Rules were old with kids, older than reason. Kids who couldn't think clearly still remembered rules. Kids who could hardly hold on to their names understood rules. Rules were there as long as they could remember. If it was a rule, it didn't have to make sense. They didn't have to understand it. It was a rule.

"It's a very big rule," I said again. "You can't hit anyone."

He turned his head toward me and it looked to me like he was trying to say something slowly. I concentrated on the shape his mouth was making. "Ma aaa . . ." Ma aaa. I put my head down to compose myself. He wanted his mother.

Finally, I looked up. "Your mom was hurt in the accident," I said. "I don't know how bad." He started blinking rapidly again and this time it was clear he was crying. I wasn't going to promise I'd find out how she was and I wasn't going to promise she'd be here soon. She could be dead for all I knew and telling the boy that would definitely not help right now.

"Look, Curtis," I said. "We need to start working on getting you out of restraints. We have a rule here. What is it?" He didn't respond, but then again he wasn't yelling. "The rule is no hitting. No hitting. Do you understand? No kicking either."

I said it over and over for what seemed like ages, but was really only an hour or so. When Curtis had stopped yelling entirely and seemed to be reasonably calm, I got up and went to the far side of the bed, moving very slowly. "Curtis, I'm going to take one leg restraint off. No kicking. It's a rule."

I wasn't sure he could handle it but for Christ's sake, what could he do with one leg? When I got closer I could see both legs were shaking slightly, whether from the injury or just the fear was hard to know. I took the restraint off and stepped back. He bent his leg up and then stretched it out but that was all. "No kicking," I said again firmly and went back and sat down in the chair. It was going to be a long morning but so far, so good.

It took less time than I thought, a few hours, to get Curtis Todd out of restraints. Ruth buzzed in and out and, although she didn't interfere, it was clear she was worried she was going to find me decked out on the floor on one of her visits.

Ruth was a hotshot when she was rested, but without sleep she went downhill faster than most. I looked back and forth from her eyes to Curtis's. Both sets looked cloudy and distracted and I realized there wasn't as much difference between the two as I would like.

"How are you doing?" I asked.

"Four admissions," she said. Since each admission took several hours, that did not make for a good night. Too, she'd been on yesterday and she'd be on all day today as well. It added up to a lot of high-stress hours without sleep. "This going all right?"

"See Ma, no restraints."

"After you leave, is he going to kill someone?"

"Uh, Ruth, why don't we talk outside," I said stepping out into the hall. "He can hear you."

She shrugged. The first casualty of sleep deprivation was sensitivity. "Well, is he?"

"No," I said. "He's clearing. He's not violent. He was just confused."

She didn't look convinced. "He broke her orbital bone."

"At least she got a rest," I said.

"I'd rather have an orbital bone."

"A few more admissions," I said, "you might change your mind."

"If I still have one. Fourteen fucking mother calls." Mother calls were calls in the middle of the night about earaches and low grade fevers and things that truly weren't emergencies. They were sandwiched in between car wrecks and child abuse cases and kids with acute, life-threatening illnesses. All of the residents hated them. Ruth peered back into the room. "Well, nothing I can do here. Medically, we're just wait-and-see."

"We're fine. Go away." She disappeared without a word.

By ten o'clock Curtis had been out of restraints for a couple of hours and hadn't killed anybody yet. In fact, he was finally dozing. Wearily, I walked the length of the hall, locking my hands together and stretching them over my head. Four A.M. was just too damned early to start the day and the rest of my day wasn't going to disappear anytime soon.

Susan, the daytime unit secretary, had taken over

the command post. She was short and stocky with a haircut that seemed to get shorter every time I saw her. She played catcher on the local softball team, which I thought was reasonable practice for fielding what came in on the pediatric unit although hockey or tackle football might be better.

"Susan," I said. "I need some help. You know the head injury in Eleven? They had him in restraints. He was a little out of it when he first came in. The thing is, there's nobody here with him. His parents were in the wreck too. The kid's got to have relatives, family friends, somebody. Social work is supposedly working on it, but you know things get lost in the cracks when they come in in the middle of the night."

"I'll take care of it," she said. "Not to worry. I'll get their tails down here and find somebody."

"Get them to check on his parents. He's getting clearer and he's asking."

"Done," she said. "You look tired. Better get out of here before somebody spots you and wants another consult."

Wearily I waved to Melissa as I headed down the hall in Psychiatry but she stopped me. "Message," she said. I glanced down at the slip of paper she held out. It was simply an extension number at the hospital and the name Zania.

"This is it?" I asked.

"She just said to call."

"Is it a consult?" I said. Susan was right. I did not want another consult right now.

"I don't think so."

"Why not?" I didn't want to call right away if it was a consult.

"Just sounded like one of yours. Secretive, didn't want to leave her name."

"Consults don't always leave their name. It could be a consult."

"It could be the White House but I don't think so. She was scared."

"Um, probably one of mine."

9

"I need to talk to you about Reginald Larsen," she said as soon as she sat down. Zania was young, in her late twenties. I had given her an appointment time right away because she had sounded so tentative I figured she would change her mind if I didn't.

"Larsen," I said surprised. That was absolutely the last thing I expected.

"I worked with him, at Boston Harbor View," she said. "They called me and told me I could talk to you in confidence."

"You're the one?" I said, confused. "What are you doing up here?"

"I'm a general intensive care nurse," she said, "and there are only a couple of intensive care units in New England, outside of Boston. And I couldn't stay in Boston, not after . . ." Her voice trailed off.

It sounded reasonable, so reasonable I forgot the first rule of dealing with sex offenders, which is that there is no such thing as coincidence.

"They said it would be confidential," she added anxiously.

"Whoa," I said holding my hands up.

"First of all, you should know that if you tell me anything in confidence, I can't use it in any way. Confidence means confidence. Just don't tell me anything with the idea that you can tell me in confidence and I can still make use of it without admitting I know it." I had been down that road before.

There was silence. "But they said . . . I mean . . . I thought . . ." Her voice trailed off.

"I don't know what they told you. You can tell me something in confidence but there's not a lot I can do with it. If you tell me and allow me to use it but withhold your name, then you know better than I whether he would figure out who gave me the information. Frankly, usually people can. If you tell me and let me use your name, then I can certainly use it, but I don't know what you're afraid of. Are you afraid of Larsen?"

"Yes, but not just him."

"Who?"

"Well, it's the hospital too."

Now I was thoroughly confused. "Boston Harbor View? Why? Why don't you just tell me what's going on and we can figure out afterward what I can do with it. Okay?"

She paused for a moment. I had clearly taken her off balance with all my caveats and warnings. I had a moment of guilt. The woman was scared about something and I had started right in with the lawyer routine. But it was important, I knew, not to let people blurt things out with unrealistic expectations of how the information might be used later.

She spread her hands out on the table in front of her and looked down at them for a long time before she spoke. It was as though she were laying her cards out and considering them. "I worked at Boston Harbor View in the intensive care unit. I did something," she said so softly I could hardly hear her. I could see the tension in her hands increase and her knuckles turn white as she gripped the table. "Well, not really. I let him do something. I mean, I couldn't believe it. I just thought there must be a reason. He was so . . . so . . ." She stopped again.

"Why don't you start at the beginning. You worked at Boston Harbor View?"

"I did. I moved here in January." She paused again. "I was afraid. Look, there are some things even the hospital doesn't know."

"Okay. Like what? Wait a minute. What *does* the hospital know?"

She took a deep breath. "They know I walked into a room he was in and he had his finger in the vagina of a woman who was on a respirator. She was drugged, of course, to keep her from fighting the respirator." She paused. "She had a head injury and an open fracture of her tibia. There wasn't any reason for him to be touching her there." She paused again. "At least I think that's what he was doing. He had the sheets thrown back and it looked like his hand was . . . he jumped when I saw him but his finger was sticking up like . . . I think he had it inside her."

I didn't say anything. My opinion of Reginald had been on an elevator going down but Zania had just cut the wires.

"The hospital knows that," she added. "I finally told them."

"What don't they know?"

She took another breath. "They don't know he was in there often. I had started wondering why he came back to the ICU so often. Once his fly was open when he left a room and I was sure it wasn't open when he went in. I think it wasn't, anyway. He made a lot of rounds on people who were drugged or unconscious. But a number of people in intensive care are drugged or unconscious and most of them had had surgery. The thing was, though, they weren't all his patients."

"But didn't other people see him?" I said. "How could he do that in an intensive care unit? You have eighty-zillion people running around there."

"Well, it's not that simple. The anesthesiologists run intensive care. And they rotate, covering each other's patients. So they're always in there, all of them. He could see almost anybody and no one would question it.

"But he was just in there too much. So I got curious and I started checking the charts. Some of those cases he wasn't involved in at all and he wasn't covering them either."

"But if *you* noticed why didn't someone else?"

"Because," she said, looking embarrassed, "my

shift rotated so I was always with different people and I think he came in mainly on my shift."

"But why on your shift?" I said. "That would make it more likely he'd get caught. If any one person knew?" It was time for me to pick up the jaw I'd dropped on the floor and start figuring it out. I still didn't know why she was so frightened.

"Because," her voice dropped again and I strained to catch it, "because I was having an affair with him. I think if anybody said he was in there too much, he'd have just said he was visiting me."

"You were having an affair with him?" I said stupidly. She had just told me that. "Did you tell the hospital?"

She looked at me like I had two heads. "I'm a single mom. I have a little girl. If I lost my job . . . I let him go in. There wasn't really any reason for him to be checking on them that much, pulling the curtains around the beds. And then if it came out I was his girlfriend I'd have lost my job. I'd have lost it if they believed me and I'd have lost it if they didn't. Either way. I couldn't take a chance. I don't know if you have any idea," she said bitterly, "what it's like to be the sole support of a child?"

I didn't, but I sure had wanted to know. I tried to think what I would have done if my sweet baby had lived and I had been in Zania's situation. Hard to say. Maybe she was right. Maybe the hospital would have fired her. At least I could see why she'd be afraid of telling them. Jesus, she'd been in a bind.

"I didn't want to believe it," she went on. "And besides, what was I supposed to tell them? That he spent a lot of time with patients? I didn't really have anything. I didn't even know what he was doing there. So I just kept telling myself it was nothing, and then that day, his finger sticking out . . . I knew. And I just couldn't let it happen . . . so I told them about that. Just that time. That was all. As far as I know, that's all the hospital knows."

"But if they know that?" I was thinking out loud. Why were they even thinking of reinstating him? But even as I spoke I thought about how famous his discovery was about to make Boston Harbor hospital. Not bad for business to have somebody on the staff make a discovery like that. And all they had against him was one person's word. Still, there were those other reports, but it sounded like they might have come later, because they did suspend him after the second.

"I told them I wasn't sure. I said maybe," she admitted. "I told them I *thought* I saw it. But, to tell you the truth," she dropped her head, "I was pretty sure.

"Look, I didn't want him to know it was me. I just wanted to give them enough to investigate. But then . . ."

"What?"

"It was weird." She glanced up at me with a perplexed look on her face. "After I saw that, I broke it off. But even before then I'd been getting these phone calls." Involuntarily she shuddered. "The voice was disguised. I would hang up, but they kept coming. I told him about it but they never came when he was there.

"Then, after I broke it off, they got worse, only,

only the voice started talking about things that only he would know. It was him. At least I think it was." She shuddered. "It had to be him because no one else knew about the things the voice said.

"Look, I could understand it better if the calls had started after I broke it off. But he was still seeing me. We were sleeping together. And he was still making obscene phone calls. Isn't that weird?"

"Yep," I said truthfully. "It's weird." But not weird as in couldn't-happen weird. Weird as in sex-offender weird. Weird as in consensual-sex-is-not-that-big-a-thrill weird. As in scaring-people-out-of-their-wits-*is*-that-big-a-thrill weird.

"I even told his mother."

"Mrs. Larsen?"

"I knew her. I mean, he took me up here to meet her when we were going together. She lives around here. And I liked her right away. So, after the phone calls got bad, I called her."

"What did she say?"

"She didn't believe it for a second. She wanted to know how I could even think such a thing. But funny thing was, the phone calls stopped right after I told her. So maybe she said something to him after all.

"I hate this. I've been afraid since this started. Afraid of what he's doing to patients, afraid of the hospital finding out I knew, afraid of not having a job and not being able to support my daughter. Afraid of everything.

"I left my job because of this. I couldn't stand by and let him do those things. And I sure as hell couldn't stop him. I left Boston. I can't believe what's happened to my life. If he did anything to hurt my daughter," she said, "I'd—"

"Why do you say that?" I said, surprised. "Is there anything at all that makes you think he would hurt your daughter?"

"No," she said. "Not really." But something in the way she said it didn't sound right.

10

"He's threatening to sue," Marv said, barely crossing the threshold of my office the next morning before he started talking. He sat down heavily in the chair next to my desk.

I bit my lip. Of course he was threatening to sue. They all threatened to sue. "Jody's father?" I asked, although I knew who he was talking about. Marv closed his eyes and nodded. He didn't look well. His face was puffy and his clothes seemed more rumpled than ever. The colors looked as though someone on a bad LSD trip had put them together. I wondered idly if he had ever treated an artist. Not for long, I'd bet.

"Do you think he's innocent?" Marv said, perplexed. "Why would he want to go to court with this if he isn't?"

"Oh, Marv. That means nothing. These people posture all the time. They think it isn't true unless they say it's true. Sometimes they say they didn't do it so many times they half believe it themselves. Who knows?"

"This is dreadful." Marv sounded defeated and I was instantly annoyed. I didn't come from a line of folks who sat around saying everything was dreadful.

"Marv," I said, "the time to get cold feet was before this meeting, not now. Now you are in this up to your neck and there is nothing to do but suck it up. Who's his attorney?"

"He doesn't have one," he said.

"He's threatening to sue and he doesn't have an attorney? This isn't serious. He's just blustering. On second thought, tell him to get an attorney."

Marv was speechless. The whole idea of telling someone like Carlson, who was already threatening to sue, to get an attorney froze his blood.

"Marv, listen. If he works through the legal system he'll be much less likely to act outside it—as in shoot out your windows some night. And, frankly, after watching him operate, I think that's definitely a possibility." I saw Marv's face and was glad I hadn't been more graphic.

The alarm seemed to animate his depressed features for a moment and then a look of helplessness settled back in. What was wrong with him? This was the way it was sometimes. It wasn't the end of the world. Nobody was dead yet. A court case hadn't even been filed. Carlson was blustering, that's all. Marv was flagging in the second quarter. Where would he be if this thing went into overtime?

"All right," Marv said, but he sat there and didn't

move. "I suppose you're right," he said again but, still, he didn't move.

"What's wrong?" I asked.

"I don't like this case," he said simply.

I sat back and looked at him. I didn't know what he was talking about. Who liked any case of child abuse? "What do you mean you don't like this case?"

Marv reached for a Kleenex and blew his nose. "I just don't like it." It was not a very articulate reply and it was coming from a very articulate man. I had learned a long time ago that when people spoke awkwardly they spoke from the heart. The more articulate the comment, the more likely it had been rehearsed and discussed and over-intellectualized until the feeling was long gone from it, dead and buried. Live affect was a groping, stuttering, stumbling kind of thing. Marv was trying to tell me something that was very alive for him, too alive for him to say it very well. "It's too close," he said, and closed his eyes.

"Too close to what?" I said with some dread. Don't tell me Marv had been abused as a child. I was well aware the studies showed there were more than 38 million molested Americans out there—more people than voted for Walter Mondale in 1984—but did Marv have to be one of them?

"Michael," he said, "you don't understand. I don't like people very much."

I laughed. "You and me both. Remember that old song of the Kingston Trio, 'And I don't like anybody very much.' Join the club. Neither do I."

"Yes, you do," he said. "Yes, you do." Marv sat up a little and looked at me. "The distance in therapy, all the rules governing objectivity and keeping boundaries and maintaining therapeutic distance, all those matter to me in a different way than they do to you. For you, they are the only things that keep you from getting involved in your clients' lives and trying to solve all their problems for them. How many times have you wanted to take someone home and mother them?"

"Only the children," I said, caught off guard, and then regretted saying it. "And that's only natural," I said defensively. "Who could see what happens to kids and not want to take them home?"

"What I'm trying to say, Michael, is that I have never once wanted to take a client home and mother them."

"You work with adults."

"That's not the point. The point is the same restraints that keep you from getting too involved keep me from leaving altogether. Without that distance, I couldn't even be there. I really don't like being close to people, not personally. My therapy relationships are the closest, most intimate relationships I have, the closest relationships I have ever had."

What? How could that be? Therapy—the distant, one-sided relationship with people who never knew you, who only knew what they projected onto you—that was the closest Marv had ever come to intimacy? I was no winner in the intimacy department but I could say for sure that I had been a lot closer to people in my life than just being someone's therapist.

"Carlson accosted me in the parking lot this morning. The parking lot. I didn't even get into work. He had already been to my office, he said. But I wasn't there so he was outside waiting for my car. I didn't even get into my office before he found me. I was completely unprepared. This is not the kind of case I want to deal with. I don't want to get out of my car wondering who is going to accost me next."

"But wait a minute," I said, perplexed. "You've had so-called 'borderline' clients before who wake you up in the night, drive by your house, call you thirteen times a day, come hours early for therapy, maybe even wait for you in the parking lot."

"Ah, but they're my *clients*. We have a contract, so to speak. I can make bargains, set limits, hospitalize them, transfer them if I have to. I have absolutely no control over this situation. How do I transfer Carlson? Or Jody's brother, who called me again yesterday? To steal a phrase from you—they are 'in my face.'" Marv grimaced when he said it. No question, Marv was not into contact sports.

I didn't know what to say to Marv. I was still blown away by the idea that being somebody's therapist was the closest he had come to intimacy. On the other hand, was I kidding myself? What about me?

"Michael, do you remember E. B. White's statement about waking up every morning torn between wanting to save the world and wanting to savor it?"

"Sure," I said, and even the thought of it made me smile. "He said it made it hard to plan the day. I've always loved that."

"I never even understood it, not until I watched you. I've never wanted to save the day. I don't even want to be part of someone else saving the day."

"What do you mean 'watch me'? It's not my thing, either."

Marv looked at me as though he expected me to laugh and admit I was joking. When I didn't, he just said simply, "Michael, you never met a windmill you didn't want to tilt. There isn't a wrong you don't want to right. You don't even like nature because it's survival of the fittest and it isn't fair." Had I told Marv that? I didn't think I had told anybody that. He sighed. "I don't want to tilt at windmills. I just like the way they look on the skyline."

I did nothing useful for the rest of the morning. Marv's words kept rattling around inside my head. Therapy was as close to intimacy as he had ever come? That was a life? You were invisible in therapy. You knew people but they didn't know you. Not really.

On a good day, it was like being an emotional voyeur. No, that wasn't fair. On a good day it was like being a reed instrument. People's pain went through the therapist and the therapist reverberated to it and it came back to the client with a little more clarity, a little more form and—like something that goes through a series of pulleys—the weight of it seemed less because it was shared. Pain was never as oppressing when someone was holding your hand.

But it wasn't a life for either side. Not even close. It was a rehearsal for life for the client, a way to learn to trust without risk. The client didn't have to trade stories or keep things even. It was her time, her space. She wasn't going to be rejected no matter what, well, unless she shot out the therapist's windows or something.

And for the therapist? It was intimacy with a

safety harness on. The therapist took no risks at all, shared nothing of her life, put nothing on the line. A sort-of, kind-of intimacy, real to a point but, as a diet, it wasn't enough to keep a minnow alive.

So why was a man as kind and as bright as Marv feeding on it? Why wasn't he out there taking his chances in the real world with the rest of us?

And what about me? Did I really tilt at every windmill I could find? I liked to think of myself as a sort of grouchy gadfly, a difficult, even inconvenient, woman. I took great pride in being difficult. It would kill me to think I was some goody-two-shoes who ran around trying to right the world's wrongs. But I had to admit that nothing, absolutely nothing, ticked me off like somebody big picking on somebody little. So maybe I did spend my life running from one windmill to the next.

But between therapy as a place to fix the world's wrongs and therapy as a place to get a pseudo-intimacy fix, Christ, I'd go with saving the world. Still, I had to face it. Either one would put me in need of a good therapist.

At 11:30 I gave up pretending to work and went to the basement where I kept my bike. I retrieved my old, dented helmet and carried my bike up the stairs to the bright sunlight outside. Sweet Jesus, but sunlight could fix anything. I climbed on and swung out onto the roadway, exuberance replacing all the pondering and obsessing.

There was a bike path around a lake a couple of miles from the hospital and I took off for it like I was racing somebody or something. I switched into my highest gear even though I was going uphill and then stood up pedaling furiously. I just needed to do something with my muscles, get them moving, get some blood somewhere besides my brain. The sweet summer air blew by as I picked up speed.

Mark Twain was right. Why did people forever describe heaven as sitting on a cloud and playing a harp? People put everything in heaven they couldn't stand on earth. If people were so fond of harps they ought to try playing them right down here on earth. We had harps here. Lots of them. There didn't seem to be a stampede to get one.

And if sitting on clouds was such a big deal, people ought to get a bunch of cotton and try it out. Imagine going to church your whole life to sit on a cloud and play a harp without ever once finding out if you liked it.

No, heaven, if there was one, would have a lot of sweet breezes and a whole line of fine bicycles just waiting for you to jump on and stables full of thoroughbred jumping horses itching to go and, God knows, a few old-fashioned rickety gyms where the doors were always open and a pick-up game was always going on and there wasn't a single ballhog-runner-gunner in the lot. Maybe somebody who passed like Larry Bird just waiting to hit you with a needle-threading pass up the middle. I might take up church for a heaven like that.

Also chocolate, fat-free, sugar-free chocolate where you could eat tons of it and not gain an ounce. But heaven had no fat. In my heaven you could eat anything and you were lean and strong and trim no matter what. And sex, a sweet, loving man who kept a little distance.

Kept a little distance. Like that play-off pass that Isiah Thomas made inbounds that ended up in Larry Bird's hands with two seconds to go and the Celtics one point behind—where Isiah said afterward, he regretted it the moment the pass left his fingertips—like that pass I regretted the words the moment they slipped into my mind.

Kept a little distance. My little brain stopped thinking how sweet it all was; it just kept repeating the phrase: kept a little distance. As in problems with intimacy. As in how different was I from Marv? I was still pedaling but more glumly now. Whose team was I playing on? Maybe I was more like Marv than I wanted to admit. On impulse, I took a right-hand turn at the top of the hill and headed away from the lake toward town.

There was a bike rack right outside Adam's office and I parked my bike without even locking it. Hey, if you can't park your bike outside the police station in a small New England town without locking it, what is America coming to? I walked in and asked for Adam. A new guy I didn't know was at the desk. He called Adam and then told me I could go right in. He started to show me, but I knew the way.

I walked through the door and shut it behind me. Adam stood up. Funny, I thought only Southerners did that. On the other hand, it might not have been because I was a woman. It might have been because he didn't know what to expect.

"Hi," I said, and sat down, glumly slumping in the chair opposite him. I still had my helmet on.

"What's up?" he said, sitting back down. It appeared I had his undivided attention.

I was silent, trying to think of what to say. Finally I started, "This thing came up . . . it had to do with something else . . . I was wondering. Do you think I have a problem with intimacy?" Well, why beat around the goddamn bush?

Adam laughed, then caught himself. I wasn't laughing.

He got that bemused look in his eyes that part of me loved and part of me hated. It softened his whole face and the lines around his eyes, which always looked pretty good, looked even better with that soft, bemused look in them. On the other hand, I couldn't escape the feeling I was the reason for the look. Bemusement was a way of laughing at someone with some affection thrown in.

"What do you think?" he asked.

I looked at him and saw that the answer was so obvious he didn't want to say it.

I got up and started to leave. At the door I stopped. "Knob-turners," we therapists called them, the last-minute comments people made because they were on their way out and wouldn't have to stay and talk about it. I was, I guess, going to make one.

I turned back around, still with one hand on the door. "All right, I'm not the easiest person," I said. "So, why do you stay?"

I saw him struggle but realized, with more relief than I wanted to admit, it wasn't because he didn't have an answer. It was because, maybe, he had more than one. Finally, he said, "Because I love you." He folded his arms and sat back. He had just thrown a hard pass, a needle-threading pass up the middle, and he knew it. Adam wasn't anybody to beat around the bush either.

I stood there for a moment trying to hold on to the ball. Maybe I wasn't afraid of big cross-country jumps and havoc under the boards and all kinds of things other people were scared of, but I was surely scared of stuff like that. I didn't drop the ball. At least I don't think I did. When I had some kind of grip on it, I just nodded and left.

When I got back to the office I brought my bike to the basement and took the back stairs up. Enough obsessing already. Intimacy, fiddlesticks. If I couldn't distract myself from troubling questions with a bike ride, work, the great seducer, always beckoned. More people drowned their troubles in work than had ever picked up a bottle. I burst into my office with energy born of a need for distraction, only to stop dead in my tracks.

A small, blue-eyed, white-haired lady sat in the visitor's chair across from my desk. "Mrs. Larsen," I said, completely unable to hide my surprise.

"Oh, dear," she said. "I hope this was all right. Your secretary, that nice young Melissa, suggested I wait in here. She thought I'd be more comfortable than in the waiting room, but I can see you weren't expecting me, my dear. Am I intruding?"

"Oh, no. Of course, it's fine. I just took the back

stairs and didn't see Melissa. No, of course. It's fine
for you to wait in here." Mrs. Larsen was well known
in the hospital because of her husband and she
would be likely to get special treatment just about
anywhere in the whole place.

"I was over here visiting some friends in Pediatrics, although there's been so much turnover I
hardly know anyone anymore. But I don't need to
tell you that. I thought I'd stop by. I hope I'm not
interrupting. I could come back another time."

"No, no, I'm delighted to see you." Which wasn't
exactly true. Worse, I had a bad feeling it was obvious to Mrs. Larsen it wasn't true. And it wasn't just
Reggie. I'd never really been at ease with Mrs.
Larsen and I wasn't entirely sure why. But every time
I saw her I remembered a dinner party at their
house to which her husband had invited all the new
faculty years ago. Something must have happened
to give me such a strong feeling about her, but for
the life of me I couldn't remember what it was. I just
never liked her since.

I sat down facing her, trying to switch gears and
collect myself. Mrs. Larsen was neatly dressed in an
expensive plaid skirt and a cable-knit sweater. She
must have been well into her seventies but her face
was lively and her eyes quick. There were certain
things about her that reminded me of Mama.
Mama's sweater might have had sequins and she
wouldn't have looked New England country but the
face had that same even and appraising look.

I was not happy about this meeting and it was
more than my long-standing lack of ease with Mrs.

Larsen. I had a sense of dread at what my report would likely do to the woman in front of me and it was growing in my stomach by the minute. She had a dead husband and only one child. I would guess she took some major-league pride in Reggie. He was all she had left. Regardless of what he deserved, it was never the offender alone who suffered the consequences. The family always took it on the nose too. I might not be comfortable with Mrs. Larsen but I felt bad about what was about to happen to her life.

"I'm sorry," I said, catching myself drifting. "I'm not sure why you're here, but I have a feeling it's more than dropping by. Please tell me what I can do for you."

"To the point," she said. "That's what Reginald always liked about you. I remember the first Grand Rounds you ever gave. I think it was shortly after you were hired. Reginald came home chuckling. 'By God,' he said, and I still remember it. 'Psychiatry has done it this time. They've finally hired someone with some spunk. She'll shake the place up.' He always had a fondness for you."

"You must miss him terribly," I replied. "I know we sure do. But I have a feeling this isn't about him. This is about Reggie Junior."

"Yes," she laughed slightly, "of course it is. And I can't tell you how relieved I am that you're the one doing his evaluation. I thought he needed someone with some history, who understood the context— and the possibilities for treatment."

I paused. I didn't have any idea what she meant by "context."

"This is awkward, Mrs. Larsen. I don't have any release from Reggie to talk to you. Does he even know you're here? I can't answer any questions about him. And I don't have the slightest clue what you know about this."

She ignored my query. "Don't worry yourself. I'm not here to ask you questions. I'm here to give you information. I believe it's generally good practice to obtain a developmental history."

"When we can get it," I said, surprised. Mrs. Larsen was there only to give me a history? I couldn't believe it.

"Well," she said. "What would you like to know? You don't have to tell me anything. Ask me whatever you like. And in any case, I know quite a bit about what's going on already. My son and I have always been close, maybe too close for his good but that's another story. I got wind from ... someone ... he was having some problems and pried out of him what was going on. But I'll leave you to talk with him about his current problems. I'm here just to give you some background."

"Okay," I said, although I was still feeling uneasy about the whole thing with no clear idea why. "What can you tell me about his background?"

"He was adopted at a year," she said. "Did he tell you that? Never mind. He often doesn't tell people. Despite his rivalry with his father, he's very proud of him, you know. Always trying to live up to him, but that's another story too.

"He had some problems, well, it was to be expected. His mother was fourteen when he was born and it was a year before she let him go. She was not, I'm afraid, a very good mother. Not many fourteen-year-olds are. And I don't know anything about his father except that he deserted the mother before Reggie was born. I don't think he was another teen, though. She said something to her social worker about his being married.

"It saved our marriage. It saved . . . well, it saved a lot of things. I had been trying to get pregnant for over a decade. Maddening. My husband was affiliated with one of the best medical centers in the country. We were able to afford the best medical care, able to go anywhere, and no one could even tell us what was wrong. I was growing bitter. I'd always planned on having a big family and was in my thirties with nothing to show for it. Then this little one-year-old was admitted to the pediatric ward. Reginald came home talking about him—one of those sad failure-to-thrive kids. He weighed twelve pounds at a year—half dead, really, when they admitted him.

"I didn't pay any attention to it. Reginald often talked about his patients. But then he came home one day and sat down in the kitchen and just looked at me. 'What?' I said. 'What is it?'

" 'She wants to give him up,' he said. We were sitting in the kitchen. I remember it like it was yesterday. I just said 'Who?' but I knew, I knew who he was talking about.

" 'The failure-to-thrive,' he said, 'that cute little guy. She wants to give him up for adoption. She says she can't cope with him.'

"I hadn't wanted to adopt. I had wanted my own

children, our children, but I was having to face the fact it was never going to happen. Reginald wanted me just to go see him. So I went over there one day after my shift. I was a cardiac nurse when I met Reginald, you know, and I continued working after we married. Anyway, I stopped by the ward that day to see him.

"He was a pathetic-looking little thing, with that radar-scanning gaze that those undernourished, understimulated kids get. But when I came through the door his eyes stopped that blank gaze and he looked at me. He really looked at me. Well, that was it." She laughed. "I'd have taken him home on the spot if I could have.

"Oh, we did it properly. Hired a lawyer for the mother to represent her. Got her counseling. But she never wavered. She'd had it with being a mom and she wanted out. She meant it too. We paid the baby's medical bills and a stipend for the mother and we've never seen her since. I hope she made something of her life, poor thing."

I had been sitting quietly but I interrupted here. "You said he had problems. Did you mean the failure-to-thrive?" I asked.

"Oh, the physical problems were gone within a year," she said. "Once we got him settled, he ate like a horse. And developmentally, well, it was barely a year before he caught up there too.

"But there were other things. He was impulsive, terribly impulsive. We had an awful problem getting him to follow basic rules. He played with matches. He got up in the night and turned on the stove.

Once we found him down the street at the playground at five in the morning and he was barely three years old. I don't know how he got the door unlocked. I had quit my job right away when we brought him home and it was a good thing. No one could handle him but me. He was just too much trouble for a sitter.

"It was all so long ago. I don't know why it seems like yesterday. We got him straight, more or less. School came along and my, that was a different story. Bright as a new penny. And the day we bought him his first microscope the acting-out just stopped. Well, most of it, anyway. After that we had to take the microscope out of his room when we turned out the lights. Otherwise, we'd find him at midnight on the floor under the blanket with it still on. Science has always been what he did best and what he loved. Which was fortunate because that was one place he and his father could definitely meet. Maybe the only place."

"No problems after that?"

"I didn't say that. I said *most* of the acting-out stopped. But he still had a problem with girls. Not young girls, always girls his own age, and who could argue with that? At least that's what I told myself. I told myself he was just all boy.

"The teachers called repeatedly. He was grabbing girls in class, feeling them up, pulling down their pants. All that impulsiveness seemed to come out in just one way. Everywhere else he got it under control but he just couldn't leave the girls alone. He never seemed to understand that the girls didn't like being grabbed and poked." Or maybe, I thought, he didn't care.

"In all fairness," she continued, "you should see what they were wearing. It was a wonder all the boys weren't grabbing at them."

It was on the tip of my tongue to comment but I kept my mouth shut. Mrs. Larsen's thinking errors in defense of her son weren't any of my business. She wasn't my client and confronting her might shut her up. "May I ask you some questions?"

"Certainly."

"At what age did he start grabbing girls?"

"Six, maybe, or seven."

"How many times did you get called?"

"Oh, Lord, between the teachers and other parents, it felt like I was in the school every other week. I don't know exactly. Frequently, that's all I can say. A couple of times a month, maybe. He was almost suspended in fourth grade. We had to pay for an aide for a while, a one-to-one aide, just to keep him in school. It was embarrassing, I can tell you that."

"How long did it last?"

"It was always a problem. Until high school, anyway. He seemed to settle down then." Or maybe, I thought, it went underground, remembering the obsessive peeping Reggie described in his autobiography.

"What did you do about it?"

"We tried counseling, but Reggie just refused to go. Said he didn't need it. Just refused." I raised my eyebrows. How could an elementary school kid in that much trouble "refuse" to go to counseling and get away with it? But Mrs. Larsen ignored the implicit question. "We talked to him about it, of course, well, I did. Reginald pretty much left the parenting to me. He spent most of his time here at the hospital. I know how much he was loved in the medical center but there was a price to be paid for that. Reggie Junior once told me the strongest memory of his childhood was the side door slamming when his father left in the night to go back to the hospital."

I left that one alone too. "How about other problems? Stealing? Vandalism? Disruptive in class? Lying to you? Staying out at night? Aggressiveness to other kids?"

"Oh, no, no, no," she said. "He really did very well, except for this one thing. He just could not seem to learn."

Which meant he wasn't a psychopath or he'd have been acting out everywhere. But he sure had a big sexual problem and an old one.

"Michael," she said, then paused. Oh, boy, I thought, here it comes. "My son may need treatment. I wouldn't argue with you there. I can make sure, believe me, that he gets it."

It was on the tip of my tongue to say that she had her shot when he was six. It was true that if she couldn't control Reggie then, she sure as heck couldn't control him now, but this was passion, not logic, talking to me.

"I'm not telling you what your report should say, but I can tell you that none of this, and I think you know this, has anything to do with his research. He

is a gifted researcher and his work can save lives. I
hope you don't cast such a pall over his career that
he can't do his work. Because I think that would kill
both of us."

"Mrs. Larsen—"

"No, hear me out. Recommend treatment if you
want. I'm sure you will. Tell him he has to be super-
vised when he sees female patients, if you must. But
don't destroy the career of the most promising researcher in anesthetics of his generation. What
would be the point? And are you prepared to take
responsibility for the people who will die if approval
of his test is delayed because of controversy sur-
rounding his name?"

I sat back and paused. I hated what I was going to
say to her and I knew she'd hate hearing it but I
could not figure out anything else to say. "Mrs.
Larsen, I once had a lawyer call me and ask me if I
could alter a report to keep from ruining a prominent architect's career. He said to me that surely I
didn't want to destroy such a wonderful career, as
though it were my actions and not his client's that
were the problem.

"I told him that when a poor man commits a sexual offense, he doesn't just lose a career, he loses
everything. He loses his job, he loses his ability to
support his family and most of the time, poor men go
to jail and rich men don't. That job may not impress
the lawyer, but it surely matters to the man's family.

"It's a slippery slope, altering reports according
to how 'important' or how 'useful' someone is. It's
not a slope I can go down. Reggie has made some

choices. I don't know all of them yet, but by the time this is over, I'm likely to know some of them. Depending on what they are, he's made his own decisions about his career."

She sighed and picked up her purse. "Reginald Senior said some other things about you too. Do you want to hear them?"

"Well—"

"He said you were stubborn as a mule and it would get you in a lot of trouble someday. Reginald is not the only one who is making choices that could affect him."

I hadn't been angry until she said that. "Those things are true, Mrs. Larsen. I am stubborn as a mule and it may interest you that it gets me in trouble just about every day. And you should know that if you'd like to complain to my chairman, you may have to get in line.

"But tell me one thing. Was this what you said to the teachers when they called? Did you ever ask someone not to report him, or not to suspend him or not to expel him because of how bright he was or how talented or because it would taint his future? Did you ever consider taking his goddamn microscope away from him and telling him he wouldn't get it back until he quit grabbing girls?"

"His father talked to you," she said, "back when you were friends. I should have known."

"No, actually, he didn't. He didn't talk to me at all. I'm just going by what you're trying to do right here in this room right now. Don't misunderstand me. I can't tell you if you hadn't done those things, he'd be different today, because I don't know that for a fact. But I can tell you protecting him from the consequences of his behavior was never going to help. It could only make him worse. It could only make him worse then and it will only make him worse now."

She stood up. "You don't understand what it's like to be a mother," she said, and the pain of her comment shot through me. It was a small community and she clearly knew how much the comment meant. "It's a mother's job to protect her child." And that hurt too. Easy for a woman who hasn't faced SIDS to tell another woman she should have protected her child.

"Not from himself," I said. "You can't protect him from the consequences of his own behavior. Sooner or later he has to pay the piper."

She clutched her pocketbook and turned to leave. At the door I stopped her. "Mrs. Larsen, may I ask you one more question? Did you really recommend me to Reggie? Did you really tell him I should do the eval?"

"No," she said, "I most certainly did not. I've known who you were for a long time. I told him it would be the worst mistake of his life."

Relief flooded over me. I wasn't Reggie Jr. and I had a hell of a time betraying the trust of people who expected me to help them. Far better for me if they saw me as the Wicked Witch of the West from the start. That I could live with.

She looked surprised for a moment at the relief on my face but I said nothing to explain it. We looked at each other for another moment. The distance between us in the room was only a few feet but it might as well have been the Grand Canyon. She had some fantasy I could save Reggie and refused to. I had a rock solid belief she'd spent her life making him worse and was still at it. Between those two there wasn't enough common ground for a mouse to walk a tightrope. There were no more pleas or threats. We surveyed the gap between us and then without a word she left.

II

"We sell fear," John Davis had said to me once, and watching Reginald Larsen on the video screen, unnaturally still and wary, it seemed clear he had bought some.

"Sit down," was all Davis had said when he and Reggie entered Davis's polygraph room. The room was basically the size of a closet, with nothing on the walls and nothing on the desk except Reggie's revised sexual autobiography and a computerized polygraph machine. On John's side of the two-person desk sat a monitor, a keyboard and cables. The cables led from the machine to the other side of the desk where sensors for monitoring respiration, blood pressure and skin conductance were conspicuously laid out in front of Reggie.

"You need to understand something about this polygraph instrument, Dr. Larsen." John sat down and patted the polygraph on his desk fondly. "I'm sure it's not as sophisticated as the machinery you're used to in medicine. The truth is, it's really a very crude little machine but, what it does, it does very well. Sort of like your stethoscope, I imagine." He stood up and walked around the side of the desk to where Larsen was sitting and stood where Larsen had to look up at him. The man who had moved into Larsen's space with such authority was a tall, lanky Southerner in a cream colored suit. He had a buzz cut and a face full of angles. He looked like a former Marine and he was.

"What it will tell me, without any doubt, is whether you're lying or not. But what it won't tell me is whether it's a big lie or a little lie. It won't tell me that." He was starting to roll into his pitch and I heard the Southern rhythms coming back into his speech. The accent had no region but when Southern rhythms started, a Southern accent was sure to follow.

"So what you need to know is that if you lie to me about anything, anything at all, if you tell me any itty bitty little white lie of any kind, I'm going to have to tell Dr. Stone that you are a *liar.* Any lie at all will trigger this little baby. No matter how small." He paused and walked back behind his desk. Reggie seemed mesmerized. He hadn't moved a muscle since John began.

"Now, Mr. Larsen, I surely—and I truly mean this," he leaned on the small desk looking straight at Reggie, "I surely would hate to tell Dr. Stone that you're a liar because there's nothing worse on the face of this earth. Nothing.

"You may think you're here today to find out what you done wrong. But that's not it. That's not it at all. Now, what I'm saying to you is very important and you need to listen up because we have got to get this straight with each other right from the start. I don't care if you raped and murdered forty-seven *thousand* people. Ain't nothing you can do about that now. But son," he leaned forward and his voice dropped so low I could barely hear it, "don't you lie to me." John paused and the silence was palpable. "Because a man who'll lie, well, he'll do just about anything."

Reggie looked stricken—and not because someone younger than he had called him "son." He opened his mouth to speak but John held up his hand, stopping him, and then got up and started pacing the small room. When he stood up, his six-two frame seemed bigger than when he had sat down. Six-two isn't always six-two. Sitting in a tiny room with someone who has a lot of say over your future, it grows considerably. John was currently looking roughly the size of Shaquille O'Neal.

"So let's get over the idea you're here today to find out what you did wrong. In fact, I got news for you, partner. I've taken a look at your autobiography and we already know you did some things you're not proud of. And I know it must have been hard for you to admit that. I respect a man who'll stand up for the things he's done wrong in his life. Anybody'd respect that.

"Hell, ain't none of us," John winked at Reggie, "I mean, you're not going to find a man who ain't done something some people think is wrong when it comes to sex." He turned his back on Reggie and threw off the next line like an aside. "I don't think

I'd trust a goody-two-shoes if I found one. Probably some kind of fairy." I couldn't help but roll my eyes. John wasn't in the slightest homophobic, but he'd use just about anything to make Reggie feel better about confessing.

"No, we're not here to find out whether you've done a few things you probably ought not to have done." A few things? As in fifty pages and twenty-five years? "We're here to answer only one question." He'd moved back toward Reggie at this point and now he leaned down, putting one hand on the polygraph chair Reggie was sitting in and one on the desk next to it. His face was inches from Reggie's. Reggie recoiled automatically but there wasn't any place to go. "Like I said, son, we're here to see if you're a *liar.*" He stood up. "That's it, pure and simple."

Reggie tried to speak again but John silenced him once more. "Now I know what you're thinking. How're you going to know? How good is that little gadget? Well, I'll tell you how good it is. It'll tell me what you're thinking. You don't believe me? Why don't we try it? Put your arm out here." Reggie reluctantly held his arm out on the school-type desk he was sitting at and John expertly started attaching the sensors. Reggie stared at the sensors on his body like they were octopus tentacles about to jerk him underwater.

John sat down across the desk and turned on a computer monitor. "Now Reggie, I want you to think of a number from one to ten and I want you to write it on this sheet of paper." He passed a piece of paper and a pen over to Reggie. Reluctantly Reggie picked it up. He looked at it suspiciously like the whole thing was some kind of trick. "Go ahead," John said. "Just write it down. Now turn that paper over and you keep it and don't tell me what's on it."

Reggie wrote something down and folded it over a couple of times, then covered it with his hand. "I don't want you to say a word. Just listen. One," John began, speaking slowly and pausing. ". . . two . . . three . . . four." He stopped and studied the monitor. "It's four, isn't it?" Reggie didn't say anything. He just sat there with his hand still covering the paper. "Could I see the paper?" John asked. Silence fell. Reggie didn't move his hand. He just swallowed hard. He seemed frozen to the spot. "I don't need to see the piece of paper, do I?" John asked.

"All right, then," he said, and moved around to take the sensors off. "Before I run the real test, I want to ask you some questions." He went back and sat down behind his desk. "Let me just take a little look at what you've written here. I looked at it before but now I want to go back over it and be sure I've got everything straight." Reggie's autobiography was sitting conspicuously on John's desk and he picked it up and started reading.

Reggie took advantage of the silence to try to get a word in. "But Mr. Da . . ."

"I'll be with you in a minute," John said without even looking up. He kept reading. He read on and on, although I knew he had read the whole thing carefully before Reggie came in. Every once in a while, he would make an "umph" sound or raise his eyebrows and take a couple of notes in a small notepad on the desk. Mostly though, he just read, turning each sheet over carefully and laying it exactly on top of the previous one.

Reggie stared at him for a few moments and then, as the minutes went by, began to look around the room. But there was nothing to look at. The entire room was as Spartan as a monk's cell. Inevitably, he came back to watch John's careful, precise reading and turning of the pages.

At least thirty minutes passed before John came to the last page. He turned the last page over, folded his hands on the desk and looked at Reggie. He said nothing at all. Reggie met his eyes for a few minutes, but under John's intense scrutiny, he looked away. Finally John spoke. "Now Reggie, I'm not here to insult your intelligence and I hope you're not here to insult mine." Silence fell again.

Tentatively Reggie spoke, but this time John didn't interrupt him. "What do you mean?" he squeaked.

"I think you know exactly what I mean and I'm going to give you a few minutes to think about it." With that, John got up and abruptly left the room.

I watched Reggie for a moment. He sat slumped in his chair and then he got up and started pacing. He never once glanced at the two-way mirror, even though he knew I was there. That one small room had become, for the moment, his entire universe. John walked into the booth, lit up a cigarette and sat down across from me.

"How's it going?" I asked.

"I don't think it's going to be a problem," he said, stretching and looking bored. "So what's up with you these days?"

"Same old, same old," I said. "Perps everywhere. Unfortunately, that means victims everywhere too. Lots of deviancy in the world. I'm never going to run out of business, that's for sure. How about you?"

He looked at his shoes. "Mary Lou's in an inpatient unit again," he said evenly. John's wife had a severe alcohol problem and had fallen off more wagons than most people had ever climbed on.

"Ah, I'm sorry. Let me know if there's anything I can do."

"You want to know something funny," he said. "After twenty years I can spot lying a mile away but not with her. I never figure it out until she's falling-down drunk."

"Makes a difference when you don't want to know," I said softly.

"Ain't it the truth," he said. We sat in silence for a few minutes watching Reggie pace. Finally, John got up and snubbed out his cigarette. "He's a sleaze," he said.

"Excuse me?"

"He's a sleaze."

"What do you mean?" At least half, probably more of the people John tested were liars and criminals of all sorts. He'd tested more murderers than I'd read about in the newspaper, so for John to call somebody a sleaze meant a little more than it would if anybody else had said it. He had quite a comparison group.

"I'll get something out of him," John said, "but he won't come clean. He's one of those onion types. You just peel them and peel them but you never get to the bottom of it. He'll flunk in the end, no matter what he admits to," he said. "Power and control. He'll withhold something, just to feel like he won."

"Just get the anesthesia stuff," I said. "I don't care about anything else. I've got to protect a source."

"Do my best," he said, and headed out the door.

John walked into the room and sat down in his chair without a word. When Reggie didn't sit down immediately, he said, "Sit down, Reggie," with a trace of irritation in his voice. Reggie immediately sat down. People didn't like irritating their polygraph examiners any more than they liked irritating, well, their surgeons. "All right," John said. "What have you decided? Is there anything in that sexual autobiography you would like to change before we get started?"

Reggie looked indecisive but shook his head no. "It's all there," he said.

John smiled slightly, conveying a good deal of skepticism, but he didn't comment. "All right, then let me just go over what I'm going to ask you on the polygraph." John settled in with his baseline questions, Reggie's name, where he lived—questions we could be sure he wasn't lying about. All that would help establish what Reggie's physiological responses were when he was telling the truth.

Then came the tricky part. John had to establish a control lie—something we knew Reggie was lying about. That way, when he was hooked up to the machine later, John could ask him the question he knew he would lie about to get a baseline for lying. "Have you ever in your life stolen anything?" he said.

"Uh, maybe when I was a kid," Reggie replied.

"Well, all kids take little things but not since the age of eleven—no, make it fourteen, have you? I mean you haven't stolen anything since the age of fourteen, have you?"

"Not really."

"I thought not. A man of any honor at all wouldn't even take a pencil home from the office that didn't belong to him. He wouldn't take a paper clip. He wouldn't borrow some paper if he ran out. You've never done anything like that, have you?"

"Well, I don't know, maybe a pencil or something."

"How many times?"

"What?"

"How many times have you taken something from the office that didn't belong to you? It wouldn't be over five times, would it?"

"I don't think so."

"You don't think so? I don't want you to guess. Give me a high number. A high number. I want a high number. You haven't taken anything from the office more than ten times, have you? I mean borrowing a couple of paper clips a couple of times might be understandable, but taking things home from the office over ten times? Well . . ."

"No, I'm pretty sure I haven't taken anything from the office over ten times."

"I don't want you to be pretty sure. Give me a high number, son, a *high* number. Let's say fifteen times if you're not sure about ten. You haven't taken things from the office more than fifteen times, have you? If I ask you if you've stolen more than fifteen

times since the age of fourteen, you can honestly answer 'no,' can't you? Hell, there are some criminals
who haven't stolen fifteen times since the age of
fourteen and they're in jail for it."

Of course, given that thirty years or so were involved, that meant that Reggie would have had not
to bring home from the office more than one pencil
every two years. Nobody could really answer "no" to
that with any confidence.

"Sure," Reggie said, "but what's this got to do
with what I'm here for?"

"I'll ask the questions, son."

I saw Reggie flush with anger but he didn't say
anything. John acted like he didn't notice and kept
going. He went over the "relevant" part of the polygraph, the questions about any sexual contact with
patients and staff not listed in the autobiography
and then he stopped. It was all part of building the
tension.

"Why don't we just get started on the real thing?"
he said. He attached the sensors carefully. He put a
tube around Reggie's chest to monitor his breathing, attached a sensor to his fingers recording gal-
vanic skin response, and a cardiograph cuff to his
upper arm recording blood volume and heart rate.
After they were attached John asked Reggie to sit as
still as possible and dutifully, Reggie complied.

I wondered if some of the effectiveness of "that
little gadget," and the astonishing number of con-
fessions that followed failing it, didn't have something to do with the way John was progressively
controlling Reggie. Early on, he had refused to let

him talk and now he was controlling even his slightest movements. The room had so little stimulation in it that John had become the entire focus of Reggie's attention and as time went on, I knew, the outside world would seem to fade entirely.

With all his sophistication, Reggie wasn't immune to that kind of pressure. John was big to begin with, but somehow Reggie seemed to be looking up to him more and more as time went on.

John ran through all the questions he had gone over with Reggie in advance, carefully watching the computer the whole time. His voice was a monotone. Reggie squirmed but held to his story. His autobiography was accurate, he said. No, he hadn't left anything out and everything in it was true. When it was done, John ran the whole thing again, and finally he ran it a third time. He always ran three charts on a polygraph and compared them.

Silently, John took all the sensors off and then sat down at his desk again. He went over the results on the computer carefully, clicking back and forth between screens, occasionally typing. I noticed he didn't offer Reggie a break. When he finished, he stared at Reggie for a few moments and then he said, "Dr. Larsen, you have made a serious mistake here today. You have sat here and lied to me, knowing there is nothing in this world that I hate more than a liar and *nothing*, and I do mean *nothing*, that I like better than seeing that one is punished to the full extent of the law." Reggie was silent.

"Let me show you something, Reggie. Take a look at this chart." John held out the chart the computer had printed out. "Now where do you see it spike?" Reggie looked uncertain but he took the chart and pointed. "And what do you see next to that? Read those numbers for me, please."

Reggie read, "R-three."

"All right, here is the list of questions that I asked you. Would you read R-three, please."

Reggie read silently and John said, "Out loud, please."

"Have you left any sexual contacts with patients or staff out of your sexual autobiography?"

"That's where the spike is?"

Reggie didn't say anything. He just kept staring at the chart.

"So you're telling me you lied to that question." Reggie seemed mesmerized by the chart. I thought I saw him swallow.

"And for what? To protect something, something that, in the scale of things that I have seen, can't be all that much—not unless you've murdered several of your patients in cold blood. No doubt you're protecting some minor sexual escapades." John's voice sounded weary. "And for that you have branded yourself a liar. And what that means is that I could never recommend, and I'm sure Dr. Stone could never recommend, that you *ever* practice medicine again."

Reggie opened his mouth to speak, then shut it again. Even from the booth I could see the indecision in his eyes. Should he fess up now? Would it help—or should he hold his ground?

"You see, Reggie. I told you from the start. When

a man is lying to me," John said, leaning back and crossing his arms, "I just can't be sure what he's done. I'm being as fair with you as I know how. I'm pretty good at what I do and when a man keeps lying to me, no matter how I put it to him, no matter how I try to make it clear I don't care what he's done, that I just care about *lying*, then I have to figure he's got something real important to hide, real important. Well, there's only one thing that's that important. And that's if he is killing people. If he's not killing people, well, hell, where's the harm? But if he's busy putting stuff in those IV's he shouldn't be, turning them on when they ought to be off," John leaned forward and his eyes narrowed, "well, that would be worth lying about."

"Oh, no," Reggie said standing up. "No, no, no. If that's what you think ... I would never ... I have never ... no, no, absolutely not."

"Sit down, Reggie," John said. "You never can tell. You're hiding something, and if that isn't what you're hiding, I can't for the life of me imagine why you'd bother to lie to me about anything else. Anything at all. Rape never left a woman that bad off. Not unless somebody beat her to death, too. Now if you're beating them half to death after you're raping them, well then ..."

I wondered idly what John said to his murderers. Maybe something like, "Hell, killing somebody isn't that bad, not if you do it quick. You didn't cut 'em up slowly while they were still alive, did you, and then mail their body parts to a relative?"

Reggie was in shock. He stood still for a moment

and then he sat down. "All right," he said. "There was a little more, but nothing like what you're thinking. Nothing like that. Some of the women were . . . maybe they were asleep or something, but I wasn't really sure," he added quickly. "I mean sometimes women pretend they're asleep when they're awake. You know, so they don't have to admit they're agreeing."

"Reggie," John said. "Maybe somebody else could get away with that story. But not you. Not a doctor. No, because you know. You know the difference in somebody who's asleep and who's awake, the difference in somebody who's unconscious and who's asleep, the difference in someone who's *dead* and who's asleep. Quit yanking my chain. It's not all and you know it."

Silence fell.

"Were they dead?"

"What?"

"I mean, if they were unconscious, I can't believe you'd lie about that. Well, hell, that's not as bad as raping them when they're awake. If they're unconscious, what's the harm in that, they wouldn't even know. But if they were dead—even if you didn't kill them—well, there's something really sick about that."

"They weren't dead," Reggie said, quickly. "Nobody was dead."

"All right," John said. "Go on."

12

I staggered out into the sunlight in a daze. Jesus Christ, the stuff people could get away with—for years and years and years. Once people trusted someone, they didn't see what they didn't want to see, didn't expect to see.

I drove over to my private practice with my head full of Reggie Larsen, and sat down to write. There was no point in putting off the evaluation on Larsen any longer. I knew what I needed to know, which was that he shouldn't be allowed anywhere near a patient. What's more, the chances increased with every mile that Larsen drove back toward Boston that he would realize I'd decide that and pull his release for the evaluation rather than having the hospital see the one I'd write. So now, while I still had a release, was the only opportunity I'd have to keep a few dozen more women from being raped while they were unconscious.

The phone rang. I decided to ignore it but I did turn up the sound on the answering machine just to see who it was. When Adam's warm tones drifted out, I changed my mind and picked it up. "Ah, Michael," he said. "Glad I caught you."

"Nice night," I said. "Sorry I had to leave."

"How's the kid?"

"Better," I said, "but I still haven't heard about his parents." Which reminded me I needed to check.

"Business," he said.

"Okay," I said.

"When was the last time you saw Sam Carlson?"

My stomach dropped. "Why?"

There was a pause. Police just naturally had an aversion to giving out information, but Adam went on, "He's missing."

"Missing? Since when? As in what kind of missing?"

"Yesterday morning, according to his wife, Sam Carlson took a rifle, put it into the car, drove away from his house and disappeared. He didn't say anything to her about where he was going. He never showed up at work and no one's seen him since."

"Have you talked to Marv?"

"Not yet. When his son mentioned you were involved, I thought I'd call you first."

"Well, the scoop is he accosted Marv in the parking lot yesterday morning but he didn't have the gun, at least Marv didn't see one. I'm sure he'd have mentioned it if he had," I said dryly. "This whole thing is over a case. Do you know about that?"

"Only what the family has told me. Crazy daughter.

False accusation of child sexual abuse. Suggested by her therapist."

"Adam, get a grip. Her therapist is Marv. Do you think Marv runs around talking people into false accusations of child sexual abuse?"

"I'm just telling you what the family told me. That's all. Now what can you tell me?"

"Nothing. Unless you get permission from them."

"You can if there's a chance he'll harm himself or others." True enough. The Tarasoff decision in California had made it quite clear there were limits to therapeutic confidentiality.

I sighed. "If I had any evidence he would harm himself or somebody else, I'd have warned somebody already."

"But taking a gun and disappearing just might change your opinion."

"It might. Oh, shit, Adam. Call Marv and meet me at Psychiatry and we'll talk about it."

I headed over to Psychiatry with hardly a glance at the fax machine. Surely, I had a few hours before Reggie got back to Boston and started thinking about what he'd told John Davis. Surely I had that much. Besides, a man with a gun took precedence over just about everything else.

The camera caught my eye first—that and the crowd. The television crew was interviewing someone right outside the main doors of Jefferson Hospital, using the hospital for a backdrop. Television crews were rare at Jefferson Hospital. We didn't see enough violence or build enough new wings to bring the TV people very often. On impulse, I pulled over and parked in front instead of heading for the employee parking lot. I just needed to know this had nothing to do with Sam Carlson and his gun.

I sat in the car for a few minutes drinking a Diet Coke and thinking. The last thing I wanted was a confrontation on TV with some irate family member, but even if this had something to do with Sam, nobody in the family except Jody knew what I looked like. I had been in the observation booth and had never met Sam or his wife.

I got out of the car and edged slowly over to the edge of the crowd, trying to get close enough to see if I recognized anyone. A woman in a lavender knit suit was talking with animation to the camera. Facing her was a young woman with a manufactured smile and a large microphone. Next to the lavender suit, looking awkward and uncomfortable, was a tall, thin man with large hands. His size didn't have anything to do with Sam Carlson, but his face did. This must be Jody's brother. He was staring at the sidewalk and looking like he didn't much want to be there. On the other side of him stood a middle-aged woman with a tight jaw and a set hairdo whom I didn't know.

But I surely did know the woman in the lavender suit.

I stepped back behind some of the crowd and peered over someone's shoulder. Maybe Sam Carlson's son wouldn't recognize me but Leila, the lavender suit, surely would. The young woman with the plastic smile asked Leila another question and held out a mike. I edged closer to catch the response.

"Yes, this has happened all over the country. Numerous people have not just been sued, they have gone to *jail,* on the basis of so-called 'recovered memories of child sexual abuse' suggested by unscrupulous, money-hungry therapists. It's a national disgrace. These people ought to lose their licenses. And I just hope, this time," she looked directly into the camera and said ominously, "it doesn't have tragic results."

"Okay," the interviewer said, and instantly the cameraman shut down and turned away to pack up. The woman with the set jaw stood hesitantly for a moment like she was surprised it was over so fast but Leila was already heading through the front doors into the hospital. I edged around the crowd and headed through the doors after her.

"Leila," I called out as she headed across the lobby. She stopped and turned.

"Well, Michael," she said. I'd known alligators with warmer smiles. Still it wasn't the smile, it was the eyes that always made the hair stand up on the back of my neck.

"You just missed our little press conference. You could have been in it," she said. I fell in step with her and we headed toward the elevators.

"And why don't I think that would have been a good idea? Got a live one?"

"As if you didn't know. You're being coy, my dear. You're in this one up to your neck."

"Really? Am I now? Who's your grim-looking traveling companion?"

"Suzy Cartwheel? She's the new head of the local AFAF. You'll be hearing a lot from her, I'm sure. Terrible case. Son falsely accused her husband of sexually abusing him as a child."

"And you testified he didn't."

"Of course."

"Ever meet the son or did you just wing this from what the dad said?"

"Didn't need to meet him. These cases are all alike."

"I see. And the new Mercedes? Or is it a Rolls?"

"Mercedes suits me fine. A Rolls would be so . . . ostentatious."

"And telling."

"Now, now."

"How's your travel schedule? Still on the road?"

"Everywhere, you wouldn't believe how many cases like this there are."

"Ah, but I would."

"You should join me, Michael. You'd be very effective at this."

"A special place in hell, Leila."

"On the contrary, haven't you heard? I'm being compared to Schindler. So little time, so many poor, falsely accused men and women, rotting in jail. A national disgrace."

"Brilliant marketing but hello, who do you think you're talking to?" Schindler. Jesus, he must be whipping around in his grave like an eggbeater.

Leila laughed. "Oh, I know you and here's what you should know. You're swimming against a rip tide, my dear, while I'm surfing my way to Oprah. You're going to be drowning in my wake."

"Doesn't make you right."

"As if that mattered."

"Did to Schindler."

The elevator came and Leila took it, but something about being locked up in a small box with Leila didn't appeal so I took the stairs to my office two at a time, instead. I tried to shake her off on the way. Swamp alligators and court whores would always be with us. Nothing to do but live with it.

I checked in with Melissa on my way by. Adam and Marv were in Marv's office, she said, and waiting for me.

"Oh, Michael," Marv said when he saw me. He seemed to be sweating although the air conditioning was working fine. "Thanks for coming. Adam here wants me to tell him about the Carlson case and there is the issue of confidentiality."

"Actually, I don't think so. I thought about it on the way over. Sam was never your client. Jody is your client and Jody can give permission."

Marv's face lit up. "Of course," he said.

"She's still an inpatient?"

"Oh, yes," he said. "I'll go up and get her to sign a release."

Marv left and I said to Adam, "I'll tell you what I know anyway. If Jody won't sign, which she will, I think you're right. Sam Carlson with a gun is a scary thought."

I gave him an abbreviated version of Jody's story complete with Carlson's explosion in the therapy session and my helplessness in the booth. "Believe it or not, this whole thing is not so unusual these days, except for one thing."

Adam had hardly moved during all this. "Which is what?" he said now.

"Most perps are pretty devious and controlled. They put on a good show of innocence. Carlson was different. Very volatile. That is one angry man and I don't think he even tries to stay in control. Never had to."

"So what's he doing with the gun, given what you've seen?"

"I don't know. Whatever he damn well feels like doing with it. He's used to running the show."

"Is he mad enough to shoot somebody?"

"Yeah, maybe. But Marv would be pretty high on his list and he didn't even show him the gun."

"Which may not be a good sign," Adam said.

"Which may not be a good sign," I agreed.

We talked for a few more minutes and then Marv showed up not just with a release but with Jody in tow. "This is Jody Carlson," he said formally to Adam. "She wanted to join us."

Jody was in jeans and a tee-shirt. Her arm was bandaged and her eyes had that hollow look people's eyes get in the bad times. She perched hesitantly on the edge of the couch. "What's this about my father?" she asked. I looked at the strain on her face and felt my heart drop. Oh, shit, she still loves him, in spite of it all, she does.

"He's missing," Adam said quietly. "He . . ." I saw Adam hesitate, then he went on, "left yesterday morning. He didn't tell your mother where he was going. When he didn't return by this morning your family called us. Do you have any idea where he might be?"

"Nope," she said quickly. "Was he mad . . . at me?"

She sounded fearful and even without knowing about the gun, it's clear that violence had crossed her mind.

Adam shrugged. "Your mother says they didn't fight. He just got up without a word, got dressed, and left."

"Actually, Jody," I interrupted, "your family has decided Marv and I are the problem. I don't think they're so mad at you right now."

Jody looked glum. "He'll make somebody pay," she said. "When my dad gets mad, somebody pays for it. Always. Each and every time."

"How?" I asked.

Everybody looked at me. "I mean, does he yell or guilt trip or hit or what? Did he threaten?"

"Oh, he hit plenty. Mostly my mother. And me some, when I wouldn't do what he wanted. My mother for nothing. Just whenever."

"Guns? Did he ever threaten you with a gun?"

"Not really. I can only remember a couple of times in my childhood when he actually threatened to kill one of us with a gun, although he did wave them around a lot when he was mad."

We all sat silently for a few minutes while I tried to figure out what to say to someone who thought waving a gun around and threatening to kill a child with it was a "not really" kind of thing. Then Jody put her hand over her stomach and said, "I don't feel well. I have to go."

Marv stood up and showed her to the door—the inpatient unit was only one floor up—then sat back down looking almost as glum as Jody had. "Leila's involved," I said to him, hesitantly. I hated to send Marv into a full blown panic attack but he needed to know. "And the news has it." Marv just sat there.

"Who's Leila?" Adam asked.

"Leila," I said, "is a social scientist. She studies, or used to, the influences of crowds on individual behavior. Did her thesis on subway accidents. You know, those cases where someone falls in front of a train and nobody does anything because everybody is waiting for everybody else to do something. That doesn't have a lot to do with sexual abuse or the reliability of memory but hey, it's close enough for folk music. She now bills herself as an expert on suggestibility. Anyway, how many grants can you get for subway accidents? Testifying as an expert witness in these cases is a whole lot more lucrative not to mention more attention-getting.

"She is now a major-league defense witness, running all over the country, testifying that *all* these recovered memory cases are bogus and people's memories can be distorted by reading a newspaper.

"She is very smart, very good at what she does and doesn't give a shit about anyone. Leila has a lot of notches on her belt."

"Notches?" said Adam.

"I don't think it's just the money," I said. "Leila's into trophies, all kinds. Outside the courtroom she's into old style male sexual ethics: anybody and everybody—male, that is—keeps score, names names."

I turned to Marv. "AFAF held a press conference," I said, "just a few minutes ago. Some reporter will surely try to contact you."

At the thought of a reporter contacting him, Marv closed his eyes. He was turning paler by the minute. Suddenly, he opened his eyes and stood up. "I don't have time to discuss this," he said, looking at his watch. "I have a client coming in." He got up and without a word walked out. Adam and I looked at each other. Marv didn't seem to have a client two minutes ago.

13

I headed back for my car thinking maybe, if I was lucky, I still had time to do the report on Larsen before he got cold feet. I'd just hightail it over to my office, get my notes and write it up. But time was running out. Any minute, Larsen could fax in a request to pull the release, and I'd be in the position of knowing an anesthesiologist was out there raping unconscious women without being able to do a damn thing about it. Therapeutic confidentiality covered everything but sexual assault of children and that seemed to be the only thing Reggie hadn't done.

I climbed into my car, finished off the Diet Coke that was still sitting there and pulled out. The signs of stress were all different for different folks. When I started carrying drinks around with me: iced tea, coffee, Diet Coke, I knew I was getting overloaded. Freud was right. We all want our pacifiers in the end. The only difference in me and my relatives was that I just kept mine nonalcoholic, but it was the same idea.

I was almost at my private practice office before the phone rang. "Michael," the voice said, "where are you?"

"Ruth? How'd you get my number?" I didn't give out my car phone number. I only bought it because Adam had thrown a shit-fit about security and the kind of work I did and threatened to buy one for me if I didn't.

"We have our ways," she said, and I laughed thinking of the expression on her face.

"So, what's up?"

"Your presence is required. Where are you?"

"Depends," I said. "Why?"

"Curtis Todd is miraculously better and going home. He pulled one of those kid things of clearing entirely. His head's good. The rest of him was always good. His mom and dad are here with various broken this and that—they don't look so good—but they're going home too and they all want to thank you."

"I'll pass," I said. "Send them my regrets and say I was tied up. Oops, maybe not tied up. Just make some excuse. Be nice about it. You can think of something." I hate thanks and besides, time was definitely going to run out on getting Larsen's report in before he had a change of heart.

"Michael," she said, "this kid wants to see you before he goes. I think he *needs* to see you. He's been telling his mom and dad all about you and they need to see you too. I'm not the shrink, but aren't you the one who's always yelling at us about 'continuity of care' and all that. So get your tail over here."

"Excuse me. What's wrong with this picture? Am I or am I not senior faculty and are you or are you not a lowly resident who's supposed to hang on my every word? It's not enough to show up at four in the morning to bail your tail out? Now you order me around? I don't want to come. Besides, I actually have something seriously pressing I have to do." I didn't much want to write an eval on Reggie Larsen but I sure did have to.

"Beside the point. Get your tail over here for this kid's sake and be gracious about it."

I sighed and pulled over. The woman was a tyrant. But she was right, I *was* always yelling at the residents about continuity of care and the kid probably did need to say good-bye. "All right," I said, "I'm coming, but this is a two minute thank you, you're welcome, I'm out of there. Remember, I don't do mushy."

The space I'd occupied in front of the hospital was taken so I pulled around back and found a temporary spot by a back door. I got out grumbling to myself and walked inside. I started to take the stairs up to Pediatrics on the fifth floor and then realized I didn't feel well enough. I was suddenly very tired and getting drowsy. Surprised, I leaned against the wall near the elevators to try to collect myself. It had come on so suddenly, I was taken aback.

I thought of turning around and going back to the car just to lie down for a few minutes and then realized how silly that was. As tired as I was, I'd fall asleep and there were people upstairs waiting for me. I swallowed a couple of times. I was beginning to salivate like one of Pavlov's dogs, which made no sense at all.

I hit the button for the elevator and the doors

opened right away. The back elevator was used mainly to transport patients to and from surgery. It wasn't a public elevator at all and wasn't busy this time of day.

I began to feel worse as the elevator inched its way upstairs and I slid down the wall and sat down on the floor, leaning against the side wall. My lungs were beginning to feel heavy and I was having trouble swallowing all the saliva that was flowing like a small river. It all seemed bizarre to me given I had been fine five minutes ago. What the hell could come on this suddenly? It didn't feel like the flu. It didn't feel like anything I knew about. I looked at the walls of the elevator and realized they were starting to close in, just like one of Poe's stories.

The buzzer sounded and I could hear the elevator door open but when I looked up the door seemed miles away. The hall beyond it was distorted, miles long and narrow like a tunnel. I struggled to my feet and got my hand in the door to block it as it was closing. This was truly ridiculous. I had a flu bug or maybe I'd had some kind of crazy allergic reaction but I *could* get off this elevator.

I staggered off the elevator and into the hall in front of the nurses' station. I wasn't moving right. My arms and legs seemed too heavy and I was too tired to cross the hall to the station. Breathing was taking all my concentration. Why did people think breathing was so easy? Breathing was a bitch. How come I had taken it for granted all these years?

I saw the unit secretary stand up when she saw me. Like a drunk, I couldn't seem to speak very well, but I could read her body language perfectly. Why did she look so alarmed? Hadn't she ever seen anyone sick with the flu before? This was a hospital, for Christ's sake. It seemed almost funny that she looked so startled. I lost the fight with the saliva and it started dripping from the corner of my mouth.

I saw her pick up the phone and heard her call for Dr. Blue to the pediatric unit. She was calling a code blue, for Christ's sake, a full-out, everybody-come-running code, which was truly ridiculous. You don't call for a code when somebody is a little sick. I went down on my knees and then realized it was too hard to stay up that high and slid the rest of the way to the floor.

I couldn't make my lungs work and it was finally dawning on me I was in big trouble when I heard feet running. I saw Ruth's face loom over me and some of the fear starting to squeeze my heart backed off a notch. Ruth, Ruth, Ruth. I wanted to say, I can't breathe. But I couldn't say it and looking at the fear in her eyes, she knew it anyway.

"Take it easy, Michael," I heard her say. "We're here." She was already picking up my wrist, feeling for my pulse while she was talking. Then she laid my head back and checked my throat. There's nothing there, I wanted to say, but I was getting tunnel vision and it took all my energy to force air into my lungs which felt like they had lead weights sitting on top of them.

I could hear the sound of more feet running and faces and knees and feet seemed to be everywhere. I could hear voices yelling but couldn't really see much anymore. I closed my eyes because they were too heavy to stay open.

I could still hear Ruth barking orders, running the code. Well, somebody has to do it, good deal it's Ruth, and then someone had my face and was breathing into my mouth but I didn't care at all because I was drifting off quite nicely, thank you.

I must have dreamed. What else could it be? When the conscious mind goes out like a light, the unconscious is free to bring up all those images that were there anyway, but just couldn't surface with all that logical yammering going on. The left brain dithered along, spewing words here and there, while the right brain quietly drew pictures that never get seen.

Except when you're asleep. Or unconscious. Then the dreams come. I floated for a while, watching them put an IV in a body below me which seemed oddly familiar, then I drifted off down the hall. I slipped through the walls, heading across the street to Psychiatry. Why don't I always take this route? I thought. It seems so simple and easy. All that elevator-stair-tunnel stuff, ridiculous. Below I saw Marv going down a back corridor, heading for an exit. I got closer and as he walked he seemed to be leaking something all over, as though he was crying, but all over. I started to speak to him but he was gone, heading for the parking lot. He shouldn't be leaving, I thought, he has a client. But it didn't seem that important. Nothing did.

Then I was somewhere else, watching a nurse check monitors at the nurses' station. There were a lot of monitors, enough that it had to be some kind of special unit. She turned and I realized it was Zania. "Zania," I started to say, "it's me," but I stopped. She had something dark around her, moving with her. He's going to hurt her, I thought, big time. First me, then her, then he's home free.

I sighed and headed back to Pediatrics. I could leave after I told her but not before. The Tarasoff ruling meant I had to warn her if somebody was going to hurt her and Tarasoff seemed to apply here just as much as there. Dying just wasn't any excuse at all.

It was easy. I'd just tell her and then I'd go. But boy, did I have bad news for my colleagues. Heaven had Tarasoff.

When I finally began to surface, there was something huge down my throat holding it open and in the background I could hear the sound of a machine droning incessantly. Even half conscious I knew the feel of big-time drugs pulling me under. Had I been fully awake I would have known they were a friend, keeping me from fighting the machine that was breathing for me, but drugs that big never feel like a friend, even when they are.

I kept fighting to get free of them but they were rolling over me like waves. Leila kept surfing above my head, riding her surfboard like the Wicked Witch in *The Wizard of Oz* and laughing hysterically while I kept trying to get a hold of that goddamn surfboard and flip her from here to Shinola. But I couldn't get anywhere near it. I just kept going deeper.

Then the sound of the machine was gone and I was in and out for a while. I was sure I saw Zania but I couldn't get awake enough to speak. Maybe I just dreamed it. By the time I was fully conscious she wasn't there. The first person I saw in Intensive Care was Adam, sitting in a chair reading a book, wearing jeans and a tee-shirt. "Hey," I said weakly, struggling to lift my head up, "where's your costume? Why aren't you working?"

"Michael," he said, getting up and sitting gingerly on the bed. He bent down and kissed me. "How're you feeling?"

"Not too good," I said slowly, every word hurting my throat. "What are you doing here?" I squeaked.

"I took a few days off. Somebody doesn't like you." He said it lightly but his eyes looked shiny and when he took my hand it felt like he wasn't going to let it go anytime soon. "I'm only here part time," he said. "I go in sometimes and Jonathan takes over here." Jonathan was Adam's best detective, a former Boston cop. He was solid and taciturn and didn't look like he gave a goddamn, but I had worked on a case with him and I knew better.

"Jeez, Jonathan too? You're taking off to baby-sit?" I wanted to muster a show of indignation but I couldn't pull off even a tiny one. Adam's presence just felt comforting. "I need a new throat," I squeaked. My throat was raw from the intubation. "What happened?" I was starting to drift again.

"You're got nine lives, kiddo. Somebody put something called ketamine in your Coke. Very nasty anesthetic. A lot of it. It paralyzes your lungs. If you hadn't been standing in the middle of a hospital when it hit you, you'd have died." He said it gently, watching me, but I had already figured out how close I'd come.

"Oh boy," I said. "I almost didn't come back." My voice was so hoarse from the tube and I was fading so Adam leaned closer to catch the words. On impulse I lifted my head and kissed him on the cheek. And then I was gone again, too wasted to say anything else, even the words, "Reginald Larsen."

It was another day before I woke up with enough energy to talk. "I came within a hair's-breadth of driving away," I said to Adam. "Somebody wanted to thank me for something and I'm not good about stuff like that. I didn't want to come back."

Adam smiled wryly. "That'll teach you," he said. "By the way, this place has been Grand Central. Marv has been in and out a couple of times a day. Carlotta's got a trial out of town, but she's been calling. Even Toby showed up."

At the mention of my esteemed chairman's name, it was my turn to roll my eyes. "He probably did it," I grumbled sleepily, "or wished he had."

"Can you talk?" Adam said. "About who did."

"A man named Reggie Larsen," I said without hesitating. "A client."

"Nothing to do with the Sam Carlson case?" Adam asked.

"No, why?"

"Nothing, go on."

"No, why do you ask?"

"Well, there was a press conference in front of the hospital with Mark Carlson, Sam Carlson's son, about fifty feet from your car when this happened."

I smiled grimly. "Leila was there too. She's a lot better candidate."

He laughed quietly. "Listen, it's a question. The family is extremely pissed at you. The son was on the spot. The Coke was in the car. We found it there afterward. And, to boot, he's a vet, so he can get access to drugs."

"He is?"

"He is."

I thought for a minute. "I can't see it. He would have had to have the stuff with him. Why would he? He wouldn't have known I would be here. Besides, why would he be that ticked at me? He hadn't even met me. Plenty of people are ticked at me, but it's usually after they've met me."

"True," Adam said. "So who's Reggie Larsen."

I told him.

14

Zania wouldn't talk to Adam. She answered the door only long enough to tell him to go away, and she wouldn't answer the phone at all. Not even when I called. And she wasn't working. She'd called in sick for the last three days, ever since I showed up in Intensive Care.

Which is why, the next afternoon, I waited until Adam left and slowly put on my clothes. It was amazing how tired and worn out my skinny little body was and how much skinnier it was than just a few days ago. I felt like shit but, I told myself, I could always come back.

"I'm out of here," I said to Jonathan as I walked out into the hall. I resisted putting my hand on the wall for support. "Thank you."

"Anytime," he said. "But, uh, from the looks of you,

you shouldn't be going anywhere. Does anybody know you're leaving?"

"You know managed care," I said. "Can't stay in unless you're dead. And then they kick you out anyway. Hell of a thing."

He looked skeptical.

"Tell Adam there was this one thing I had to do. I'm fine. Really. More or less, anyway." Jonathan didn't look happy as I headed off but there wasn't a whole lot he could do except call his boss.

I'd called Melissa for Zania's address, which she had filled in when she came to see me, and I headed straight for her house. She'd rented a house in the country; this might not have been the best idea if she was afraid of being stalked. But maybe she wasn't. Maybe when she left Boston, she thought she had left Reggie behind for good.

I got into the car but was too tired to start it. I put my head on the wheel and waited for a few minutes until I got enough energy to turn the key over. Jesus, it's amazing what a little thing like nearly dying can do to you.

The house was an old farmhouse set on a side road near the interstate. The curtains were drawn and the house looked closed and quiet. The garage door was shut so I didn't have any way of knowing whether Zania was there or not. In some ways it almost didn't seem to matter. I just had to try. I paused on the doorstep realizing something had changed in me, but I'd have to think about that later.

When I raised my hand to knock I felt like I'd stepped out of "The Listener," an old poem I'd loved as a child. "Tell them I came, that I kept my word," I wanted to say, but of course I just knocked and said, "Zania, it's me, Michael."

There was no answer. "Zania, let me in. I need to talk to you." I knocked for a few more minutes and was beginning to think she really wasn't there when the door opened abruptly.

She looked at me for a moment and then said, "You look like shit. What are you doing out? They shouldn't have let you out this soon." Zania didn't look that good herself. Her face was shadowed and her eyes were dark.

"I'm better."

"You don't look better."

"Thanks," I said, "but, hey, considering the alternative . . ." I tried to say it lightly but there was nothing light in the atmosphere. "Can I come in?"

"I don't want to talk about this anymore," she said. Suddenly there was a howl from behind her. She turned for a moment and I slipped past.

"I'll only be a moment," I said, walking over and sitting down firmly on the couch. I was so tired I was grateful to be sitting and it would have taken a lot to get me up right away. Zania glanced at me briefly, seemed to realize that and shut the door. She walked over to the source of the howl and knelt down.

There was a toddler on the floor, maybe sixteen months or so. She had wispy blond hair that fell just below her ears and the brightest blue eyes this side of Paul Newman. She was trying to pull up a "blankie," a worn and threadbare infant blanket that looked like she had carried it around for the last millennium or so. Unfortunately, she was also standing on it, a fact that made

it impossible for her to wrench it free. She was screaming at her dilemma without any recognition of her own
contribution, not unlike a number of adults I had treated.

Her mother said, "Robin, let me . . . ," but Robin
screamed so much louder that Zania backed off.

She tried again to show Robin she was standing on
the blanket but Robin glared at her with such a fierce
look that my first thought was the emperor Nero could
not have done better. The look would have stopped a
tank. It certainly stopped her mother.

Another mother would have picked up all twenty-
five pounds of Robin and moved her a foot or two
whereupon the whole problem would have disappeared,
but Zania just stood watching helplessly from the side-
lines.

Robin gave one more furious yank and managed to
pull the blanket from under her foot, which knocked her
over. She sat down abruptly on her diaper-cushioned rear
and stopped crying in surprise.

"Feisty," I commented.

I had fallen in love instantly but Zania just shook her
head and said tiredly, "That's one way of looking at it."
She sat down in a chair opposite me but I was still looking at Robin.

"Is she always like that?"

"Only seven days a week."

"How do you handle her?"

"Oh, mostly I just give her what she wants. It's not
worth the fight."

I started to say that would make things interesting by
adolescence but didn't. Nobody asked me. I was there
for something else entirely.

Reluctantly, I pulled my head back to the business at hand. "How are you doing with this?" I said softly.

"This? This what? You mean the fact that I almost got you killed? I feel like shit. But I never, I never thought——"

"Zania, you didn't nearly get me killed. What are you talking about?"

"If I hadn't told you——"

"Zania, Reggie never knew I talked to you. If he was the guy, he did what he did based on what I got from him. Not you." She didn't look convinced but I went on.

"May I ask you some questions," I said, gently. "This doesn't make a lot of sense to me. People don't do things like this out of the blue. Not unless they have a lot bigger problem than I know about. You just don't start trying to kill people at his age. Is there anything else you're not telling me? Did you ever have any unexplained deaths in Intensive Care when Larsen was around? Anything that didn't add up?"

Zania was silent for a minute. "Are you kidding?" she said finally. "You can't accuse a man like Reginald Larsen——"

"Zania, I'm not accusing him of anything. Just bear with me, think about it."

She shrugged. "It's hard to say," she said evasively. "Just about everybody who comes in the unit *could* die, that's why they're there. And a lot of them do."

"But *when* they die is another story. Did you ever have anybody die after one of Larsen's visits? Anybody who was getting better? Anything that didn't make sense?" Maybe I was reaching but if the best predictor of future behavior was past behavior, the best predictor of past behavior was present behavior.

"Not really," she said and her voice trailed off. She looked down, almost guiltily, I thought.

"What?"

Just then Robin howled again and we both looked over. She had a small music box and was trying to open it from the hinged side. Since she was pulling on the side which was fastened, nothing was happening. Undeterred, she just kept pulling and yelling. Goddamn it, that box *would* open. I couldn't help smiling. Robin's approach to life seemed all too familiar.

Zania ignored her and turned back around. "This is ridiculous. You can't say something like that about a man like Reginald Larsen. Nobody would believe that."

"I don't know who would believe he tried to kill me but that's not the point. The point is, if he tried to kill me, you gotta ask the question of whether it's the first time." I felt like saying, "Duh, hello, you know damn well he tried to kill me so what are you being so squirrelly about?" But I didn't. I just said, "Which brings me here. Zania, he's got a lot more reason to fear you than me."

"Don't be silly. What are you saying?"

"Zania, with me, he can at least hope I'll stick with confidentiality, although I guess he didn't. But you don't have any reason to keep quiet about him at all. None. And you only told the hospital a fraction of what you know. All you told them was that you thought you might have, maybe, seen one incident, and then said you didn't really see it, you came in afterward and you weren't sure. And he doesn't even know you told them that much.

"As far as he knows you're sitting on a powder keg of information that could destroy his career, none of which he thinks you've shared. You know he was in the unit all the time when he had no reason to be, that he was always going into patients' rooms and shutting the door. You know he had an affair with you and came in mainly on your shift. Which looks pretty deliberate to an outsider. Not to mention the incident you saw with the patient. Reggie surely knows if you told what you know his career would be over."

"Are you serious? You're saying he could try to hurt me?" There was enough fear in her voice to put goosebumps on my arms. I felt like Alice in Wonderland, lost in her lack of logic. Why hadn't she figured this out? But people didn't see what they didn't want to see, couldn't bear to see.

"Well, he could," I said tentatively.

"Kill me? He could kill me? I can't believe that. That's ridiculous. Reggie would never try to kill me."

I was silent. I wanted to ask why not but it sounded harsh. Finally, when I couldn't think of any other way to say it, I gave up and said, "All right, why not?"

"Well, he's a physician, for Christ's sake. He wouldn't try to kill anyone."

She saw the look in my eyes and said weakly, "Well, we don't know for sure he tried to kill you. It could have been somebody else."

"If you think it was somebody else, why have you

been crying? Why have you stayed home for the last three days? Zania, you've got to get real about this. You can't somehow pretend that Reggie Larsen would try to kill me and not face the fact he could try to hurt you too."

"He wouldn't try to hurt me," she said stubbornly and I could hear an undercurrent of something like panic, rising just under the words. "I have a little girl. He knows that. What would happen to Robin?"

"People who kill people don't worry about things like that. It's just not on their agenda. Come on, Zania. How many times have you seen a killer worry about how it would affect anybody's relatives? But you don't need to panic about this. If you tell the hospital what you know, he won't have any reason to kill you. Once it's out, it's out. He's not into revenge. Besides, it would look even worse for him if you died under suspicious circumstances after you'd blown the whistle on him. You're only at risk as long as he's trying to keep you silent."

Zania stood up again. "I can't do that," and this time her voice had risen to the point that Robin stopped pulling and stared at her mother. "You don't understand anything. You don't know anything. Get out of here. You're scaring me to death. I don't have to listen to this."

"Zania, please—"

"Right now. You've got to go. I'm really busy. I don't have time for this."

Stunned, I got up. There was no way to argue. She was too scared to think or plan or do anything but push it all away. I wanted to say, "Hey, listen up, does it mean anything you've got my life in your hands, too?" But that definitely wouldn't help. If she wouldn't tell to save *her* life, she surely wouldn't tell to save mine.

I got up and walked out. There wasn't anything else to do. At the car I turned and looked back at the house for a moment. I wished to God my life was in Robin's hands and not her mother's.

15

I headed home and then changed my mind. There was one person who knew something that might help. And surely he'd tell me now. On the way over I thought about how to approach him. I'd be mature about this. I'd ask him politely, and if he refused to tell me, then and only then would I threaten to break both his thumbs.

"Michael," Marv said, as he opened the door and the warmth in his voice felt like balm to my tired little body and soul. "Thank God. Come in, come in. I went over to the unit this afternoon but you were gone and no one seemed to know where you were. Surely you didn't go AWOL, my dear, not after what happened? By the way, Carlotta called. She's looking for you too."

"There was something I had to do," I said. "Do you have time for me to visit? I've got something I want to talk with you about."

"I've always got time for you," Marv said. "Stay for dinner?"

"Only if we don't order in," I said. "I'm a little low on trust right now. And no Cokes."

Marv laughed. "I think I can whip up something if you're not too fussy."

"It's one of the few names I've never been called," I replied.

I sat down gratefully on Marv's overstuffed couch while he went off to the kitchen for drinks. I was so tired I felt like going to sleep on the spot. "What's happening with the Carlson case?" I called out to him.

"Timely question," Marv replied. "Jody and I have a meeting with her brother, Mark, tomorrow."

"Why?" I asked, closing my eyes for a moment.

Marv poked his head out the door. "He insisted. His father still hasn't turned up. The family is getting increasingly concerned that something's happened to him."

"How is meeting with you going to change that? Does he think you know where he is or you have him stashed away somewhere?"

Marv shrugged and his head disappeared back into the kitchen. "I'm not sure what he thinks. He just asked to meet with me and Jody. I don't know if their mother is coming or not. This time I want to set up some rules up front. I don't want a repeat of what happened last time." I could hear the shudder in his voice.

"Probably he wants Jody to drop the whole thing and apologize publicly," I offered, "and ask Dad to please come home, all is forgiven and, besides, there's nothing to forgive, it never happened anyway. That's certainly what the AFAF would advise him. Demand an apology and threaten to sue the hell out of you both if she doesn't give it to him. Then if she does apologize, use that publicly as proof of 'another' false report."

Marv brought the drinks in and sat down. He said nervously, "Do you really think they'll sue?"

In a heartbeat, I thought, but I didn't say it. I'd had enough of scaring people for one day. "It depends," I said. "Who knows?" Other than me and Leila and the entire Association for Falsely Accused Families that had a policy of suing anytime, anyplace, anywhere. If I knew the AFAF, they'd be praying Carlson had killed himself. Just think of the publicity. Leila had practically predicted it on camera, which she knew would make her look very smart if he did.

"Do you want me to come?"

"You don't look well enough, my dear. Why don't you just take it easy for a few days."

"We'll see," I said. "I'll come if I can." Although Marv wouldn't admit it, he looked so grateful that I decided to drag my tail over there tomorrow morning if I could get it moving.

"Well, enough of that," Marv said. "How are you?"

I stirred my iced tea slowly for a moment. "I need," I said bluntly, "to know what Reginald Larsen Senior said to you that made you think I shouldn't see his son." I sipped my iced tea and looked at Marv.

Marv looked at me and blinked a couple of times and I could see the wheels turning. "I should have told you," he said. "No, I couldn't have. I didn't . . ." He sighed. "Well, too late now." He sighed again and settled back in his chair. "All right. It was back when Reggie Junior was doing his residency, in Texas. There was a scandal; he was accused by a patient of improper behavior during an exam. Or something like that, it's been so long, I've forgotten the details.

"In any case, they were considering what to do—as you know, it's terribly difficult to remove a resident in his last year—when the head of the committee started getting anonymous phone calls, threatening him and his family." I thought immediately of Zania and Robin. By age fifty there really was nothing new under the sun. Whatever Reggie was doing now, he'd likely done before.

"To make a long story short, the calls were traced to Reggie, and he was thrown out. Thrown out with no recommendation whatsoever. I believe he went into the army. They were fairly desperate for physicians at the time. No other residency would take him.

"His parents were distraught. They wanted recommendations for treatment. I gave them some but I don't know if Reggie ever followed through. I really didn't want you to take the case."

"Why not?"

"He had a history of acting out impulsively. Given that and the residency episode . . . well, it's obvious, isn't it? He functions poorly under pressure and has an underdeveloped superego combined with limited ego strength and a significant degree of impulsivity. That did not bode well, particularly in the light of the specialized evaluations that you do, which, I believe, involve a great degree of stress. Certainly, Reggie might have matured since residency but given the kind of difficulties you were alluding to, I was fearful he hadn't."

I sat back in my chair. "Let me get this straight. You were afraid I'd pressure the shit out of him and he'd lose it and do something rash, like he did back in Texas, that is, unless he had grown up a little in the meantime."

"Exactly," Marv replied. "Perhaps I felt a little protective of you, given some of your recent experiences. You've run into several clients with poor boundaries recently."

I smiled. Sometime back, someone had tried to strangle me and someone else had tried to shoot me and I guess you could call that poor boundaries, although my Southern genes would simply say they were "sum bitches."

Marv started to add something when the phone rang. "Hello," he said. He listened silently for a few moments. "No, of course, you aren't interrupting me. I want you to call when you need to."

He looked at me and shrugged as if to say he couldn't do anything about it and took the phone in another room. It was clear he was on a crisis call and I knew that might take a while.

I got up and started wandering around the room, looking randomly at Marv's art work. There were several pieces I didn't remember seeing and after a few minutes I realized there was something different about them. It took a minute before I started to realize what I was seeing.

When Marv finally hung up, I didn't sit down right away. "Marv," I said, "when did you get this lithograph?"

He walked over. "Oh, that," he said, "I picked that up last October at a little gallery in New York. Every once in a while they get in something wonderful that I can afford. Most of their things I can't touch."

Wonderful was one way of looking at it I suppose. I

moved on, looking for the things that weren't familiar. "What about this little fresco type thing?"

"Ah, the mother and son? You won't believe it. I found it in a flea market on my way through London."

"Which was?"

"This spring. When I was coming back from Russia."

I wandered into the dining room still looking. "What about this statue on the hutch?"

"I've had that," Marv said. I looked at it for a moment. Maybe I was wrong.

"It's been here all along?"

"No, I didn't have it out. I've had to start rotating things. I've run out of room."

I wasn't wrong. I sat down and I tried to think about how to say what I wanted to say when the phone rang again. It was the hospital asking Marv if he wanted to talk to a client of his who had come in on emergency. Marv glanced at me and said the on-call person could deal with it. I wondered what he would have done if I wasn't there. Gone in, I thought. He wouldn't have just talked to them on the phone. He would have gone in and spent the evening working.

"Michael," he said, "I'm sorry for all the interruptions. I really have been distressed about what happened to you and whether I should have said something or not. I know Adam's working on the investigation but if there's anything I can do, anything at all, please let me know."

"Thanks," I said. "I really appreciate that, but never mind that for now. Can I move some of your art works around just for a moment?"

Marv looked surprised. "Move them around?"

"Just for a moment."

"Of course, but—"

"Just bear with me." I got up and slowly took each piece that Marv had bought in the last year and laid them in a line leaning against the wall. I put them in order of when he got them. And then I went back and got several of his old pieces and put them right before the new pieces.

"Take a look," I said.

Marv looked at me and then at the art. He looked puzzled for a moment and then I saw his eyes cloud over. "No," he said. "I don't see what you mean."

"But you must," I said. "Marv, look at it. Your art is a Rorschach. You're burning out. You need a life. If you don't want a lover, at least get yourself a pet, a Doberman or something." I saw the look in Marv's eyes. "All right, never mind the Doberman, a goldfish, whatever."

"With all due respect," he said frostily, "I don't know what you're talking about. As for the art, it really isn't your thing, Michael. Why don't you just come have dinner and talk about these difficulties with Dr. Larsen."

I stood rooted to the spot for a moment in disbelief. Nobody was listening. Zania wouldn't listen and Marv wouldn't listen and yet I'd bet my chances of a gym-filled heaven I was right. Reggie Larsen had every reason in the world to kill Zania, and he'd already demonstrated he was capable of it. And the art Marv had bought in the last year told him everything he needed to know about what was wrong with his life. Everybody was walking along the path with their eyes six inches in front of their toes and nobody wanted to look up for fear of what they'd see. I just hoped it wasn't true of me as well.

16

I thought about going back to the hospital but I couldn't bear it. I thought about going to Adam's but I didn't want to. What I wanted to do was to go home. I wanted to be in my own tiny little A-frame listening to the sound of the stream running through the backyard, and maybe sit in the hot tub soaking my wounded spirit. No doubt people would question my sanity, given how isolated the place was, but home was calling me and I was going.

When I got there, there was a car I recognized sitting in the driveway and a dark dome-shaped object I didn't recognize sitting on the lawn. I pulled in and walked over. "There's a tent in my front yard," I said.

Adam stuck his head out. "Greetings," he replied.

"What is a tent doing in my front yard?"

"It's neat," he replied. "Take a look. Sierra Designs. Two people, four pounds. On sale at REI."

"Adam."

"Would you have let me in?"

"Well, to visit maybe, not to park."

"That's why there's a tent in your front yard."

"Get serious. You can't just put a tent on my property. I could call the police."

"Yes?" he said.

"You're not funny." I sat down cross-legged on the lawn. "What are you doing here?"

"Why don't we go in and talk?"

I looked at Adam's face. "What's wrong?"

"Larsen," he said.

Adam didn't seem to be in a hurry to talk about it. He hadn't eaten so I pulled out this and that, all the time worrying about what he had to say. Finally, we sat on the deck watching the clouds race across a full moon and I couldn't stand it anymore. "So what's up?" I asked. "Shoot."

Adam put down his cup. "Reginald Larsen has a new girlfriend, a nurse, and she says he arrived back in Boston almost exactly three hours after the polygraph ended. She is adamant about it and insists he stayed with her the rest of the afternoon and evening."

"She's lying."

"Likely, but she is a nurse, an upstanding member of the community. She's had no problems with the law. A jury would believe her."

"His last girlfriend was an upstanding member of the community and she covered up all kinds of things for him."

"Doesn't help. Plus, there are no fingerprints on your car, on the Coke can, on anything. And no one that we can find who was in and out of the hospital about that time or listening to the press conference remembers your car or anybody going anywhere near any car. They just didn't notice."

"Well, there wouldn't necessarily be fingerprints. If he was careful he only had to lean in the window and drop something in. He didn't even have to pick it up." I sighed. "So what now?"

"Nothing now. There's nowhere to go with it."

"What do you mean there's nowhere to go with it? He can't just get away with it. He tried to kill me. He damn near did kill me."

"Michael, there are a lot more unsolved homicides out there than people know about."

"Is it that easy? That fucking easy to get away with killing somebody?"

"Sometimes," he said. We both fell silent.

"Jesus Christ," I said. "Jesus fucking Christ." I was pissed as hell but there was a ball of fear rolling right behind the anger. "You know I think I counted on getting him on attempted homicide and the whole problem would just go away. I must have because I am ripped beyond belief."

Adam didn't comment. "So what happens now?" I asked. "Do you think you're just moving in here?"

"For a while, yes. Either in your house or on your lawn."

"I don't think so," I exploded. "Forget it. You're not doing either."

"Michael," he said and I was surprised by the gentleness in his voice, given my outburst. I had wanted a fight but Adam wasn't buying. "You're living on luck. On luck alone. This is the third time since I've known you that something's happened that could have killed you. People run out of luck," he said simply.

I started to speak but he interrupted me, "No, listen for a minute. How do you feel about runner-gunners?"

"They piss me off. I can't stand playing ball with them."

"On the basketball court you are the best team player I know. You will pass up a perfectly good shot if you spot someone cutting through the middle. But in life, you are a runner-gunner of the worst sort. You want to take every shot yourself. I've stood by twice while you fooled around with getting yourself killed and you never even thought about passing the ball.

"Think of it this way. I'm tired of sitting on the bench and I play this particular game better than you do."

I opened my mouth to say something, then shut it.

"So I'm here. So throw me out of the house, I'll stay on the lawn. If you throw me off the lawn, I'll pitch the tent by the road. I've had it with being shut out. You turn into a crazy lady every time something dangerous comes along. You're going to get yourself killed and I'm tired of standing around waiting for it to happen."

His words went through me like a shock wave. They were what my mama would call the gospel truth, the word with the bark on it. The truth was always tough. I knew all kinds of things about lying. I was used to people lying. But the kind of truth that was spoken from the marrow of the bones was a different thing altogether. I opened my mouth to speak and then shut it again without saying a single word. I had nothing left to say.

* * *

By ten the next day I was sitting in Marv's office with Jody Carlson waiting for Marv to fetch her brother Mark from the waiting room. I was still feeling shaky but I couldn't help smiling thinking about the long, silky night with Adam; there were some medicines hospitals didn't dispense. Suddenly, I thought of something. "Jody," I said, "this thing about your father being missing. Where do *you* think he's gone?"

"I don't know," she said. "I never used to know where he went. Nobody ever told me anything."

"What do you mean you never used to know where he went? Has he done this before?"

"Oh, sure," she said, "but—" Jody was interrupted by Marv opening the door. Jody froze and looked down as Marv and her brother walked into the room.

I stood up. "I'm Dr. Stone," I said, reaching out to shake hands.

Mark Carlson was a tall, good-looking man in his late thirties with sandy-colored, thinning hair. He was neatly dressed in slacks and a shirt and he had a kind of singular neatness about him that looked like he appreciated an orderly world.

He shook hands with a firm grasp and nodded at his sister. "Jody," he said, then looked away immediately. He knows, I thought, somewhere deep down he knows and he's not deceitful enough to look her in the eye.

As we all sat down Marv turned to me and said, "I explained to Mr. Carlson that you'd be joining us." He said it firmly without any pause for argument.

"Now," he went on, "I want to be very clear about one thing from the beginning. This will be a civil meeting. An entirely civil meeting. If there is any shouting or berating of anyone by anyone, I will immediately terminate this meeting. Is everyone agreed to that?" I looked over at Marv appreciatively. Clearly, he had learned his lesson the first time and wasn't going to let this be a repeat. However depressed he was, he had rallied himself to get through this.

"There won't be a problem," Mark Carlson said quietly. "My father is the one with the temper."

He must have seen the skepticism in both my eyes and Marv's. He went on sheepishly. "I want to apologize for yelling at you on the phone. I'm sure even Jody will back me up when I say that's not my usual behavior."

"Very well," Marv replied. "Jody?"

"It'll be okay," Jody said. She was sitting very close to Marv as though for support. She didn't look directly at her brother but only glanced over occasionally.

"Well," Marv said, turning back to Mark. "What brings you here today?"

Carlson took a deep breath. "I've been thinking a lot about this," he said, turning to speak directly to Jody. "I am sorry I yelled at Dr. Gliesen on the phone but I haven't changed my mind about how I feel about this. I don't know why you want to tear up the family this way but it has to stop. It just has to stop. It makes Dad crazy. You know how he gets when he's upset. And you know what happens to Mom. And then she's on the phone to me three times a day crying about it.

"You just can't keep doing this, Jody. I've got a family to take care of. I've got to work. You don't feel the repercussions of this, but I do. Look, I don't know what went on when you were a kid. I was in the same family and I never saw anything. But even if something did happen, it was a long time ago. You just have to get on with your life and let it go. You're messing up everyone's life."

Jody looked stricken and pulled her feet up under her on the chair. We all waited for a moment but she seemed to be fighting tears. When she didn't speak Marv spoke instead. "Mr. Carlson, assume for a moment that sexual abuse occurred. Assume for a moment that it has left Jody impaired enough that she can't work or go to school, that she becomes so depressed and suicidal that she endures repeated hospitalizations. If those things were true, think about what you're asking her to do."

"It's nothing new," Jody said angrily to Marv. "He just wants me to go on pretending nothing's wrong to save everybody else's ass. Dad's a royal pain when he's pissed. He's right about that. Mom bitches and moans behind his back and doesn't dare say anything to him and makes everybody else miserable. So keep Dad happy. That was always the message. My job was to keep Dad happy."

She turned to Mark and her voice started rising. "So how did I get to be the sacrificial lamb? What about you? How come he didn't pick on you? What about your daughter? How about sending her into Dad's room and telling her to keep Dad happy like Mom used to do to me." Jody started crying and curled up in a fetal position on the chair.

My breath caught in my throat. Why hadn't I thought about this before? "Wait a minute," I said. "You have a daughter?"

Carlson didn't answer for a minute. "Yes," he said finally when no one else spoke. "I have two children, a boy and a girl."

"How old is the girl?"

He paused again. "Eight," he said, then added quickly, "But my family has nothing to do with this."

"Given what Jody has claimed your father did to her—and at about the same age—have you ever asked your daughter if her grandfather has been inappropriate with her?" I persisted.

"Are you serious?" he asked, his voice skyrocketing.

"Mr. Carlson," Marv said, "we all agreed—"

"What? Now you want me to drag her mind in the sewer like my sister's? What is wrong with you people?"

"You don't have to be graphic with her," I said. "And you don't have to upset her. Ask her if her grandfather has ever done anything that makes her uncomfortable, anything she's thought of telling you about. Ask her if he's ever scared her or asked her to keep a secret. If she hasn't been abused, she'll just think you're talking about his temper."

"That's ridiculous," he said. "My father would never . . . He knows . . ." He looked up and saw all of us looking at him. No one spoke for a moment. "That isn't necessary," he said at last.

"Mr. Carlson," I said, "strange things do happen in this world. Every offender I have ever seen has had someone close to him who loved and trusted him and thought he would never do such a thing. Nobody here is suggesting anything harmful to your daughter. For her sake, just ask her. Ask her if he's ever scared her, if he's ever asked her to keep a secret. Given that you have a sister who says he abused her when she was about the same age, don't you owe her that much? You'll never forgive yourself if he abused her and you didn't bother to ask."

"I can tell you the answer right now," he said stubbornly. Funny, I thought, he doesn't want to go back and prove us wrong. He doesn't want to ask her, no matter how nicely, no way, no how. And there's only one reason for that. He just isn't sure of her answer.

"I'd rather you wait until you ask her," I replied softly.

No one spoke. Carlson looked like he had run into a brick wall and I couldn't escape the feeling we weren't it. Finally, he said, "There's nothing I can do here, is there? I'm wasting everyone's time." He was trying to sound gruff but he couldn't quite pull it off. He sounded more worried than anything. He glanced over at Jody. "You're not going to listen. I don't know why I even bothered to try." Jody was still crying quietly and didn't look up.

"Depends on what you want, Mr. Carlson," Marv replied. "I think Jody is available to talk with you. I can't speak for Jody but I think that she'd like to have a relationship with you. I think she could use some support right now. She needs someone in the family to talk to about what happened. And she needs someone to believe her.

"But if you're only here to tell her to keep it to herself, no matter what the cost to her, I think you heard her answer to that."

"I don't want to hear what happened," Carlson said. "I don't want to hear what she *says* happened," he added quickly. He looked at his watch. "I should be going. I don't think this is going to help. I'm sorry. I had some idea maybe we could just get past this and go on." His voice seemed more resigned than angry. He stood to leave and Marv rose to join him but I interrupted. "Mr. Carlson, just one more thing. Has your father ever disappeared like this before?"

"No, not really."

"What does 'not really' mean?"

"Well, nothing like this."

"What *has* he done?"

"Nothing really. He's gone away for a day or two but not this long."

"He's disappeared for a day or two without telling anybody?"

"Once in a while. Not that often."

"Did you tell the police that?"

"It really wasn't necessary. It's not the same thing. It's never been this long, really."

"Where did he go?"

"What?"

"Where did he go? When he got back, what did you find out about where he had been?"

"I don't know." Carlson looked uncomfortable. "I don't really know." He looked at his watch again. "I'm sorry, but I need to get back to work." He shut the door.

I looked after him for a moment. It was a bad idea to be on the South's side in the Civil War, a very bad idea. There was no way on earth to justify fighting for slavery and despite all that junk I was taught growing up in a Southern school about the war being fought over economics, it was fought over slavery, pure and simple. But no doubt there were some loyal and decent kids who became cannon fodder who were on the wrong side.

My opinion had changed about Mark Carlson. In person, he didn't strike me as Dad Junior. He struck me as a foot soldier, fighting in the trenches on the wrong side of a bad war. And denial ain't just a river in Egypt; it's a uniform that people like Mark Carlson wear day in and day out, a heavy, uncomfortable uniform, all wrong for the weather, but one he had to wear if he was going to keep fighting.

I said nothing but Jody seemed to be thinking along the same lines. "Sometimes," she said, sitting up and reaching for a Kleenex, "I think what my mother did to him was as bad as what my father did to me."

"What do you mean?" Marv asked.

"He was the man. He was the one. She turned to him for everything. She'd call him at school when she was upset and he had to come home and take care of her. I'm talking elementary school. He never played sports or anything in high school. He always felt he had to go home and take care of Mom. She'd wake him up in the night and cry and carry on when Dad stormed out. He used to sit up and listen for hours to her. Sometimes he was so tired the next day he fell asleep in class and the teachers would complain. And she never took responsibility for it. She just let them think he was staying up late on his own. She still does it. She talks to him every day.

"Funny thing, though." Jody blew her nose. "He's not a bad father. He doesn't do anything like that to his kids. I always wanted to be closer to him but no dice. He was always so focused on keeping Mom happy he had no time for me. Nothing else mattered."

"Do you think your father could have abused his daughter?" I asked. "He got a little upset when I raised that."

"He'd better not have," Jody said. "My brother will have a shit-fit if he did. I may be expendable but I don't think his children are."

Walking out I saw Mark Carlson hanging up the pay phone in the main lobby. I nodded to him and kept going but I heard him call my name. Surprised, I turned around and waited for him to catch up.

He looked awkward but determined. "I meant to say something in there. But things . . . well, they always get out of hand with Jody." He took a deep breath. "Leila told me you were in the hospital, that someone tried to kill you." I stared at him. Good old Leila. I hated clients knowing anything about my private life.

"I just wanted to say . . . I'm sorry that happened and I hope you don't think any of us . . . anybody in my family had anything to do with it."

"Why would I think that?" I said coolly. I knew he probably meant well but I had a major-league aversion to discussing my private life with clients.

"Well, she told me that it was ketamine . . . I'm a vet . . . We use ketamine all the time, I was just afraid you thought—"

"I never thought you or your family were involved," I said, but for the first time a little bit of doubt started creeping in. If vets use ketamine all the time, it wasn't just Sam I had to worry about, it was anybody in his family. But that still didn't make any sense. I had to be very low on anybody's hit list in that family.

"It was a hell of a choice," he added, "but probably you know that already."

"Why do you say that?"

"It's very lethal," he said. "Very. And extremely fast. You're quite lucky to be here." I knew that already so I wasn't sure why hearing it shook me up but it did.

We said our good-byes and I turned to walk away but only got a few feet before I stopped. Mark Carlson was heading off in the other direction when I called out, "Mark." He stopped and turned around. "One more question. What are the chances that somebody could have done that impulsively?"

"Impulsively? No, no," he said walking back. "At least I wouldn't think so. It was too good a choice, and nobody except a vet would be likely to be walking around with ketamine in their pocket. No, it was carefully chosen. Somebody had to think this through and go to some trouble to get it. No, I don't see how it could have been impulsive."

I walked slowly to my car and got in. The problem was, why would anybody have planned to attack me? That didn't make any sense, not any sense at all.

* * *

I hadn't been back to my private practice office since this started but I knew the fax from Reggie Larsen was there and it was. I picked it up and read it. Read my lips, it said in legalese. I'm withdrawing permission for you to talk about my case with anybody. I'm withdrawing permission for you to release a report about me to anybody. I'm withdrawing permission for you to even *think* about my case or look at my case file. I'm withdrawing permission for you to even remember you ever had a client by the name Reginald Larsen. It didn't use those words exactly but that was the idea.

"Fuck you," I thought. On impulse I picked up the phone. Maybe I couldn't talk about why he came to see me but some things had happened that were totally outside the evaluation sessions.

"May I speak to Margaret Jones?" I said. "This is Dr. Stone speaking."

She came on the phone almost immediately. "Yes," she said, "this is Margaret Jones."

I felt the first qualms of guilt. Was this violating confidentiality? Probably. "Good morning, Dr. Jones. This is Michael Stone. I'm letting you know that Reginald Larsen has rescinded his release of information and therefore I will not be at liberty to send you my report or discuss the case further with you."

"Really?" she said, sounding genuinely surprised.

"I'm afraid so."

"Interesting," she said thoughtfully. "He asked for a meeting and I'm seeing him this afternoon. I was hoping he was going to tell me the evaluation was done and the report would be in shortly. We couldn't begin to reinstate him without an evaluation and time is so much of the essence here."

"Why is that?" I asked. I had never entirely understood the time pressure in this case.

"Oh, didn't he tell you? His article on his new research is coming out this month in the *New England Journal of Medicine.* The media gets advance copies and they've already started calling. I was hoping to have this settled one way or the other before the frenzy started."

"Ah," I said, "I see," and I surely did. Reggie was about to attract a storm of media attention. Not a good time to be in the middle of ethics charges.

"Oh dear," she said. "I'm not sure where we go with this now."

"So sorry I can't help you," I said. "Just one more thing. I don't want to alarm you or upset you but something came up that Dr. Larsen did not tell me and did not come out of my direct evaluation of him. I can't tell you any more but I do have a question for you. I feel I have to ask it given what's at stake." I paused, then took the plunge. "Have you had any unexplained deaths in the ICU in the past few years, deaths that you felt were untimely or unexpected, deaths that you were suspicious of?"

The pause was so long I wondered if we had been disconnected. "Good Lord," she said finally when she had caught her breath. "Are you saying—"

"I'm not saying anything," I replied. "But I have to ask this question."

"But you're implying—"

"I don't want you to jump to any conclusions. It's just something that needs to be checked out."

"My God," she said, "what a thing to say. What a thing to imply. I'm sure we haven't—" and then she stopped midsentence. I held my breath. She was thinking of something, I'd bet on it. "I'm sure nothing like that . . . ," she said finally, but her voice sounded weak and shaken.

"Will you check on it?" I asked.

"Do you have any evidence to make a charge like that?"

"I'm not making a charge." I sighed. It was clear I'd have to tell her something. "Someone tried to kill me," I said. "By putting ketamine in a drink. Now, that's not the usual choice for the kind of people I usually deal with. I don't have anybody else on my caseload right now who'd know about ketamine or how to get it or how fast it acts or how lethal it is. And I don't have anybody else whose major-league career could be . . . shall we say . . . affected, by a pending evaluation of mine."

"Oh, my God. I'm so sorry. But even so, even if that were true, even if it were, what makes you think—"

"It's a little late to be starting this sort of thing. If, hypothetically, someone were willing to kill to silence someone, you just have to ask the question of whether anyone else had ever been a threat. And what happened. That's all."

I could hear the wheels turning, spinning wildly, was more like it. "I'll get back to you," she said. "Or maybe I won't be able to. I don't know . . ."

"One more thing," I said. "You mentioned a nurse whom you said made a confidential, anonymous report that Dr. Larsen didn't know about. If she has information that important about him, she could be at risk too, hypothetically speaking, of course." If Zania wouldn't listen to me, maybe she'd listen to Margaret Jones.

"I'll get back to you," she said quickly, "if I can."

I had surely poked a stick in a bees' nest. The alarm bells would be going off all over the upper echelon of the hospital. The Chairman of the Board was probably the first call; unquestionably the hospital's lawyer was the second. They'd better have an EMT on hand when they tell the lawyer what I had asked.

17

"Michael," the voice on the phone said, "you're still alive. And you have the balls to nearly get yourself killed while I'm up in the Northeast Kingdom prosecuting a very stupid minor-league drug case. I take that personally."

"What, Carlotta? The drug case or me almost getting killed?"

"Screw all that. Are you well enough to go sailing?"

I looked at the phone in shock. "First of all, Carlotta, it is nine o'clock on a Saturday morning. What are you doing up?"

"I've been up for hours," she laughed. "Hank got me up."

Hank was a judge Carlotta had been seeing for about a year. I had been watching this thing grow and I wasn't going to be surprised if he moved in.

I wasn't sure how I felt about it. I liked Hank, but

when men moved in, women friends definitely took a backseat. I hated to see Carlotta become a "couple," with all the baggage that entailed. I had a guilty moment thinking I was being a bit hypocritical since Adam was living in my house. But that was just temporary, I reminded myself. I was not in a relationship. Okay, so I slept with him, sometimes, occasionally, whatever. That didn't make it a relationship.

"Hank's got a murder trial next week and he's going to be working all weekend," Carlotta added. "And besides, I want to take a look at you. Fatten you up. They tell me you weigh eight pounds."

"Ah, I'm all right. Talking about Hank is more fun. He got you up? No doubt he was up early working on the case. Let me guess. He was consulting you on points of law?"

"Noooooo, I'd say not, although there was definitely a point involved."

"But he was seeking your input?"

"No, I'd say I was seeking his."

I laughed. "Well, I certainly hope you didn't do anything illegal."

"Depends on which state you're in. Did you know oral sex is illegal in Georgia?"

"Everything's illegal somewhere in the South. Don't forget I grew up there. So what's this about sailing?"

"Why not? It's a fine summer day. I checked the weather station. There's a ten to fifteen knot breeze blowing and no bad weather ahead. The boat's in Portsmouth, less than two hours if *you're* driving, more than two and a half for the rest of us. Are you all right? Are you up for this?"

"You bet I am. One thing though. Overnight, right?" Carlotta knew I hated to take the boat out, sail it around in circles, then go right back to the same harbor we came from. I liked to cruise, which meant spending at least one night in a harbor we'd never seen before. If you were going to go, you might as well go.

"Where the wind blows us," she answered. "Come on over." I hung up and looked down at the phone. Carlotta was already part of a couple. Why was she going sailing? Because Hank was working. Would she have gone sailing if Hank had been home? No, she would not have, not unless he came along.

I hated this couple thing. Couples tossed their friends whatever scraps of time were left over from The Relationship. Friends became fillers, a way to keep from missing an absent partner, or a way of saying, "I don't have to sit around waiting for you." Slowly, inevitably, The Relationship wasn't just on the table: it became the centerpiece. It became the sun around which everything else revolved.

But what the hell? I'd done the same thing to Carlotta in my time. The one thing about friendships—they endured. One thing about relationships—mostly, they didn't. And besides, I might be selling her short. Nearly getting killed might be enough to compete with The Relationship even if Hank hadn't been busy.

Knowing Carlotta, she really did want to check me out. Fatten me up and touch base to make sure my head was in reasonable shape. Carlotta liked to nurture. I got restless with all that nurturing but I could put up with anything for a chance to sail. It was a compromise we could both live with.

Adam was up and gone. Who knew where? Grudgingly, I'd given him a key the night before so he could come and go without being locked out. What to tell him? I settled on a brief note, "I'm gone. Be back Sunday." Should I explain more? But why, I thought resentfully. I hadn't invited him to stay. The truth was, I was delighted to get away. Adam made me so damned nervous living in my house.

I walked out to the car. All right, maybe I fled to the car. I always keep a travel pack there so there was no packing to be done. I like the feeling of being able to put the phone down and get into the car and go. I'd had moments when I had been driving home from work and, on a whim, headed for the local airport and a flight home to the coast of North Carolina. I don't have houseplants and I don't keep pets. All I need to do to leave is lock the door.

My travel pack includes enough clothes to travel for a million years. What do you really need to travel? Two pairs of shorts, three tee-shirts, one pair of long pants (you wear the second), two shirts with collars, one black stretch-velvet dress, a sweater, a bathing suit, five pairs of underpants, two bras and a few toiletries. If the place requires a coat, you shouldn't go. Of course, everything is wrinkle free and everything washes out in the sink and dries by morning.

Lately I'd gotten expansive and thrown in a pair of sandals. That wasn't as simple as it sounds because of my 250 rule. I never own more than 250 things. I'd been right up there at my limit and I had to figure out what to get rid of before I bought the sandals. After all, I couldn't just throw in my regular pair. The whole idea was to keep everything in the travel pack ready to go, which meant having duplicates.

That was the only tough thing about a travel pack. I used up thirty items of my 250, counting toiletries, on something that mostly sat in the car. But it was definitely worth it. Carlotta could have called me on the way to the grocery store and I would have simply turned around and headed for her house.

On the way over I considered whether I should have expanded the note to Adam a little bit. Maybe I should call and leave a message. The whole thing was very confusing. "Fuck 'em if they can't take a joke," I finally told myself. I kept my eyes on the road and never even glanced at the phone.

Carlotta had a boat. Not just a boat, a thirty-five-foot Dickinson, a big old wooden, heavy weather sailboat. Her aunt Sally died several years ago and left it to her. Aunt Sally loved two things in life, her Dickinson and her niece Carlotta. Well, there were those cigars.

I had known Aunt Sally for years—after all, Carlotta and I had been friends since college. She had lived at Mattapoisett on Cape Cod and Carlotta and I used to go down and sail with her on weekends. She had the boat rigged for single-handed sailing and at eighty-five she was still taking it out by herself. At least by then she had given up night sailing.

Carlotta was relieved at that—she had always

been expecting to run into a twenty-foot steel buoy some dark night—but I wasn't. Night sailing with Aunt Sally was an experience unlike any other.

The wind would be kicking the waves into foam and the night would be pitch black. Aunt Sally would be standing at the wheel in a bright yellow slicker because of the spray. Her eyes were so bright and her posture so lively you could mistake her for a twenty-year-old in the darkness. And she'd have that boat hauling ass. Carlotta's face would be so pale I could see it from ten feet away in the dark. But it was perfectly safe. Aunt Sally knew every buoy and every rock in the waters anywhere around Cape Cod.

Well, maybe not perfectly safe. Aunt Sally liked to *sail*, which meant to her not using the motor unless you had to. She never had to. I had seen her tack back and forth out of a harbor so narrow a five-year-old could throw a rock across it, and even then no one on board had dared suggest to her she use the motor. People used to gather on the shore to watch Aunt Sally sail out of a harbor like that even in broad daylight. On a dark night, in a thirty-knot wind, in a tight harbor with boats moored like cars in a parking lot, well, Chuck Yeager would have fallen in love with Aunt Sally.

Sailing with Carlotta was pretty tame compared to Aunt Sally, not that Aunt Sally was entirely gone. Both Carlotta and I knew she was still there, sitting in the cockpit, wearing her inevitable L. L. Bean boat shoes, smoking her cigars, reading the tide tables like some folks read the daily newspaper. Her presence on the boat was still so strong you couldn't climb on it without feeling you needed to ask her permission to come aboard.

Carlotta came out of her house loaded with duffels. She put them into the back of my car and went back and forth for an eternity carrying duffels and bags. I didn't offer to help.

"Carlotta," I said when she was finally in the car and we were headed out. "Is Hank joining us?"

"No, why?"

"Perhaps we're entertaining the entire population of Southern Vermont."

"Give it a rest, Michael. There's plenty of storage on the boat."

"There isn't enough storage on Donald Trump's yacht for that amount of stuff. You have four duffel bags of clothes for one overnight."

"Some are foul-weather gear."

"Foul-weather gear is on the boat."

"I brought some more."

"It's Ralph Lauren, isn't it? You brought Ralph Lauren with you again, didn't you." Carlotta had a thing about Ralph Lauren sheets, about Ralph Lauren anything.

"What's your problem?"

"He's a rip-off artist. He makes L. L. Bean look-alikes and charges quadruple."

"It's my quadruple."

"I am never traveling with you."

"So, don't."

We fell silent. It was an old argument but I could never let it rest. I loved lean and fit and fast. I didn't like encumbrances. I liked simple and I hated "stuff." I hated traveling with it, living with it, wearing it.

But I also loved Carlotta dearly and Carlotta loved "stuff." She wore dangling bracelets. She wore make-up on sailboats; she traveled with more "stuff" than Elizabeth Taylor.

Actually, Carlotta never knew how much self-restraint I exercised. I glanced over at her nails. They were green with what looked like designs painted on them. Whatever self-restraint had temporarily silenced me evaporated.

"Carlotta, you don't go to court with those things, do you? Half the judges in Vermont have never seen anything like that. They'll cite you for contempt."

"No, I did them this morning."

"You did your nails to go sailing?"

Carlotta gave me a withering look. "They lied to me," she said. "Pretty clearly you're back to your old self. They told me you were a complete wreck. What a joke. But if you don't pipe down, there will be a second attempt on your life." With that, she pulled out a book and ignored me for the rest of the trip.

There was a light breeze rippling the water when we arrived at the harbor. We both got out of the car and just stood there for a moment, watching the boats bob on their moorings. The breeze was strong enough to blow my hair back and I could smell the salt in the air. Exhilaration rose in my chest like a tide.

Without a word, we started unloading the luggage. I relented enough to help Carlotta carry the bags to the main dock, mostly because I was too excited to wait for her to do it. We found her little wooden dinghy on the dinghy dock and launched it. The dinghy was an anachronism. Boats as big as Carlotta's tended to have rubber rafts these days with small outboard motors. But it would have seemed like sacrilege to either of us to motor out to Aunt Sally's sailboat. And the rowing was a ritual for us both that separated sea from shore.

I picked up the oars. Lordy, I do love to row. From the first stroke, I feel like I'm home. I stretched forward, bending my knees and then straightening them as I pulled the oars through the water and leaned back. My body fell into the rhythm with a kind of relief. My head may tolerate sitting in a chair all week but my body hates it.

As the dinghy bobbed through the water, I laughed out loud remembering the several times I'd run solidly into boats, buoys or moorings while rowing. The problem with rowing is that you're going backward and I always got so carried away I would forget to turn around and look where I'm going. I needed a Carlotta sitting there steering for me. She made no comment at the laughter. She was used to my crazy behavior on the water.

The little dinghy bobbed gamely through the waves and I watched the shore slowly recede. It couldn't recede fast enough for me. We rowed across the harbor to the outer edge of boats where Carlotta kept hers and pulled up to *Aunt Sally*. The only major change Carlotta had made on the boat when she got her was to rename her. Aunt Sally had called her *Uncharted,* which neither Carlotta nor I ever understood and Aunt Sally wouldn't explain. Clearly and unmistakably the boat should be called *Aunt Sally.* She was Aunt Sally's alter ego when she was alive and all that was left of her now that she was dead. Besides, it allowed both of us to talk to her without admitting we were talking to a ghost. Everybody talks to their boats.

"Aunt Sally," I said when I first grabbed her side and spun the little dinghy around. "We're back. Permission to come aboard."

We picked up the "stuff" from the dock and headed out to open sea, unabashedly motoring. I could practically hear Aunt Sally sputter but too bad. "Hey," I said out loud to the criticism I could feel just hovering in the air. "We're just the bench team. What do you expect?" It was an old argument with Aunt Sally that had started right after she died.

We turned the boat in the wind to raise the sails as soon as we cleared the harbor. We might motor a little when we needed to but the rhythm of motoring was all wrong for a sailboat. Actually, there was no rhythm to motoring at all. Motoring was like driving a car over the water. Never mind the wind or the current or the waves. Motoring meant not paying attention to any of the forces around you, just driving as though you were on concrete. And that wasn't even mentioning the noise of the motor. You couldn't hear a sea gull when you were motoring, not if he used a megaphone.

All in all, motoring was to sailing like instant coffee was to brewed hazelnut, like masturbation was to sex. Personally, I had always secretly wondered if stinkpotters—as we sailboat people generously called motorboat folks—had some strange form of brain damage. Maybe they were the people advertisers had in mind when they wrote those memorable words: "the look and feel of real plastic."

The breeze was kicking up so Carlotta and I unclipped the mainsail and put on a smaller one and a working jib. Between us and the hydraulic winches we raised the sails and tied them down. I pulled in the main sheet and cut the motor. The sail caught the wind and the boat leaned into the water and took off like the thoroughbred she was. Aunt Sally always did love to sail.

It was Sunday evening before we got around to talking about what had happened to me. Carlotta had tried a couple of times but I had cut her off. I just wanted some time free of the whole mess.

But Sunday rolled around all too soon and both of us were pensive. Shore was calling and it was impossible to ignore it forever. I looked out over the water. The bright red sunset was tethering the boat to the shore with golden lines. Lulled by the glow of the gold, the sea had settled into a vast smooth expanse. The occasional duck left a long wake on the slick surface.

"So, why'd he do it?" Carlotta asked.

I shrugged. "What do you know about it?" I replied.

"Pretty much what Adam knows and what the police reports say. I've been assigned to the case by the County Attorney's Office."

"You mean you got yourself assigned."

"I mean I got myself assigned."

"I don't know," I replied. "Beats me," I said. "Flipped his wig, I guess, over flunking the polygraph and blurting out more than he meant to.

"Except for one thing. I ran into a vet," I said. "He'd heard about this. Good old Leila at her usual discreet best. Anyway, she told him it was ketamine and he seemed to think it was too carefully chosen to be impulsive. It seems it's a particularly lethal substance and he pointed out it was unlikely anybody was just walking around with it in their pocket. Whoever did it thought through what to use. Larsen would have had to bring it with him and why would he have done that?

"So I don't get it. Larsen had no way of knowing he'd flunk the polygraph. He had no way of knowing he'd confess to a bunch of stuff. I mean if he thought he was going to flunk the test and confess and he was going to kill me over it, why didn't he just refuse to take it? Plus, what was he going to do about John Davis? Kill him too or just assume he'd keep his mouth shut?" It occurred to me for the first time that maybe I should call John Davis and warn him about this, just in case.

We both sat there glumly for a moment. "It doesn't make any sense," Carlotta said slowly, "unless he had it with him for some other reason."

"As in what? I'm the only target he went after. Nobody else was driving my car. Or even sitting in it." I thought for a minute. "Uh oh," I said. "Uh oh, I've got a bad feeling about this." Carlotta looked at me. "I *wasn't* the original target. I wasn't even the reason he came up here.

"What have you always heard me say about sex offenders?" I asked. Carlotta shook her head. "That there's no such thing as coincidence. How many times have I said that when a sex offender moves in across from a school, it is *never* a coincidence."

"True," she said, "but—"

"I never really questioned why Larsen drove three hours for an evaluation. He just said his mother lived up here. But it could not be an accident that he came where Zania was. It's never an accident. Larsen didn't come up here because I was such a great evaluator or even to see his mother. He came up here because of Zania. He's been worried about her all along. He came to see me because he'd have an excuse to be in the area, an excuse to be driving back and forth."

"Which means," Carlotta said thoughtfully, "he probably didn't follow you to the hospital. Could be he went there with the ketamine looking for Zania. Zania was the one he expected to find at the hospital."

"And it would have been easy," I said. "He knows his way around a hospital, especially this one where his dad worked. He would have found her, met her for a cup of coffee, anything to have contact with her in some quiet sort of way, then slipped the ketamine into her coffee and walked her outside to talk. Or anywhere. An empty office for twenty minutes would have done it. That stuff is very fast and it shuts everything down." I was silent for a minute, remembering just how fast it shut everything down.

"Anyway, it's available in a hospital so Larsen had no reason to think they would ever have looked outside the hospital for the killer. Not in a million years. As far as he knew you'd have been interviewing everybody on the ward. They'd have been checking medication supplies and asking who had access and who had a grudge against her. They'd have turned the hospital inside out. But there was no way to think they would ever have even looked at a guy three hours away who nobody knew anything about."

"But," Carlotta said, "you knew about him—and the connection. You could have told them."

"But Larsen never knew that. Zania approached me in confidence. I never told Larsen anything about her. I never confronted him with anything she said. And the hospital never told him anything about her. They wouldn't even tell me who she was. She called me. He never knew I'd ever met her.

"Which raises the question of what she knows," I added. "It has to be something pretty important."

"As in you don't think digitally raping a woman in a coma is important?" Carlotta asked sharply.

"In terms of destroying him," I replied, "maybe, maybe not. That was subject to interpretation. There was no way to prove he had done it. He could have said Zania imagined it. He was just adjusting the covers for the patient and Zania made some hysterical leap. He could even have said she was seeking revenge because he broke off the affair. Who's to say? There wouldn't have been any evidence. The

patient was unconscious so she wasn't going to give
a statement. It was his word against Zania's and he
had a whole lot more status than she did. You want
to go to court with a case like that? 'Jilted girlfriend
makes sex charge against prominent physician' or
'Nurse with a grudge accuses doctor, makes sex
charge.' And if the hospital fired him on that evidence, they'd have surely found their tails in court.

"No, I think it was something that was much
more of a threat than that. Something that could be
proved."

"So why go after you at all? Why not stick with the
plan? She was still much more of a threat. I know
how you get yourself in knots with this confidentiality stuff. If he pulled the plug on the eval you
couldn't have told anybody anything unless he was
molesting children."

"I don't know. Maybe he *was* disoriented from
flunking the polygraph and panicky when he saw
me at the hospital. God knows whether he developed some paranoid fear that I was there to see
Zania. The sight of a press conference couldn't have
helped. It would just have reminded him how bad it
would all be if this came out. Hell, I don't know
why."

"You might be right," Carlotta said. "About all of it.
Let's say you are. But my problem with this is that it
doesn't bring us one iota closer to proving he did
it. Not one iota." I didn't answer her. The truth was,
there wasn't going to be any way to prove it. And I
didn't want to talk about that.

"What now?" she asked. "You're the shrink. Say

it's true. Will he count his lucky stars he didn't get caught this time and call it a day?"

"No," I said. "I don't think so. But I don't think he'll go after me. I just had to do with the panic of the moment. But there's still Zania. She lives alone, just her and the most adorable toddler you have ever seen in your life. Larsen still has no reason to think we know anything about her and she still represents whatever threat to him she did before."

Carlotta looked glum. Neither of us spoke but the same thing was on both our minds. Without a word Carlotta got up and started packing. Slowly, I got up and followed her. Finally, when all was done, Carlotta sat down and started in again. "All right," she said, "what are we going to do about it? The state police aren't going to camp on her lawn. A restraining order doesn't do any good when someone's trying to kill you. Not to mention he hasn't even threatened her, so we couldn't get one. As far as the police are concerned, this is all guesswork. Besides, the state cops don't even have enough people to patrol the highway. And Twin Rivers, where she lives, has one part-time police officer for the whole town."

I didn't reply. Finally, I said, "I could contact Reggie. I could tell him I know all about Zania and if anything happens to her I will publicly accuse him of killing her, no matter how she dies."

"Except," Carlotta said, "it doesn't sound like he does very well under pressure. How do you know he'd back off? He could just as easily do something rash to both of you."

"Well, what else then? She won't even talk to

Adam. I can talk to her maybe, but trust me, she's not somebody who likes to be frightened out of her wits. This isn't going to make her mad; it's going to scare the bejesus out of her. She doesn't have that stubborn thing. She has that ostrich thing. And while we sit here floating around, watching the ducks, he could be knocking on her door. He probably is knocking on her door." Which, of course, is what both of us were thinking.

"What about that old movie trick?" Carlotta said. "What if she tells him if anything happens to her she'll have a sealed envelope delivered."

"That kind of thing works," I said, "when you don't have a toddler he can threaten. All he'd have to do is get ahold of Robin and she'd cough up every sealed envelope in the known universe. And so would I."

"Then her only way out is to contact the hospital and tell them what she knows," Carlotta said firmly. "If she doesn't tell everything she knows, then she's still a target."

"Oh, that's good," I said. "Tell someone who can't stare down a feisty toddler that she needs to stand up to a homicidal psychopath. That should go down well. 'Hey, I know you don't like to cross the street if there's a car in sight but just stand out here right in front of this tank going full speed and hold your hand up. I'm sure it'll stop. At least I think so. But in case you think you have any peace of mind left, let me tell you that if you don't stop it, this tank is surely going to sneak up behind you and do something that will close your throat and paralyze your lungs and no matter how hard you try your lungs

just won't work and the air will just stop coming—' "
I stopped abruptly and looked at the water for a few
minutes. I shook my head. "Jesus, where did that
come from? Sorry."

"For what?" Carlotta said gently.

"I don't think I'm over this," I said, surprised.

She rolled her eyes, then laughed and shook her
head. "Jesus, Michael, you're a trip."

Neither of us spoke. There was a dinghy to be
rowed in and a long drive and craziness at the other
end of it, and I, for one, had no stomach for any of
it. "You know what?" I said. "I have to go back and I
need to go back but I don't want to go back."

"Well, I never do but then I could live here. You
surprise me. You're usually hyper by now and ready
to take on the world, even the Reginald Larsens."

"Not this time." I paused but Carlotta didn't say
anything and Aunt Sally didn't comment so I went
on. "It's a whole bunch of stuff. There's another bad
case going on. Marv has wandered into some territory where he didn't belong and he got his and a
client's ass kicked from here to Shangri-La. I couldn't
stop him and now I'm caught in the middle of it. I
hate being in a car wreck when I'm not driving."

"I know," Carlotta replied. "You'd rather make
your own. It doesn't sound nearly as bad as almost
getting killed. What's new about getting your ass
kicked? You don't even play basketball with people
your own size." Carlotta thought the fact that I
played pick-up games with people who had fifty
pounds and six inches on me was a sign of demen-
tia. "Sure this doesn't have to do with Adam?"

"What about Adam? Everything's fine with Adam," I said quickly.

"Sometimes I think you get more nervous when Adam tries to get close to you than you do when somebody tries to kill you."

"That's ridiculous," I said indignantly. And it was. It was true, but it was still ridiculous.

I could tell Carlotta wasn't going to help on this one so I shut up. What else could I say? That sometimes I got tired of violence and craziness and perps who run over everyone in sight? That no matter what happened in the confrontation session with Jody and her father, nothing was ever going to give Jody her childhood back? That in the real world people like Reggie Larsen won a whole lot of the time and there was a real possibility he'd kill either Zania or me or both of us and get away with it? And failing that, the least that would happen was that we couldn't touch him and he'd go his merry way, raping women deep in the trenches of anesthesia and I'd spend the rest of my life knowing about it and unable to do a goddamn thing.

How many things like that did I have on my conscience already? Men who had walked in off the street with no charges against them who had told me they were sexually attracted to children but denied ever molesting one. I knew and they knew I knew that they were lying through their teeth. They were child molesters plain and simple but there wasn't a goddamn thing I could do about it. Then there was the university professor who liked to choke his dates unconscious while raping them but the woman who told me wouldn't report him. I knew about the moderator of the town meeting who had raped two children in front of each other while singing them a song. One was dead from suicide and the other was a woman who didn't think she'd be believed and who had panic attacks when she heard that song.

Something in nearly dying had knocked some of the wind out of me. I could see the windmills out there but I was tired of charging them. On the other hand, I still didn't like the way they looked on the skyline.

I called Zania from the car but she wasn't home. I checked the hospital and confirmed she was working. This would keep till tomorrow. Even I knew that making someone hysterical while they were working in the ICU wasn't the best idea. It would seriously augment a reputation for insensitivity that I knew needed no augmentation.

There were two messages on the machine when I got home. I hit the play button and listened to Mama's exasperated voice—Mama always took it personally if you weren't there to take her call—and Adam's puzzled tones. Mama demanded to know where I was; Adam just said simply he'd got my note and he'd stay at his house until I got back.

I replayed his message idly and realized I was listening for annoyance. If he was annoyed, I could get pissed and I'd a whole lot rather feel pissed than guilty. I laughed when I realized what I was up to. I hated feeling guilty worse than anything in the world but Adam didn't help me out. He just sounded worried.

I called Mama first. For me, she was easier. Mama and I had been in the ring countless times before and we had each other's moves down pat. "Well, where have you been, girl? I thought I'd never get ahold of you."

"What? You've been calling? This was the only message."

"Well, I thought I'd get you sooner or later." I could hear the criticism hovering in her voice, but over what? The world centered around Mama, that was over what. Mama had wanted to reach me and I hadn't been there. End of story.

"Mama, I've only been gone a couple of days. So I'm back."

"Well, you are never there when a body tries to reach you." She'd gone one sentence too far and predictably I took the bait.

"Oh, come on, Mama. You sit around waiting for the phone to ring? So I've got a life. What's up?" Mama never really called to chat. One of my relatives must be in jail or pregnant or dying of cancer or could be one of them killed someone. I had a diverse group of relatives.

"Well, it's your cousin Wilbur. You know he bought that marina out by Harker's Island, mortgaged everything he owned to do it. He's been scraping by ever since."

"Yeah, I remember."

"Well, he thought he had it made when he bought that thing. But it was harder to make a go of it than he thought, don't you know. He's had a lot of business but nothing big, just little repairs and things. Then this big yacht comes in, coming down the Inland Waterway from New York to Florida. Wilbur said the thing was tore up. He don't know what happened to it but the motor was in a state. He said it hurt him just to look at the hull it was so bad. Looked like the damn thing had run into something big.

"Owner wouldn't really say what happened. Just said he'd got the boat at a bargain and knew it needed some work. Wilbur didn't think he was on the up-and-up with him but it weren't none of his business.

"Well, it needed some work all right. Wilbur put twenty-five thousand dollars of work into that damn thing. Took him two months of having his whole crew working on it day and night. He was fair about it. He told the boat owner all along the way what it was costing. But he kept saying, 'Go ahead. Do whatever it takes,' like money was no object. Money was falling out of trees. Acting like a big shot, don't you know."

"And?" Where was this going? Nowhere good for Wilbur, I had a feeling.

"I'm getting to it. Just hold your horses. Wilbur got up Monday morning and that son of a bitch had took off in the night. Soon as the boat could go. He just climbed on her and took off. Left Wilbur high and dry. Didn't pay a penny. Goddamn son-of-a-northern-carpet-bagging-bitch."

I ignored Mama's hostile references to the North; I had grown up with them. Not that they didn't register. Mama's constant hostile references to the North might have something to do with why I lived there.

"Oh, shit," I said. "What a shame." And it was. Wilbur was a nice guy but a little naive. "He didn't get any of it as he went along?"

"Not a penny. You know Wilbur. He'd believe anything they say to him. The guy kept telling him he'd settle up when they were done. Took off the day right before Wilbur finished."

"Oh, I'm sorry, Mama. That's awful. What's Wilbur going to do?"

"Well, he went to a lawyer, a' course. He went up to see Claude on Main Street but the truth is he doesn't really know anything for sure about that guy."

"What do you mean? Nothing?"

"Well, not really. He don't even really know if he's got the right name. He knows the boat, inside and out, but that don't help him much."

"Oh, Christ."

"That ain't even the worst of it. Claude says if they do find him, they're going to have to sue him back in his home state, wherever the hell that is, and it could take two years and most of the twenty-five thousand to do it. So, what kind of help is that? The best the law could do for him is to wait two years—if anybody can find that son of a bitch—and then get whatever crumbs the lawyers leave after they're done getting their cut."

Mama didn't like lawyers. Never had. Daddy had been a lawyer and I was never sure if he had been an exception or not. "Oh, shit," I said again, "is Wilbur going to lose the business?"

"Lose the business?" Mama said, surprised. "Of course not."

"Why not? You said he was barely getting by."

"Well, we're going to have to get his money back for him." Mama said it slowly as though she was talking to a total idiot.

"What do you mean 'we'? There's not a whole lot I can do to get Wilbur's money back. There's not a whole lot you can do, for that matter." I paused but Mama didn't speak. "Is there?" I said tentatively.

"Of course there's something we can do. There's always something you can do." If Mama had a motto, it would be, "There's always something you can do." I got a sense of unease in my stomach. Sometimes the things Mama thought you could do weren't anything I thought you could do. "I wouldn't let that son of a bitch get away with this for hell or high water."

"What are you going to do?" I asked flatly.

"Why, it's just like those goddamn Yankees to come down here and think they can run all over people. They act like we're stupid or something." Which would be, I had to admit, a mistake. Mama was a lot of things, many of them less than admirable, but stupid was not one of them.

"So what are you going to do?" I said again.

"I don't think I'm going to tell you. You've taken on airs since you've gone up there and I don't know if you'd approve of people doing something more than handing their money over to a lawyer."

"Is it legal or illegal?"

"What kind of question is that?" Mama snorted. "What do you take me for?" I noticed she hadn't answered the question.

"Mama, I am not going to come down and bail you out of jail."

"Well, that'll be the day that Billy Lewis puts me in jail."

She was right about that. Billy Lewis, our current sheriff, had gone to school with me and knew Mama all too well. Mama would have to commit an ax murder in front of him for Billy to put Mama in jail. This was the South, after all, where "he needed killing" was a viable defense.

"I'll tell you this much. I'll fix his butt."

I thought about it. "Mama, there isn't anything you can do legally and the law takes a dim view of hiring men to beat up on people or whatever you're thinking of."

"Beat up on people? How the hell would that help Wilbur? You've been living up where the sun don't shine. It's froze every brain cell you ever had. You better come down here to God's country and thaw out. I'm disappointed in you, girl. You ought to know your mama would come up with something better than that."

She had me stumped. What the hell could she be thinking of that would get Wilbur's money back?

"All right, Mama, you're going to do what you're going to do. So do me a favor. Make that one phone call to Claude, not me." I was pissed at her for being coy. It wasn't like her. Mama usually pointed to left field before she swung the bat.

I hung up annoyed, stared at the phone for a minute and then dialed Adam's office. I was already worked up over Mama as I dialed but Adam deserved the heat, I told myself. He had no business worrying about me and fussing over me. I could go where I damn well pleased. I definitely did not have to check in with him. Just because he lived in my house didn't mean I had to spend the weekend with him. So why did he want to know where I was? It was none of his damn business.

"Adam Bower," he said, answering, and for a second I saw him with the moonlight shining on his shoulders in the hot tub. It tripped me up and I lost my voice. "Hello," he said, again. I cleared my throat and got my voice back, more or less.

"Hi," I squeaked, not the firm kick-ass-hey-what's-it-to-you kind of voice I'd planned.

"Michael," he said dryly, "you're alive."

I had a lot of retorts. I could have said, "What's it to you?" I could have said, "I'm gone one weekend and you give me shit?" I could have said, "So?" I could have said, "Just because you're living in my house doesn't give you the right to run my life." I could have said a lot of things. But none of them came to mind. "Dinner?" was all I said, meekly.

Later in bed, sleep and I had a falling-out. I looked over at Adam who seemed to have no such problem. Men are a lot like computers: one big power surge and they're out for hours.

I drifted in and out, images of Larsen flitting through my head. He was forever putting something in a cup that Zania was forever raising to drink. The pictures pulled me to the surface like mosquitoes in a tent. Then the image shifted. I saw the floor of the hospital, felt the cold tile pressed against my face and saw feet rushing toward me. In the background the sound of a respirator droned on. As I drifted deeper my throat closed and my lungs wouldn't work and I woke with a startle, breathing hard and frightened.

Adam stirred beside me at the startle and his eyes opened quietly. I turned on my side to face him and he put his hand on my shoulder to steady me until my breathing slowed. I looked at his face, the lines softened by the unconscious caverns he had left behind. "You're not just here to protect me," I said sleepily. "You came to hold me."

"Whatever," he said carefully.

18

In the morning I tried to figure out the best time to contact Zania and the best way I could pitch this thing. I knew she'd been working all night and catching her when she was exhausted wasn't likely to make hearing what I had to say any easier.

So swallowing the idea that Larsen could be standing outside her door, I decided to wait and go by in the afternoon. I'd get only one shot at this and I needed to do it right.

It was the sensible thing to do but all through the day, running back and forth from meetings to seminars, I fretted about whether the sensible thing was the wrong thing. Who knew if today was the day Larsen would decide to finish things up.

By three, I was mercifully back in my office for a breather. I was going over messages when the phone rang and I jumped so high I nearly liberated my coffee cup from the desk. Oh, sweet Jesus, don't let it be anything wrong with Zania or Robin. I should have gone over this morning. I should have gone over last night. But the voice on the phone was a stranger.

"Dr. Stone, this is Doug Griffen," a man said smoothly. "I'm a reporter from *People* magazine. I'd like to speak with you about Reginald Larsen."

"What?" I asked, standing up so abruptly the chair tipped back. "What did you say?"

"I am doing an article on Reginald Larsen," the voice said, calmly, "and I have been told by sources in the hospital that he is seeing you for a psychological evaluation. I was wondering if you'd like to comment on that."

"You must be joking," I said. "Surely you know that no therapist can comment on any patient or alleged patient. If this man was my client I couldn't tell you that and if he wasn't I couldn't even tell you that."

"You should know," Griffen said, "there are some very bad rumors surfacing in the hospital about Dr. Larsen. Let me explain how this all came about. I just went there to do a story on this new miracle anesthesia test which they say might save twenty thousand lives a year. We've got an issue coming out on the new pioneers in medicine and this seemed like a natural.

"So I just started poking around trying to warm up the story. You know, human interest stuff. Who is he? What are his hobbies? What he's really like? I was looking for some warm, fuzzy anecdotes about working till all hours, years of dedication, that sort of thing.

"Then it turned out he was on leave. Okay, I thought, rest after labors, long vacation, whatever. But something just didn't smell right. Everybody was so tight-lipped. And nobody had anything *good* to say about him personally at all. Nothing.

"So a source turns up. That's all I can say. But it looks like a good source to me. Now, actually, there's more than one. They're coming out of the woodwork. I've had two calls since the announcement."

"What announcement? What are you talking about?"

"You didn't hear?" he said. "The hospital has accepted Dr. Larsen's resignation."

"What? As of when?"

"As of nine o'clock this morning, Dr. Stone. I would say someone isn't keeping you informed. Dr. Larsen is leaving to pursue his research interests, that is, if you believe the joint statement he and the hospital issued. He's withdrawing from clinical work entirely. Which doesn't make any sense, does it? Hospitals have all kinds of research types on their staffs. With a discovery like this he could stay on the hospital staff and do full-time research. He'd have research grants up the wazoo. Plus nobody mentioned where he's going, which is to say, he's not going *to* something, he's going *from* something.

"And that brings me to you, Dr. Stone. Off the record. What's wrong with this guy? Why is he seeing you? Does he have some kind of problem? Drugs? Alcohol? Or does he have some *other* kind of problem that's more in your line of work?"

"Off the record?" I said.

"Off the record," he agreed.

"Off the record, my eye," I replied, nearly yelling into the phone. "Ten to one you're tape-recording this. There is no such thing as 'off the record' when talking to you good ol' boys. Read my lips, good buddy. I could not tell you that Prince Philip is or isn't a client of mine. I couldn't tell you that Elvis Presley is or isn't a client of mine. I cannot make any comment about whether anyone living or dead is or is not, was or was not, a client of mine in this lifetime or in any previous past lives. No comment." I slammed the phone down. I hated it when those good ol' boys lied to me like that.

I stood for a moment, my hand shaking on the phone. This was big trouble. Why didn't people like Larsen ever have a clue? If you want to screw around, don't get famous. If you want to get famous, don't screw around. It wasn't rocket science. They didn't have to be moral. Just a little paranoia would work wonders.

Still standing, I picked up the phone again and dialed Margaret Jones. Would she take my call? "This is Dr. Stone," I said, trying to keep my voice calm. "Could I speak to Dr. Jones?"

The secretary was gone only for a moment. "I'm sorry," she said, "Dr. Jones is tied up right now. She doesn't know when she'll be able to get back to you."

I resisted an impulse to yell at the secretary, who had nothing at all to do with any of it, not unless she was one of Griffen's sources. "Give her this number," I said, rattling off my home number. "Tell her to call when she can."

"Son of a bitch," I said, hanging up the phone and starting to pace. "Son of a bitch." They'd cut Reggie a deal. He'd resigned, no problem, and I'd bet Bill Gates's weekly income that in exchange they would not forward anything, not *anything* to the licensing board. That's the way it worked. Otherwise, why would he resign if it wasn't going to help him?

And it was probably my fault for scaring the bejesus out of the hospital. Investigating Larsen for sexual improprieties was one thing, but the bad publicity and the liability the hospital would have if he'd actually killed someone was another story altogether. I knew from experience hospitals thought about those things—a lot.

And it sounded to me like they weren't so sure he hadn't because before Margaret Jones heard from me, there wasn't any talk of working out a deal. Not until they got an eval and knew what they were dealing with. So why this sudden deal if I hadn't hit some kind of nerve?

The hospital was going to quietly let this whole thing go away and it would be off to the next one for Larsen, no doubt in a distant state where it would be unlikely that any rumors would follow. He'd arrive as the conquering hero, fresh with his discovery, and start raping unconscious women all over again.

In the meantime, there was still Zania and she could still upset his chances for fame and fortune.

And from her side, things had just gotten worse: there was no longer anyone to tell. The hospital wouldn't want to hear it. Case closed. She could go beg the police to get involved but that was even more intimidating than telling the hospital.

The press would love to hear it, of course, and they would surely find her. Anybody at the hospital who knew about me surely knew about Zania. The leak was somewhere very high, maybe on the ethics committee itself. Sooner or later Reggie had to hear the press was onto him and looking for Zania. I grabbed my car keys and headed out the door, but I didn't get very far. As I opened the door I almost collided with Melissa.

"There's someone here to see you," she said.

"Who?"

"Mark Carlson."

"What? He just stopped by? Tell him I can't talk to him right now."

"I think you'd better."

"Why?"

"Because he's crying."

I cursed and turned around. "All right," I said. "I'll talk to him for a minute. Just a minute."

"Mark," I said, standing up and reaching forward to shake hands when he entered the door. "I really only have a moment. There's something urgent I have to do."

He didn't seem to hear me. He tucked in his shirttail even farther than it was already. He straightened his tie although it didn't need straightening. He was blinking rapidly and he started to speak but nothing came out. "Sit down," I said gently, relinquishing my keys. "What happened?"

"I'm sorry," he said finally. He was speaking so quietly I had to lean forward to catch the words.

"Sorry for what?" I said.

"But how could he? How could he?" The voice was plaintive and the rapid blinking didn't slow. He was in shock.

"Your daughter?" I asked.

"I asked her. I mean, I thought it was ridiculous but I asked her anyway. I just asked if her grandfather ever told her to keep anything secret from us. I saw the look in her eyes. It hit me right in the stomach. I was in the army and someone took a swing at me once in a bar. He caught me right in the stomach. It felt like that. I'll never forget the look in her eyes."

I took a deep breath and tried to put Reggie Larsen aside for a moment. Mark Carlson had woken up one morning and opened the curtains to find a whole different landscape outside than had been there the night before. He had gone from being a resident of the land he lived in to being a stranger. Nothing was the same and nothing ever would be the same again.

"Is she going to be okay?" he asked. He blew his nose noisily. It looked like tears had been coming haphazardly for a while. "I need to know. That's why I came. Leila said you treat children who've been abused. Is she going to be okay?"

He meant, of course, was she going to be like Jody but he didn't want to say it. And the real answer was, who knew? "I don't know her, Mr. Carlson," I said gently. "I've never met her. But lots of kids who are abused do fine, maybe most of them if their family supports them. What does your wife say about this?"

"She went crazy," he said. "She's never liked my father. She's always said he was nothing but a bully and she's hated the fact that I talk to my mother on the phone every night. She says she isn't nearly as helpless as I thought. I've always felt caught between her and them.

"She went completely crazy. She started screaming and yelling that none of them would ever set foot in her house again or she would take the children and leave. She says she'll see him in jail. She says she'll see him in hell. I think she means it."

"What did your mother say?"

He looked down. "I called her right away. I needed to talk to her. She said the most unbelievable thing. She said Cindy got the idea from Jody, that she was just trying to get attention. I tried to tell her that Cindy didn't know anything about Jody. We've never told her anything about what Jody says my dad did. I told my mother about the look Cindy gave me. Then she started shrieking that she was tired of all this stupid uproar over a little sex. That sex wasn't a big deal and everybody was trying to make it a big deal and what about her? Did I ever think about how she felt? Why didn't I think about her? She started yelling that I didn't care about her any more than my father did, that he was off screwing his little chickie and she was there alone and nobody cared about her . . . It was incredible."

"His little chickie?"

"That's what she said."

"Who was she talking about?"

"I don't know. That's the first I've ever heard."

"She knows where he is?"

"I don't care where he is. But wherever he is, he better stay there. I'm not sure I could kill him but I think my wife could."

19

It took another hour before I could get out of the office. Mark Carlson was grieving the loss of a safer, better world than the one he was living in and it was not an easy grief. He had spent his life stretching himself thin trying to protect his mother and explain away his father and the sister he had sacrificed to do it had now metamorphosed into his daughter. Somehow he thought his father would never betray him or his family that way, but of course, a guy who'll screw his daughter will screw his grandchild just as fast. The real Golden Rule was, "If they'll do it to others, they'll do it to you."

Betrayal always left a wake. It was probably the reason they shot spies. Deception was just too crazy-making. Soldiers announced who they were. Everybody knew they'd kill you. The one good thing you could say about an enemy soldier was he never asked you to trust him. There was no bond with him, and without a bond, there was no such thing as betrayal. The one thing about spies, they pretended to be someone they weren't, someone you could trust.

So it was after four before I found myself on the road to Zania's house, hands clutching the wheel tightly with some sort of primordial dread at what I'd find. "This is ridiculous," I told myself. "Maybe Larsen's a risk to her but if he is, he's going to be a risk tomorrow and the next day and the next day. What am I going to do? Worry every day for the rest of my life as long as they're both alive?"

The old farmhouse looked peaceful enough and Zania's car was in the driveway. Surely by now she'd be up. I wondered idly who watched Robin while she worked and slept and whether she'd picked her up yet.

No one answered my knock, but I could hear music playing. I knocked again and when no one came, I started around back. I wasn't leaving without knowing everyone was okay or I'd worry about it all night.

As I walked by the windows I saw Zania sitting in the kitchen. She seemed to be swaying to the music. It was dreadfully loud and I wondered how a toddler dealt with that much noise. I knocked again on the back door and not sure she could even hear that, I tried the handle and opened the door enough to stick my head in. When Zania saw me, she startled and I realized she really hadn't heard me. She just stared at me for a moment and then got up and walked out of the room into the dining room. The music died and she came back in.

I had stepped inside in the meantime. "Hi," I said, uncertain of my reception.

"What do you want?" she asked, sitting down again at the kitchen table. Her speech was slurred and I suddenly realized that she was drunk.

"Just to talk," I replied, walking over and sitting down across from her.

"It's not my fault. I tried. I really did."

"Tried what?"

"You don't know what I'm talking about, do you?" She swayed slightly.

"No," I said truthfully, "I don't have a clue."

"Never mind," she said and picked up a glass in front of her.

Just then Robin walked in and said firmly, "Want juice."

"Oh, Jesus," Zania said, looking at Robin. "I don't have any juice."

"Why don't I see what you've got," I offered. I had the feeling Zania did not want to get up. I wasn't sure she could get up again. Without waiting for an answer, I went over to the refrigerator door and opened it. To my relief there was apple juice and I got some and poured it for Robin. When I turned around Zania had her head on the table. I handed the juice silently to Robin, who clutched the glass with both hands and wandered back out.

"How much are you drinking?"

She didn't answer for a moment then she lifted her head. "Not that much," she said.

"Every day?"

"No, not every day. No. Why would you say that? Who told you that?"

I picked up the glass in front of her and smelled it. "Rum?" I asked.

"None of your business," she said, putting her head back down again.

"So who's looking after your daughter while you're drunk?"

"She's fine."

"You're here alone? This is it? No one's here? No one's coming to take care of her? This is a problem, Zania. This is a big problem. You can't look after Robin this way." Just then the phone rang. Zania ignored it and so did I. When it finally stopped ringing, the answering machine came on and Reggie Larsen's urgent voice electrified the room.

"Zania," he said. "This is Reggie. I know you're there. I really need to talk with you. Right away. It's important, Zania. I've got something you'd be interested in. Please call me back right away. It's urgent." He left his number and hung up.

I was so surprised that for a moment I couldn't speak. Zania just closed her eyes. "You're still seeing Reggie," I said incredulously.

"Not really," she said.

"What does 'not really' mean?" I asked. "Not really? Have you lost your mind, Zania? You know damn well he tried to kill me. Doesn't it compute that he is dangerous? Dangerous to *anybody* who gets in his way? What is wrong with you?" I blurted out.

"I'm not seeing him," she said. "It's not like that."

"It's not like what? What is it like?"

"I'm not sleeping with him," she said.

"Oh, that helps," I said. "Zania, what is going on here? What are you doing with Reggie? What does he mean he's got something you'd be interested in, as in what?"

Zania didn't answer and I finally gave up. "I am calling Child Protective Services," I said. "You are too damn drunk to take care of a child. She could turn on the stove or put a plastic bag over her head and you wouldn't even notice." I started to get up when Zania lifted her head and grabbed my arm.

"No, no, no," she pleaded. "Don't do that." She started to cry and she held my arm so tight it hurt. "Don't. They'd take my daughter. I'd lose her. I can't lose her."

I put my hand over Zania's and sat back down and just held it there. "Zania," I asked gently. "What are you hiding? Are you in trouble with booze?"

"I'm in trouble with everything," she said. And then it hit me.

"Something you'd be interested in?" I said. "Drugs? Is Reggie supplying you with drugs?" Anesthesiologists had been known to have problems with drugs. Reggie wouldn't be the first who'd been tempted by the warehouses of painkillers he had access to.

She let go of my arm. "I don't know how he knew," she said. Suddenly, she seemed more sober. The threat to call Child Protection had frightened her out of some of her drunk, anyway. "It's in my records. Maybe he got them somehow."

"What's in your records?"

"I got caught. Five years ago. For drugs. Those goddamn drugs. I had to go through rehab or I'd lose my license—for good. Then what? Then what would I have done?" She rubbed her eyes, still sleepy. "Jesus, I was scared. I was so scared. I had to have urine screens for two years before I could even apply to come back.

"But I did it. I did it all. And it was good. It really was. It was a good thing. When Robin came along I was so damned grateful it had happened. I didn't touch anything through the entire pregnancy. Nothing."

"So what happened?"

"He knew I'd tell you. Maybe it was me, I keep thinking." She sat up tiredly and yawned. "He was up seeing a patient one time and I made some offhand comment about a drug the patient was on. I said something about it would fix anybody's troubles. I remember him looking at me. I thought then he knew but he just called later and asked me out. So I thought I was wrong. Now I think I was right the first time."

"He offered you drugs?"

"Not right away. We dated for a while. He pulled out some grass early on. Well, grass isn't a big deal. That's what I told myself anyway. And then later on he offered me some Percodan. The funny thing is I didn't really even want it. I just went along with it because I was so caught up in him. Jesus, he was so fucking nice and so smart and, yes, he was so fucking rich. I kept thinking what a good daddy he'd make for Robin. So I didn't want to lose him and I went along with it. Jesus, what a mistake."

There was nothing to say to that. "So now you know," she went on. She sighed and I realized she wasn't going to last much longer. She yawned again. I couldn't tell if she was about to go to sleep or pass out but it would be one or the other. "I couldn't tell the goddamn hospital what he was up to for fear he'd tell them about the drugs. And to tell the truth, once I climbed back into them, I was scared of losing them. That's when the booze started. I couldn't always get the drugs. Booze was better than nothing."

"Did you ever break off with Reggie?"

"Not really. I quit sleeping with him and I even moved up here and tried to break it off. His mother helped me get the job. She said she wouldn't tell him but . . ." Zania shrugged. "Before I knew it Reggie was back on my doorstep with some Demerol and some Percodan and, yeah, I let him in. So now you know." Her voice started fading and I leaned forward to catch her words. "I'm a lousy mother and I don't deserve to have her but I can't live without my daughter. She's all I have." She started to cry again and reached for the glass in front of her but I grabbed her arm and held it.

"It's Robin or the drugs," I said. "You choose."

She looked at the glass for a minute and then she let it go. I picked it up and walked over to the sink and threw the liquor down the drain.

"Do you have anyone who can come take care of Robin tonight?"

She shook her head. "Nobody?" I asked. "What about her sitter? I'll drop her off."

She shook her head again. "She's out of town," she said. "At her mother's. She left after I picked Robin up."

"Friends?"

She shook her head again. "I don't know anybody that well," she said. She put her head down again and I thought for a minute she had passed out.

"All right," I said finally. "I'll stay and look after her tonight. I've got some stuff in the car. You're still too drunk to take care of her. Tomorrow we'll make a plan." Zania would have to go back into rehab and God knew how she'd manage that, but tonight wasn't the time to talk about it.

"Zania, just tell me one thing."

She lifted her head. "What?"

"You told me that whole story about being so scared of him?"

She sighed. "It's true. I am scared of him."

"But you let him in anyway? You let him feed you drugs?"

Zania stared at the spot the glass had been in as though if she stared at it long enough she could bring it back. "You don't do drugs, do you?" she said. "Nobody who does drugs would ask me a question like that."

I walked into the other room looking for my charge. I had hardly heard a peep from Robin since I got there and I realized belatedly that was probably not a good sign. I found her mother's pocketbook open on the living room floor and lipstick smeared all over the couch and the rug, but no Robin. The front door was open and I ran outside, knowing that even slow country roads have cars, but Robin was sitting in the garden digging in the dirt.

I squatted down beside her and got hit immediately with the aroma of dirty diaper. "Come here, sugar," I said, picking her up. All children are named "Sugar" in the South up until the age of five at least. She yelled and struggled when I picked her up but changing diapers is one of those death-and-taxes things in the kid world—nothing to be done about it. She kicked so hard I held her on my side with her legs kicking out into space behind me and marched back inside.

Later, much later, she fell asleep with her thumb in her mouth after an endless reading of the same book. Toddlers like the same things: the same song, the same book and the same caretakers. Robin had eyed me suspiciously all night but except for her fervent objections to the diaper changing, she had tolerated me reasonably well. Dinner and a bath and the fifth reading of the same book had mellowed her. She snuggled closer as she fell asleep, the two of us curled up in her twin bed like refugees from a larger world.

I watched her face in the moonlight for a few minutes. Children's faces never looked as lifeless in sleep as adult faces did. Robin's small face had as much life force in sleep as it did when she was awake, only the live presence was maybe easier to see when she was still.

Funny, the grief didn't clip me until then. I had played with her, fed her, changed her, bathed her and put on a small flannel nightgown without once asking the question that now seemed unstoppable: would my small, sweet Jordan have looked like this, talked like this, smelled like this if SIDS hadn't hit her like a hammer?

They say sometimes the dead look like they are

sleeping but dead children don't. None of the life force is there that swam just below the surface of Robin's skin, shimmering so strongly you could feel the impact of it with your eyes shut. Misery rose in my chest until I could feel it spread down into my palms.

I got up slowly and walked carefully down the stairs, holding on to the wall all the way. Grief attacks always made me feel fragile, like I could slip just walking. Bridges disappeared and everything was disconnected. Getting from one room to another, from one second to the next, all seemed like a big deal. Paths had to be made; streams crossed. Grief was a 900-pound gorilla and he packed a hell of a punch.

One thing was for sure. There was a child upstairs who hadn't got hit with SIDS: a feisty little tiger of a girl who was as alive as Jordan was dead. One way or another I'd have to find a way to get her mother off those goddamn drugs and out of Reggie Larsen's frantic, lethal hands.

20

It was late when I heard Zania say, "Oh, Jesus." Then I heard the sound of footsteps and the bathroom door open and shut. Finally, she tiptoed gingerly down the stairs, holding her head in one hand and the wall with the other. "Oh my God," she said. "Oh, my God." She sat down on the last stair. "I'm sorry. I'm so sorry. I'm not like this. Really, I'm not. You must think . . ." Her voice trained off.

"How are you doing?" I asked softly. I had a feeling anything above a whisper would sound like I was yelling to her poor hungover brain.

She put her head in her hands. "Like shit. Where's Robin?"

"Having oatmeal. She's fine."

"Oh, Michael, I'm so sorry. I'm so very sorry."

I didn't respond to that. "Do you remember last night?"

"Most of it. All of it, I think. I hope."

"Reggie called."

"I know." She sighed. "Son of a bitch. I know you won't believe this but I was trying to stay away from him. I thought if I drank I could get by without anything else."

"Maybe not the best idea," I said mildly. Zania knew it already so there was no point in haranguing her. I turned back to the kitchen. "Coffee or tea? We need to talk."

Zania followed me in and sat down glumly. Robin stopped eating and climbed down and then up into her mother's lap. Zania wrapped her arms around her and the two of them rocked back and forth slowly.

I fixed some coffee for Zania and tea for me and then I sat down across from her. "Zania," I said. "I don't understand what's going on here. I nearly got killed out of this. I'm pretty sure you could get killed and the crazy thing is, I'm not even sure why. So now I need to know the worst of it. What do you know about Reggie that has him so freaked? Because I'm pretty sure it's something more than you've told me."

"You don't know the worst."

"So what is it?"

Robin had had enough cuddling and she wiggled out of her mother's arms and went back to her oatmeal. Zania looked bereft without Robin in her arms. She finally folded them across her chest and hugged herself tightly.

"When I came to Boston," she said finally, "I had nothing. I mean nothing. I didn't have a suitcase. I didn't have a coat. I had Robin in my belly and that was it. I had twenty-two dollars in my pocketbook and I only stopped because I ran out of gas and was afraid if I spent my last twenty on gas, what would I eat?"

She laughed quietly. "Which is pretty funny when you think about it. I wasn't going to eat very long on twenty-two dollars anyway. But I wasn't thinking past the next meal."

"What were you running from?" I asked.

"A man," said, shrugging. "What else?"

I suppose she was right. What else, indeed? "What kind of man?" I asked.

She didn't answer but I could see her eyes scanning back and forth like people do when they are remembering something. When she picked up again, it didn't seem to be an answer, at least not a direct one. "After a while I couldn't look in a mirror. It sounds funny now but it's true. It wasn't what you think. It wasn't the bruises or the stitches or any of that. I just didn't recognize myself. I lost any sense of who I was. I don't know how to say it. One day I passed a mirror and glanced up without thinking. My first thought was who was that woman and then I realized it was me.

"I didn't know how my life turned out that way. I didn't know why I married him in the first place. He was crazy jealous and he had knocked me around a couple of times even before we got married. He said it was just because we weren't married and after we got married it would be different. It was different all right; he was right about that—it was worse.

"He brought the drugs. But the truth was I was glad enough to take them. It made the beatings easier. I wasn't really there half the time. But he'd disappear for days, weeks sometimes, and then the drugs would too. That's when I started taking them from work."

"From the hospital? How?"

She glanced over. "It's easier than you think. They monitor them, of course, you know that. They count them and check them against what the doctors have ordered and what the chart says the patient's been given and they count everything that's left. It's all supposed to add up. But who gives them to the patients? The nurses do. And nobody's standing over us to make sure we really give them.

"So sometimes I didn't give them and sometimes I gave less than the doctor said. It wasn't all that hard."

She saw my face. "All right," she said. "It was a lousy, crummy, horrible thing to do. What do you think? I know that."

She sighed and got up. "Let's go sit in the living room. I don't know what to tell you. You want an explanation for all this and I don't have anything but bits and pieces."

Actually, all I wanted to know was what she knew about Reggie Larsen that made him frantic but I bit my tongue. Zania was the one who wanted an explanation for all this and she was the one who only had bits and pieces. "You're doing fine," I said, getting up and following her. "Talk about it any way you can."

She paled when she saw the lipstick all over the couch and rug but she didn't say anything. She just turned away and sat down in a rocking chair by the window. I dragged up a chair and sat across from her.

"I wasn't a very good mother last night."

"Nobody's a good mother when they're drunk."

"You must have wanted to kill me. You stayed here all night?"

I shrugged. "Zania, it wasn't that big a deal and, to be honest, I did it for Robin, not for you. I figure grown-ups can take care of themselves, but a toddler can't. So you don't owe me anything for that and I hope you don't use the whole thing as an excuse to beat up on yourself and make yourself feel worse and worse until the only answer is a drink. Just keep going. What finally happened?"

"Just what you'd expect," she replied. "I got caught. Too many patients complaining about not getting their meds. I think the Nursing Board would have just thrown me out for good but everybody on the floor knew I'd been coming in to work black and blue. Maybe somebody told them and they took pity on me.

"Anyway, they suspended my license but said I could reapply after two years if I got drug counseling and had clean urines the whole time. Boy, that got my attention. I knew if I couldn't make a living I'd be under his thumb forever. So I did everything just like they said.

"Karl didn't exactly help. He liked having me dependent on him for the drugs but I wouldn't take them after that no matter what he did. The beatings got real bad. Real bad. He got on this kick about 'breaking' me. I think I'd be dead by now if I hadn't gotten pregnant. He didn't want the baby and he tied me up and beat me in the stomach to make me abort. But I didn't. She was too strong for him." She stared away for a minute and the scanning came back and she shuddered.

She looked over at me. "That was it. That was the end. All of a sudden everything got real clear. How dare he beat my baby? Maybe I was worthless but she wasn't. She wasn't at all. So I left. I had gotten my nursing license back so I could work again and I just got in the car one day and drove for twenty hours straight. Didn't tell anybody where I was going. I didn't even know until I got there. Left everything behind, everything. Had my pocketbook and a sweater and that was all. He never found me. The truth is, I don't even know if he tried."

I interrupted. "Do you have family anywhere?"

"Nope. Mother died of breast cancer before I ever met Karl. I haven't seen my father since I was twelve and I was it for kids: my father used to say I was the one mistake he made. My grandparents are all dead. There's really nobody," she said.

"You did that all by yourself?" I was incredulous.

"Had to. Yeah, it blows my mind too." For a moment a fleeting expression of pride replaced the worry and the fear. "But I didn't know what else to do. He was not going to beat my baby. That was not going to happen."

It was unbelievable. A line from Richard Selzer floated through my mind, "For I know it is the scarred and the marred and the faulty who are subject to grace." This woman had grace, indeed. Damaged enough to let a man nearly beat her to death, where the hell had she found the courage to draw the line at her baby?

"I don't get it. How'd you do it? Where'd you start?"

"It was something. I don't ever want to have to do it again. Try showing up in a strange city pregnant with no money and nothing but the clothes on your back. I slept in the back room of a 7-eleven for a while and worked there. God bless the manager. He let me stay. He must have felt sorry for me. And he never came on to me or anything although I half expected it. Then I bought a tent with my first paycheck and lived in a state park outside of Boston that first summer. I couldn't afford anything better and I was afraid of the fleabag hotels."

"A tent? You didn't go to a shelter?"

"The funny thing is it never crossed my mind. I didn't know where any were. I just never thought about it. Sometimes now I can't believe I made it through.

"But I did and I stayed clean and sober and things were going better than they ever had in my entire life. And then I met Reggie. Jesus, I wish I'd never met Reggie.

"I was nursing again. I was out of a tent and into an apartment. I was still clean and sober and had been since Robin was born, since I got pregnant really. Robin was about a year old then and she was just great, so gorgeous. We were doing really good. Robin didn't have any of the problems she would have had if I had kept doing drugs. You'll laugh but I had just put up mirrors. It's true. It was almost a year after she was born before I could put up a mirror in the apartment."

"Then Reggie showed up."

"Did he ever. Bowled me over. He was wonderful at first. Why are men always wonderful at first?" She paused and rocked for a few moments, thinking.

"I don't have any excuses. When he offered me the drugs I took them. I just wanted him to like me. I was afraid if I didn't take them, he'd know something was wrong, that I had a problem. I don't know why I did it. Maybe I just wanted the drugs."

"Does Reggie have a drug problem?"

"I don't think so. That was the funny part. As soon as I started taking them, he stopped. He only did them a couple of times with me in the beginning. That's when I first began to wonder what was going on.

"But I didn't wonder much because it was amazing how fast I was right back into them. I don't think I ever faced it. I think I always told myself I only took drugs because Karl beat me. I don't think I ever faced how damned addicted I was. Am, I have to say. Am addicted. I *am* addicted. That's important, I think. I have to say 'am.'

"Anyway, Reggie. At first I thought he was coming into the ICU to see me. He'd just check on a few patients while he was there. But after a while he spent less time with me and more with the patients and eventually it got pretty clear he wasn't there to see me. Then this awful thing happened. This really horrible thing happened."

She didn't just pause. She stopped cold and rocked for a while. "What horrible thing?" I ventured finally.

She didn't answer. "What horrible thing?" I said again.

"There was this woman," she answered finally. "A young woman. She was in a coma. Well, you know, nobody knows these days how much people are aware of when they're in those things. She'd been in a car wreck and she had a head injury and a bad open fracture of her tibia. She'd been in a coma for a while. Seemed like a nice lady from what her family said. They came in every day and they were really devastated.

"Anyway, they'd done some surgery on her leg and Reggie had been her anesthesiologist. After a few weeks there wasn't any reason for her anesthesiologist to still be checking on her, but he was still coming every day, mostly late at night or early in the morning when the family wasn't there. You know how it is in the ICU. The family has to stay in the waiting room and they're only allowed in for a few minutes at a time. If they were there, he'd just come back.

"She was the one I told you about, the one that he had his finger in. But I didn't tell you the rest. I didn't break off with him then like I said I did. I told myself I was imagining things, that I had a sick mind.

"Then one day, she started clearing. She just woke up. That's the way it is sometimes. Actually, they were thinking she ought to wake up. Her head didn't look that bad. I saw the activity on the monitors. Reggie was in her room. It seemed like he was always in her room back then.

"Anyway, I came rushing down the hall and came flying through the door just in time to hear her say, 'I know . . .' That's all she said, 'I know.' She was looking right at him. I don't know what she meant. She could have meant anything. But I know what he thought she meant because I still remember the look on his face. It was so . . . stricken, sort of, and trapped.

"I don't know what she said after that because I rushed out to call her doc and tell him she had woken up. That's when it happened."

"What happened?"

Instead of answering she got up and walked over to Robin, who had come in trailing an entire roll of toilet paper behind her. Neither of us had noticed and Zania didn't seem to notice now. She just scooped her up and held her tight, toilet paper and all. She sat down again and tried to rock her but Robin started to squirm and wiggle out of her arms immediately. Zania gave up and let her down. Without Robin, she started nervously rocking. "So what happened?" I asked.

"I don't know. When we all got back, she was dead."

"Dead?"

"Nothing they could do. Deader than a doornail."

"From what?"

"Nobody was sure. Looked like a stroke. The family refused an autopsy. All I know is I saw those CAT scans. I know I'm not supposed to know anything about it because I'm just a nurse but there was nothing going on in her head which should have caused a stroke like that. She was a young woman. I'm telling you it didn't make sense."

"What did the doctors think?"

"Nobody was sure what happened. They wanted to do an autopsy but the family wouldn't let them. That's all I know."

"I don't get it. Why do you think Reggie was involved?"

"All I know is Reggie was standing there when I left and she was fine. When I got back she was dead and he was nowhere to be found. I never told them about that."

She saw the surprise on my face.

"I couldn't tell them. I had no proof that he was there. And there were the drugs. I wasn't doing them at the hospital but I was sure if they knew I was on drugs again I'd lose my job. Reggie could have told them about the drugs. Said anything. Said he stopped dating me because of it. Said I made up a ridiculous story implying he had something to do with this woman's death as revenge.

"Don't you see? It would have been my word

against Reggie's and look who he was and who I was.
I was an ex–drug addict who'd already lost her nursing license once. He was Mr. Golden Boy big shot
who everybody said would win the Nobel Prize
someday. Not to mention who his father was. He
could have said I begged him for drugs and when
he wouldn't give them to me I made up a story to
get back at him. I didn't know what would happen. I
had Robin to support.

"It was horrible. I didn't know what to do. I
thought if they did believe me they might even call
me an accomplice because I hadn't reported him
earlier, when I should have, when he was in there all
the time for no reason.

"I couldn't even prove a crime had taken place. I
didn't know for sure a crime had taken place. But if
it hadn't, why did he leave? I tell you there were seconds in between. If she had a massive stroke or
something like that, why wasn't he trying to help
her when we got back?"

"Wait a minute. I don't get it. How could Reggie
kill her without leaving a mark in just a few seconds?
What are you talking about?"

"Jesus, Michael, you're naive. There are all kinds
of things he could have done."

"Like what?"

She shrugged and ignored the question. "That's
when I broke it off. I couldn't bear to be around
him after that. It just reminded me. I saw that
woman in my dreams for months. I still see that
woman in my dreams.

"And that's when the calls got worse and I figured

out they were from Reggie, just like I said. That was true. Everything I said to you was true. I just left some things out."

I remembered what my old mentor in deception, Goldstein, always told me, people left things out a lot more often than they lied. But murder, it seemed to me, was kind of a big thing to leave out.

Zania took my brooding silence for skepticism. "It's true," she said. "All of it. I can prove it, sort of. I kept a diary."

"What?" I said, startled.

"A diary."

"What kind of diary?"

"I've always kept a diary ever since I was a teenager but I left them all behind when I left Karl. But I started right in again. It helps me think things out."

"Can I see it?" I asked.

"The current one or one of the ones when I was back at the hospital?"

"The hospital."

She was gone only a few minutes and when she returned she was holding a stack of books with bright covers, the kind that are bound like books but come with blank pages. She opened several until she found the one with the right dates and handed it over to me.

I opened it at random and started reading. It was obvious right away she was a journaler, one of those people who spend more time writing about their lives than living them. Anaïs Nin was one and there were thousands of ordinary folk without a smidgen of her literary talent who had the same passion for recording every nuance of their day. Zania's literary talents would fill a thimble but her eye for detail filled volumes.

She included what she ate for lunch and what the weather was like and where she had her hair cut. Her entries were long on detail and short on meaning. But the same detail that made most entries tedious made the sections about Reggie electric.

She had kept track of every time he had come into the ICU, or so it seemed. She talked about the patients he saw, not always by name but always by date and usually with enough information to identify them. It was the eighty-year-old with the stroke that came in on the fifth of November, the teenager who fell off the roof who came in in July.

Even from a brief scanning, it became quickly apparent that Reggie had visited only women patients and then only ones who were unconscious or delirious and somehow cognitively impaired. Nobody was ever going to believe Zania made all this up, not if these people matched these dates. She would have had to have made it up at the time and it just wasn't credible that she would have planned to "get" a physician in this way for months and months and months, almost a year in this journal alone.

The journal was damning. A prosecutor or a medical board would think they had died and gone to heaven if they got evidence recorded at the time of the events that was this concrete and detailed. Zania had what John Dean had, only he knew it and she didn't.

When I could get my breath back, I said, "Does Reggie know about this?"

"About my diaries?" I nodded.

She thought for a minute. "I don't know. When I was sleeping with him he knew I kept a diary. I couldn't go to sleep without writing in it. And he once asked me if he was in it. I said, 'Sure, I always put down my boyfriends,' but I don't know if he knew I wrote down his coming on the wards. I don't think so. At least he never said if he did."

"Zania," I said, "you cannot keep these here. You absolutely cannot. May I take them with me? I want to go through them and think about what to do next."

"Michael, please don't do anything that will cost me my job. You can't show those journals to anybody. The drugs are in there."

A riptide of irritation swept over me and I struggled to keep it down. "Somebody is dead," I said evenly, "who maybe shouldn't be. And I was almost dead. And I don't wanna be. And you are somewhere on the list of people who could be dead. And Robin needs you not to be.

"And I don't even want to think about whose life is up for grabs if he keeps practicing. What happens when the next patient threatens him? So get a grip, Zania, and think about what's really important here."

She didn't say anything. "Take them," she said finally. "And don't even tell me what you're going to do with them. I don't want to know."

21

All the way home the journals sat on the seat beside me. I kept looking at them like they were a fellow passenger. Somehow I didn't want to touch them, there was so much misery inside.

I got out of my car with the journals in my arms and walked into the house. I hadn't showered at Zania's and I wanted to shower and change before work. I stood in the shower a long time as though the water could wash out of my head all the ugly things I'd heard that morning. Somebody needs to invent a shower for the mind, not just the body. Abruptly I turned the water off and walked out to the phone. I called an old lover and found him, luck be, in his office. "Jack," I said. "Got a minute?"

"Michael," he said, "long time no see," and for some reason I was pleased to hear the old warmth still in his voice.

"I've got a quick question," I said. "Doc wants to kill someone, an inpatient. On impulse. No time to plan. She's coming out of a coma and the nurse has gone to call her regular doctor so he's only got a few seconds. What could he do?"

"Jesus, Michael," he said. "That's a hell of a question. Don't tell me this is real."

"Could it be done? I mean, it just looked like a stroke. There was no autopsy so nobody knows for sure."

"How do you know anybody did anything? She was in a coma?"

"Yea, but her head didn't look that bad and she was a young woman. They weren't comfortable with it at the time. Could it be done?"

There was a pause. "Sure," he said finally.

"How?"

"Lots of things. The simplest is just inject the IV with a syringe full of air."

"That's all?"

"That's all it would take. Air bubble would either stop the heart and cause a heart attack or block the carotid artery and cause a stroke."

"That's all it takes to kill someone in a hospital?"

"We don't publicize that kind of thing, but yeah, that's all it takes."

I drove to work thinking seriously about becoming a Christian Scientist.

I called Adam at work to tell him about the journals but he'd gone to Maine to pick up a prisoner. I was just hanging up when I was surprised to hear the door to the waiting room open and shut. I wasn't expecting anybody

so I got up and walked out to see who was there. The
man standing in the waiting room was more than six feet
tall and so good looking I felt my mouth go dry. He had
sandy-blond hair and the kind of chiseled features that
made cigarette companies drool just thinking about bill-
boards. There was a hint of JFK around the eyes and a
lot of Clint Eastwood in the chin. I realized I was staring
at him and finally picked up my jaw and walked over.
"Are you looking for someone?" I said.

He smiled and every one of his teeth had to be
capped: God didn't give anyone teeth like that. "I'm
looking for Dr. Michael Stone," he said.

"I'm Dr. Stone."

"Doug Griffen," he said, holding out his hand, "*People* magazine. I called."

I took a step back involuntarily, ignoring his
hand. "What on earth are you doing here? I can't
talk to you."

"Actually, I didn't come to talk to you," he said.
"I'm looking for a woman named Zania Thompson."

He was watching me closely when he said it and
he caught the alarm on my face.

"You're good," I said.

"Thank you, ma'am. Just trying to be sure I'm on
target. But as long as I'm here, do you think we
could talk a little? I don't know who you've been
dealing with but when I say something is off the
record, I mean it's off the record."

"You're not that good."

"Maybe not." He just stood there for a few moments, looking at me and not saying anything. "Just
out of curiosity, what would it take for you to trust

me? I can give you references, people you can call who've dealt with me."

"I don't think that would help much. You're only going to give me the ones you haven't betrayed."

"So what then?"

"Uh, Mr. Griffen, I don't know who you've been dealing with but I don't talk about clients even to people I trust. It's a little thing called ethics. And as far as trusting you, I trust people just fine—when I've dealt with them for about twenty years."

"Doesn't sound too bad," he said, smiling. "I need to call on an expert from time to time. Sometimes I need to know something about your field."

"Well, it so happens I need to call on a reporter from time to time," I replied. "Sometimes I want to get a story out that doesn't involve a client of mine."

"You're on," he said, handing me his card. "I'll be back."

"Not on this one," I said firmly.

"Oh, I don't know," he said, "you might just want to know what I know—before it goes into print."

"Good point," I said. "Speaking of which, how far have you gotten? Have you talked to Larsen yet?"

"Not yet, but I've got about a zillion calls in to him. Man seems to be avoiding me."

"Who wouldn't?"

"A man who had nothing to hide."

"Listen, if Mike Wallace came through the door, even the Pope would take the back way out."

"Maybe the Pope should. But I'm not Mike Wallace. We're *People* magazine, remember. We do up-beat stories."

"Not this time."

"No, not this time." He stood looking at me for a moment. "I don't suppose I could talk you into dinner." His smile made my stomach knot. "Nothing about work," he said, casually.

"I hate it when you lie to me," I replied.

"Could be interesting," he offered.

I shook my head. "You got me once already. I can't take chances on this one."

He turned to leave but this time I stopped him. "Just curious," I said. "What stopped you from being an anchor?"

He turned around and grinned sheepishly. "An unfortunate tendency to stutter under the lights."

When he left, I went back to my desk and sat down glumly. Jesus Christ. The press had found Zania Thompson. Did Reggie know that? Had Doug Griffen mentioned her in his phone messages to Reggie?

I picked up the phone to call Zania and then put it down. How dirty would journalists play in search of a story? Pretty dirty, I'd bet. I'd had one experience of having my phone tapped already and I didn't want to take a chance calling on this line.

I grabbed my keys and walked out to the car. Would I spot a tail? Not hardly. I was a therapist; I knew zilch about tails. Why the hell hadn't they taught us something useful in graduate school? I drove over to Psychiatry slowly, looking behind me all the way. I didn't see anything, but what did that mean?

I took the stairs two at a time and said to Melissa, "Is Marv free?"

"He's in a meeting in the conference room."

I jogged down the hall and stuck my head into the conference room. Toby stopped in midsentence and heads turned toward me. "Marv," I said, "could I see you for a second. It's urgent."

Marv got up and hurried out. Toby picked up where he'd left off. Nobody seemed alarmed; psychiatric emergencies were pretty common in Psychiatry.

"What is it?" he said anxiously the second he was outside, but I was already walking toward his office.

"Nothing about Carlson," I replied and I could feel his tension ease. "I just need some help."

I walked into his office and closed the door. "Can I borrow your car?"

"Of course," he said, and went over to his desk to get the keys. "Is something wrong with your car?"

"No, I'm just afraid I'm being tailed by a reporter."

"This isn't anything dangerous?"

"No, no, reporters don't kill you for a story. They just momack you to death."

"Momack?" he asked.

"Sorry, Southern speech. Harass, make your life miserable?"

He gave me the keys. "Anything else I can do?" he said uncertainly.

"Nope, here's my keys. Car's parked in G if you need it. Thanks," and I was gone.

I stopped by Melissa's desk on the way out. There was no one in the waiting room. "Can you trade shirts with me?" I said. "Right now, quickly?"

She looked up from her typing for a long moment. "What, you don't like your shirt?"

"Not exactly, I want to throw a reporter off."

She sighed, "This isn't in the job description," but she was already getting up and heading for the restroom as she said it.

"It comes under 'other,' " I said.

"Your 'other' is a little different from everybody else's 'other.' "

"Makes life interesting."

"Winning the lottery would make life interesting. Working with you just makes it weird."

I pulled up in front of Zania's house and was surprised to see a dark blue Volvo sitting in the yard. I almost didn't get out of the car. If Doug Griffen had beaten me there, there wasn't a whole lot of point in my going in. In fact, it would likely make matters worse if he got direct proof of a connection between the two of us. Then I noticed the plates, Vermont plates. Unless it was a rental car, it wasn't him. I got out of my car and looked inside it. There was a woman's scarf on the seat and too many miles on the odometer to be a rental car. I'd take my chances.

I knocked on the door and Zania came to the door looking calm and reasonably cheerful, so I let out the breath I'd been holding. Her visitor obviously wasn't Griffen; it wasn't any reporter or she wouldn't be looking like that.

"Hi," she said, and opened the door to let me in without asking why I was there. Spending the night seemed to have changed my status in the family.

The visitor sat primly on the couch and after the first surprise at seeing her, I realized this could be a good thing. If anybody could control Reggie Larsen, it was his mother.

"Mrs. Larsen," I said uncertainly. She looked up, and some kind of storm flickered through her intense, blue eyes and then was gone. The bland, social mask slid back into place like a heavy, well oiled door closing.

"Michael," she said, nodding. "So good to see you. There's something I've wanted to say to you. Do sit down."

I sat down dutifully across from her while Zania went off to pull Robin off a tabletop.

"I want to apologize," she said, "for my behavior the other day. It was dreadful, really, and you were absolutely right. Of course, you have to be objective and impartial about this. I wouldn't argue with that for a second. I don't know what I was thinking. I just get so upset about Reggie and his future. But you're quite right, my dear. There is nothing I can do about it. I can only hope you forgive me."

"That's quite all right," I said. "Mothers aren't supposed to be impartial." She didn't mention why she was there and I didn't ask. Probably she was there to try to do with Zania what had failed with me. Little did she know it wouldn't matter in the slightest.

There seemed to be nothing more for us to say to each other and silence filled the room while we both waited for Zania to finish wrestling with Robin. Mrs. Larsen picked up her tea and sipped it quietly, filling the silence gracefully with the small ritual.

Zania came back in and said cheerfully, "Coffee or tea, Michael?"

"Nothing for me," I said. I saw relief briefly on Mrs. Larsen's face and realized she was hoping my visit would be short. Zania sat back down. She seemed comfortable around Mrs. Larsen in a way I had never been. Maybe they had bonded, I thought, over their mutual frustration with Reggie.

I took a deep breath. "I came to tell you something, Zania," I said. "And it's probably good if both of you hear it. A man from *People* magazine contacted me about Reggie a few days ago. I refused to talk to him, of course, but then he showed up in my office this morning, asking for you by name." Mrs. Larsen stiffened. Zania had picked up her coffee cup and it tipped sideways so much it almost spilled.

"Zania," I said, "you're going to spill." She looked at the cup, then righted it and put it down. Her hand was shaking. "How did he know about me? What does he know? What does he want?" Her voice was rising as the questions flew. "I don't want to get involved in this," she wailed.

"I don't know what he knows," I said calmly. "And you don't have to talk to any reporters if you don't want to. But they're likely to come here and pester you so you need to have a plan.

"There's a leak somewhere high up in the hospital, possibly in the ethics committee itself. Well, hell, he admitted it. I have no clue what they've told him. I didn't tell him anything, of course, nothing. But he'll find you. You can find anybody on the Internet these days, even get a map to their house. He'll be here on your doorstep, sooner or later."

I sat back and looked at both of them. "The cat's

out of the bag, one way or another. I don't know exactly what this guy knows but for sure he knows some things. He knows there's a problem. He knows Reggie's resigned." I caught the surprise on Mrs. Larsen's face. Interesting Reggie hadn't told her that. "If he doesn't know why, he'll find out something about it. A good reporter could cut and paste what he knows now and come up with something intriguing. And I think this one is probably very good. Any way you look at it, it's going to be enough for a major scandal."

"Thank you for telling us, Michael," Mrs. Larsen said quickly, recovering smoothly from her initial shock. "I think that Zania and I can probably sort out how to handle this, that is, if you want my help, dear." She looked over at Zania. Zania just nodded numbly. Mrs. Larsen looked back at me and it seemed to be a direct invitation to leave.

I hesitated. I was sure that whatever Mrs. Larsen had in mind would be in Reggie's best interest, but would it be in Zania's? It made me nervous to think of Reggie's mother as her chief adviser. If Reggie had killed someone, his mother might well talk her into an obstruction of justice charge or even an accessory after the fact. "Zania might be better off with an attorney," I said carefully. "She may need some legal advice somewhere down the—"

The sound of a car pulling into the driveway interrupted my comments and I stopped in midsentence. Zania turned pale and slumped back in her seat. I jumped up to look out the window but then stopped dead in my tracks when I saw who it was.

"Is it him?" Zania said, referring to Griffen.

"Different him," I replied.

I walked over to the door and opened it just as Reggie raised his hand to knock. "Come on in," I said. "Everybody else is here; you might as well be, too." I had no fear of him with his mother there. I had seen killers a lot colder than Reggie Larsen stopped dead in their tracks by their mothers.

Reggie didn't look at either Zania or me but walked directly over to his mother. His jaw was set and his face looked determined but he didn't look at all surprised. "What are you doing here?" he demanded.

"What are *you* doing here?" she replied. "What happened to your appointment?"

"I canceled it," he said. "I knew you were up to something. Mother—"

"I'm just visiting with Zania," she said, starting to rise and picking up her purse. "But I can see there's no point in continuing just now. Why don't we go, Reggie? We have some things to discuss."

Reggie ignored her request. "This is none of your business," he said bluntly, and we could all feel his anger fill the room. "I don't want you involved in this."

"Now dear," she said, sitting back down slowly. "I was just trying to help. Why don't we . . ."

Reggie gritted his teeth and said carefully, "We have gone over this and over this, Mother. I do not want your help. I am tired of your help. I don't want you running my life. I'm a grown man."

He didn't seem to notice or care that Zania or I were there. I wondered what could possibly have led up to his being so willing to make a public scene. The Larsens were Waspy, blue-blood New Englanders and New Englanders did not make public scenes. In the Larsens' social circle the scene unfolding in front of us just did not happen.

I glanced over at Zania who looked as embarrassed as I was. Robin toddled in and we both gratefully turned our attention to her. She picked up Zania's coffee cup and said "Drink?" looking up at her mother.

Zania started to speak when Mrs. Larsen turned, breaking off with Reggie, and said, "Now dear, caffeine isn't good for babies." She reached over and took the cup out of Robin's hands and put it down.

Robin started to screw up her face to scream and Zania said quickly, "Oh, it's okay." She picked up the cup to give it to Robin. "I let her have a sip now and then."

Mrs. Larsen reached forward and grabbed it from Zania. "No, no, *no*, my dear," she said. "Let me give her some of my tea. Coffee isn't good for children."

Slowly I stood up, staring at the half-empty cup she had snatched out of Robin's hands. I could feel my throat close in memory.

"Mrs. Larsen," I said, "what's in the coffee?"

She didn't speak but there was irritation and worse, no surprise on her face.

I looked back and forth from her to Reggie. "Are you in this together?" I asked.

Reggie looked at me and then at his mother. "What are you talking about?" he said.

I looked over at Zania. "Are you all right?" I said.

"No," she said, and her face was turning pale. "I'm not feeling very well." She put her hands over her stomach and put her head down between her legs to get it lower than her heart.

I bolted for the phone. Reggie made no move to stop me. He just turned to his mother and asked, "What's going on here?"

Mrs. Larsen sat very still with her chin up. "I don't know what she's talking about," she said. "Are you sick, Zania dear?"

I called 911. "This is an emergency," I said, then realized I was talking way too fast and tried to slow down. "A woman's been poisoned. Lethal dose. Maybe ketamine." I hurriedly gave them directions and turned to find Reggie frozen, staring at his mother. Zania slipped off her seat to sit on the floor and Reggie finally stopped staring and walked over and knelt down beside her. Calmly, he took her pulse.

"Lie down," he said.

"What is this, Michael?" he asked.

"She used ketamine on me," I replied. "It's probably the same thing."

Reggie stared briefly at his mother again, then turned back to Zania.

"Don't listen to her," his mother said to Reggie. "She's talking nonsense. We need to leave, Reggie, right now." Reggie ignored her. "Whatever is wrong with her, it's none of our business. She's a drug addict. She could have taken anything."

Zania's breath started coming in short rasps. "Was it ketamine?" Reggie asked.

"I don't know what you're talking about," his mother said.

Zania started to cry and curled up in a fetal position against the stomach cramps. Reggie left her and strode over to his mother, grabbed her by the shoulders and lifted her bodily right out of her seat. "Tell me," he yelled, shaking her.

"Reggie," she said, "you're hurting me. Put me down this second." For the first time her voice lost its control and there was real fear in it.

I grabbed her purse that was sitting on the couch, "Pockets, purse," I yelled. "She had to bring it in something."

Reggie dropped his mother and stuffed his hands into the pockets of her blazer while I opened the purse. Inside the purse were three empty vials. I snatched them out and gave them to Reggie. He barely had to glance at them. "Jesus Christ," he said.

"I did it for you," his mother pleaded. "For you. So you could do your work."

"All you ever did for me," Reggie said, turning back to Zania, "was make my life completely and totally miserable for as long as I can remember."

Zania's breathing was sounding worse and worse. She had no breath left to talk and her eyes were panicky. Robin was still standing next to her and frightened by what was happening to her mother, she started to cry.

Reggie ignored Robin and knelt beside Zania. "It's going to be all right," he said, soothingly. "I can keep you going until the ambulance gets here. Now listen to me. The ketamine will paralyze your respiratory muscles temporarily and you won't be able to breathe but I will

take care of you. I promise you I won't let you die."
Zania barely nodded. Tears were rolling down her
cheeks. She was swallowing repeatedly and I knew why,
remembering the saliva that had just started flowing in
my mouth. I went over and picked up Robin, who was
crying even harder and reaching for her mother.

"Reggie," his mother said, raising her voice to be
heard over Robin. "What are you doing?"

"I'm taking care of a patient," Reggie replied. "In
case you've forgotten, I'm a doctor."

She got up and stepped forward. I quickly stepped in
front of her, holding Robin away from her on one hip. I
couldn't do much for Zania Thompson but I could damn
sure keep a seventy-year-old from getting in the way.
"Stand back," I said.

"Reggie," she said, and this time she was pleading.
Her face was losing its control and there was a funny
light in her eyes that made me want to look away. Why
hadn't I seen that craziness before? Surely it had been
there, behind the rigid mask. But I had, I remembered. I
had seen it once before—at a dinner party. "Think of
what you're giving up. Think of it. She's the only witness, the only one. Think of the lives you can save."

"I'm going to save this one," he said, "right here and
now." Just then Zania stopped breathing and Reggie
calmly started breathing into her mouth. He raised his
head after a few seconds and started rhythmically pushing on her chest.

"Despite everything you taught me," he said quietly,
more to himself it seemed than to anyone else, "I am
still my father's son." Quiet or not, there was no mistak-
ing it: it was the word with the bark on it.

Mrs. Larsen must have heard it too because she gave up and sat down abruptly in the chair. There were no cards left to play, I thought. End of a long, decades-long war. All kinds of alligators eat their children, even some of the human ones, and some of them tell them how much they love them while they're doing it. I turned my attention back to Robin to try to soothe her when Mrs. Larsen suddenly leaned forward and without any warning picked up Zania's coffee cup and drank it in one swoop. I hadn't expected it and I wasn't in time to stop it.

"Now," she said, triumphantly, the strange light in her eyes having won out entirely. "I need you too. You can't save both of us. Who are you going to save, your mother or your little drug addict?" I was staring at her open-mouthed. I never expected anything that hysterical out of her although thinking of her eyes, maybe I should have.

Reggie was entirely focused on Zania and didn't even look up. "What'd she do?" he said to me, while he pushed on Zania's chest.

"She drank Zania's coffee," I replied. There was silence in the room except for the sound of Reggie working. He bent over to breathe into Zania's lungs again, then straightened up and continued pushing on her chest.

"Michael," he said, "do you know artificial resuscitation?"

"Yes," I said, "more or less."

"Good, when my mother keels over, would you please keep her from dying?"

"Reggie," his mother screamed, "I'm your mother. I could die."

"Yes," he said, "you could, but if I have to triage, I'm going to save a twenty-something woman with a small child over a seventy-two-year-old woman with a heart condition. That's just the way it is, Mother. Now lie down before this thing cuts you off at the knees and you fall down and break a hip."

Mrs. Larsen seemed to freeze and the look on her face was painful—not defeated, more bewildered. She couldn't understand what Reggie was saying, what he was doing. The narrative line she had lived her life by— despite all Reggie's attempts to get her to stop—the sense she had made of things, had come down to a test, an easy one for her. She had put it all on the line, confident that Reggie loved her as much as she loved him, that he would choose her and his career over everything and everybody. After all, she had done so much for him.

There seemed to be nothing left for anyone to say and we all just waited. Mrs. Larsen just seemed lost and she suddenly looked older than her seventy-something years. Reggie continued to breathe for Zania and keep her heart going, smoothly and professionally. I eyed Mrs. Larsen, wondering just how much artificial resuscitation I remembered, and thinking it wasn't all that much when, to my relief, the sound of an ambulance started rising gracefully in the distance.

The medics were surprised to find two patients instead of one and there was an initial scurrying and flurry of activity, but in an incredibly short period of time they had both patients loaded and took off, tires screaming and sirens blazing. By the time they got her into the ambulance, Mrs. Larsen was feeling her handiwork. It didn't look pretty. In her seventies she had less vitality than either Zania or I and a heart condition to boot.

Reggie didn't ride with them. He told them he'd drive

in separately but once the ambulance took off, he just sat down and looked like he wasn't going anywhere. We were alone except for Robin, who was clinging to me now and sucking her thumb. She was still whimpering and crying a little but the excitement seemed to have exhausted her and she lay mostly quiet in my arms. "Has she done anything like that before?" I asked.

"Threatened it," he said. "Not all that infrequently, but never did it." He looked deflated and depressed. "My house wasn't what most people thought it was. There was a reason my father worked all the time."

"I know," I said. "All through this, I've been remembering a dinner party I went to at your parents' house."

"Umph," he said. "She'd have been on her best behavior then."

"Sort of," I said. "But I remember she was telling stories about your father—I don't remember exactly what, running the boat aground, that sort of thing—but I remember he was the brunt of all of them. They were supposed to be funny but they weren't really. Every one of them seemed to put your dad down and I think it made all of us a little uncomfortable. Your father just didn't seem to notice or, if he did, he put up a good front.

"But what I forgot was I came around the corner from the bathroom and your mother was standing in the doorway with a tray of something and she was looking at your father, who was laughing. He was sitting with some students and they clearly adored him and he looked happy for a moment, but the look on her face froze me.

"There was this light in her eyes, just like today—she had that same look today while you were working on Zania—and it was so clearly malevolent. I remember looking at him and looking at her and thinking that she hated something: hated him having a good time, hated him, I don't know. I don't know how to explain it. She didn't look angry. She looked cold-blooded, like she meant him harm.

"I stepped back and waited until she left before I went in. I didn't want her to know I saw it. I think I knew then that something was seriously wrong with your mother."

Reggie didn't say anything for a long moment and then he spoke. "I never knew if she loved me, although she said it, God knows, enough. She had this way of fastening on you like you were her left arm and about that much entitled to your own life. And if she didn't get her way, she pulled out all the stops."

I sat down with Robin, who had fallen asleep, and we sat in companionable silence. It was, I knew, a momentary oasis. There were endless pressures that loomed once we left the quiet of Zania's house for the ICU. This whole thing would generate a storm of media attention, not to mention we hadn't even begun to deal with the police part of it. "The press are on to you," I said, putting off the real question I wanted to ask, wondering if I could trust the answer, wondering what the point was of asking it if I couldn't trust the answer.

"I know," he said. "*People* magazine, of all things."

"They know about Zania," I said. "I don't know how."

"Really," he said, but it didn't sound like he cared.

"Just so you know. They didn't get it from me," I said. "Or from Zania."

"Doesn't matter," he said. "It was bound to come out sooner or later."

"I have to ask," I said, finally. "Not that you have to tell me. Not that I know I can believe you. And a lawyer would tell you not to answer it. But did you kill that woman in the ICU?"

Reggie sighed. "I know who you're talking about," he said. "Zania used to hint around about it when she was stoned. She must have said something to my mother, too, since I'm guessing this has something to do with that. What do you think, Michael? Do you think I killed her?"

I paused and thought about it. "I don't know, Reggie. People do crazy things when they are desperate. On the other hand, you didn't hesitate to save a life today and I'd say this was a pretty desperate time. It's a hard call. Somebody could argue that you did it because you had a witness and you couldn't get rid of me too, not easily anyway. But I don't think so. I think you'd have saved Zania, no matter what. But in a different situation with a woman you didn't know? A moment of blind panic? It's a hard call."

"What kind of life am I living," Reggie muttered, "when everyone, even my own mother, thinks I'm capable of murder?" He didn't sound argumentative though, just tired.

"You can think what you want," he said finally. "But I'm not a murderer. I remember that day like it was yesterday. I thought I was caught for sure. All she said was two words—'I know'—and my blood turned to ice. I couldn't breathe I was so frightened. I bolted from the room. I spent the next few hours waiting for the police to knock on my door. It was horrible. When nothing happened, I went back to

work the next day still expecting the worst and that's
when I found out. I don't know what happened to
her any more than anybody else did. Probably she
had a blood clot break loose from her leg that mi-
grated to her brain or her heart. She had a bad
open fracture. Did you know that?

"But whatever it was I was glad. It's a terrible thing
to say but the relief made me giddy. I even stopped
for a while after that. I told myself I'd never put myself in that position again. But I did, somehow I did.

"You don't understand, Michael. In my mind, in
my mind, I was just fooling around a little with a few
patients and it was no big deal. They were all asleep
or confused. They wouldn't even remember what
happened if they ever knew it in the first place. All
the covering up—just little white lies, no harm in
them. I didn't think it was such a big deal. But murder? Murder never even crossed my mind."

I stood, silently rocking Robin a little in my arms.
White lies. The hand under the white sheet where
safety should have been. I remembered waking up in
the hospital clutching the sheet and feeling a huge
sense of relief when I saw it. It sure beat the hell out
of lying on a linoleum floor waiting to die. Safety lay
in the white sheets—unmistakably hospital sheets—in
the IV drips, in the noise of the respirator breathing.
But what safety lay in the white sheets for all those
women coming in from the car wrecks or the explo-
sions in the brain or the fall in the bathtub, already
made more helpless than the threat of a gun or a
knife could ever have done? The hand that pulled
back the sheets wasn't there to keep them safe.

White lies. I ought to know that as well as anyone, coming from a place where the worst thing that could happen to you was to look out some night and see a man wearing a sheet standing on your lawn.

Still the white lies he told probably kept Zania alive—not the ones he told to others, the ones he told to himself. He never really faced how bad what he was doing was, and murder seemed to him a world away.

Did he cross that line? Did he kill that woman? I wanted to believe him. Hell, I did believe him even though there was no way I would ever know for sure. But I had seen him take care of Zania and in that moment he had looked like a real doctor to me. In the end he was his father's son, that much was clear, and because of that I'd give him the benefit of the doubt. Not that I could do anything about it either way but Reginald Larsen, Senior, I said silently, this one's for you. I let it go.

22

I walked across the waiting room and held out my hand. "Good to see you," I said. "Come on in."

He walked through the door and as I closed it I said, "I'm sorry about your mother."

"What a fool," he said quietly, sitting down. "You don't take ketamine with a bad heart condition in your seventies. I guess she thought she was invincible. Or maybe she really wanted to die? What do you think?"

"I didn't really know your mother, Reggie, but I'd say she wasn't thinking too rationally about the consequences at the time. She was not a well woman, that's for sure."

Reggie merely nodded. He had lost weight since I saw him last and he looked almost as tired and depressed as he did that day, the day his mother got carted away in the ambulance. I hadn't seen him since. "Are you all right?" I asked. "What's happening to you?"

"Nothing good," he said. "The goddamn media have crucified me. I don't know if you've been reading about it."

"A little," I said.

"Complaints have come out of the woodwork since the article. People I've never met are accusing me of molesting them."

"I doubt that," I said.

Reggie didn't answer. "Are you going to keep your license?" I asked.

"My lawyers aren't optimistic."

"You've still got your research."

"Yes, I do," he said. "I never wanted to work for a pharmaceutical company but it may be my best option. They don't seem that bothered by the publicity."

"With the amount of money you'd make for them, probably not," I said. "It's the right option," I said. "You can't see patients, Reggie. You'd do it again."

"I'd like to think I've learned my lesson."

"I'd like to think so too but it isn't true. It went on too long. It'll come back. You need treatment; you know that."

"Is that why I'm here?" he asked, sounding bitter. "So you can gloat over my demise and tell me I need treatment?"

"Whoa, Reggie," I said gently. "I'm not your mother; your mother's dead. I'm not gloating over anything. In fact, I have a lot of respect for your saving Zania's life. But you're right, I've got no business telling you you need treatment. If you don't know it by now, my telling you won't make any difference. And it's not the reason you're here. You're here because of Zania."

"Zania?" he said. "What about her? She's about to be released. She's fine."

"Not exactly fine," I said. "She has a big-time drug addiction which you helped foster. She needs inpatient care and her insurance will only cover part of it. She needs someone to take care of Robin while she gets treatment. I'm thinking she needs a full-time nanny and she needs some money to live on because she's probably not going to be able to work full time for a while."

Reggie just looked at me. "You've got some responsibility here," I said. "She was clean and sober and working when you met her and you deliberately hooked her."

"Look," Reggie said. "Zania is a sweet kid but she was a drug addict before I met her. I'm not responsible for that."

"A recovering drug addict," I said. "Until you handed her Percodan."

"You know the figures, Michael. Most of them relapse sooner or later. It was just a question of time."

I gritted my teeth and struggled to keep my voice calm. I knew in my head that saving Zania hadn't turned Reggie Larsen into a saint or even a reasonable person but I was still disappointed.

I went over to my desk and started piling journals that had been sitting on the floor on top of it. Reggie looked perplexed for a moment and then he stood up and walked over to look at them curiously. He became very still when he realized what they were.

"Zania has quite an eye for detail," I said. "Do you want me to read you some entries?" I opened a book at random, flipped through a few pages and found an entry. "'July 12,'" I read. "'Reggie came in at 10:30 P.M. and headed straight for the 23-year-old girl who fell off the snow mobile. He pulled the curtains around the bed and stayed for—'"

"Stop," Reggie said. "This is blackmail."

"No," I said. "No, it isn't. This is saving your ass. Because this is a preview of the exhibits that Zania's attorney will be using in the civil case against you if you don't suddenly grow some sense of responsibility. And if you think you have troubles now, you just wait until patients who haven't reported you recognize themselves in these accounts. How many lawsuits do you want to fight, Reggie? Fifty? A hundred?" I was pissed and it showed. Well, I was never that good at hiding that sort of thing anyway.

"What do you want?"

"I want a check written out to Zania Thompson that is so big she won't even think about suing you." I didn't mention that Zania paled at the thought of taking Reggie Larsen to court and had no intention of suing him. "And that means it had better be big enough that she won't change her mind later and decide she could have gotten more from the courts."

Reggie looked one more time at the journals and sighed. He reached for his pen.

We were all sitting at Marv's glumly watching the television screen. Leila, in yellow this time, was dazzling in her analysis of the "toll" the "incest machine" was taking on innocent families, the latest example being this terrible tragedy with the Carlsons. Suzy, the

local head of the AFAF, sat next to her and I noted she
was still using the same hairstylist, the one with stock in
a hair spray company.

The host of the local call-in show, a man who
sounded like he had been studying Peter Jennings
tapes—same rhythm to his language, same inflection—
sat between them. Neither Mark Carlson nor any member of his family was there but that didn't stop Leila
from dissecting the case.

"Still missing," Leila emphasized. "An example of—"

"She irritates hell out of me," I said. "She knows. She
was in close contact with the family. She knows Mark's
daughter reported abuse too."

Marv just shook his head. "I am gravely disappointed
in her," he said.

Carlotta said, "I don't get it. Doesn't she know Mark
or his wife could just call up and make a total fool of
her?"

"What she knows," I said, "is that they won't go
public in order to protect the privacy of their little
girl."

The phone rang in the studio and the first caller
praised Leila lavishly and then went on to say his es-
tranged wife had engineered a false report of abuse to
cut him off from visitation with their daughter. Leila
sympathized. Suzy gave him information about contacting AFAF.

"But this is unethical," Marv protested. "They don't
have any way of knowing whether that man sexually
abused his daughter or not."

"AFAF has never screened for abusers," I said.
"Didn't you know that? When you ask them how they

can be sure that *all* of the people who join are innocent, they tell you how much money their members
make a year and how middle class they all are."

"But, that's incredible," Marv said. I rolled my
eyes at his naiveté. Just then a caller electrified all
of us.

"I'm Sam Carlson," the voice said, "and I want to
tell you, you got it right this time."

"Mr. Carlson," the moderator said, "is that really
you?"

"You're goddamn right it's me," he said. "I used
to think you news people were full of shit but you finally did your job."

"He's drunk," I said.

"He doesn't sound drunk," Marv said.

"He is," I said. "He's the type that doesn't slur
their words. He's habituated to the stuff."

"Sh-h-h-h," Carlotta said.

"Mr. Carlson," the moderator said, "are you all
right? Everyone's been worried about you. Where
are you?"

"None of your goddamn business where I am. I
get tired of living with that fat cow every once in a
while, you know what I mean."

Leila's posture stiffened and she couldn't keep
the alarm off her face.

"Well, Mr. Carlson—"

"The bitch called me," he said. "Goddamned
cunt, yelled and screamed at me about that little
shit of a granddaughter who's now jumped on the
bandwagon, accusing me of abusing her. I'm going
to sue the fucking lot of them."

"How is he able to do that?" Marv asked. "Don't they beep that kind of language?"

"It's live," I whispered. "Really live. Local talk show isn't big enough to have time delays, which is how they beep things."

"Sh-h-h," Carlotta said again.

"Is that your wife?" the moderator said, bewildered. "Your wife called you?"

"Of course, it's my wife," Sam said. "Who the hell else do you think I'm talking about?"

"She knows where you are?" the moderator blurted out.

"Oh, she knows," he said. "She knows when she wants to know. I told her before, she don't treat me right, there's always someone who will."

"Uh," the moderator said, "Dr. Jenkins, do you have any questions for Mr. Carlson?"

Leila just shook her head but Suzy ventured forth, "Mr. Carlson, this is Suzy Cartwright. I'm the chair of the local Association for Falsely Accused Families. You are telling us you are innocent of these charges, is that correct?"

"Goddamn right, I am," he said. "I didn't do nothing she didn't want me to and that's a fact. Not a goddamn thing. I'm the victim in this, you know what I mean. If anybody was abused, it was me."

"Abused by the false charges," Suzy said quickly.

"Hell yes, abused by the false charges," Sam replied. "Teenage girls today, hell, with what they wear, they're just asking for it. They're just asking. What's a man to do?"

At that the moderator finally recovered enough

to intervene. "Thank you very much, Mr. Carlson," he said smoothly and flicked a switch. "A man *claiming* to be Sam Carlson has just called the studio," he said. "I want to reiterate we have no way of knowing if that really was Sam Carlson. We'll be right back, after these messages."

There was a God, after all, and she gave Sam Carlson a bottle of whiskey and turned on the TV.

"Was that really Sam Carlson?" Carlotta asked.

"Oh yes, that was Sam," I replied.

"You're sure."

Marv and I both nodded. "Marv met with him, remember, and I watched through the booth. Trust me, that's his voice and that's his style."

"He's not going to make a very good representative of the AFAF."

"If I had my way," I replied, "I'd make him the poster child for the AFAF. I hope the *public* makes him the poster child of the AFAF. Say what you want, Sam Carlson is AFAF."

Carlotta said her good-byes and I started to but Marv asked me to stay for a minute. He looked like something was on his mind so I agreed. He came back from seeing Carlotta out and sat down in a chair across from me.

"Jody went home today," he said. "She's staying with her brother and his wife."

"Um, not bad."

"Not bad at all. I got to meet his wife for the first time. A very nice lady, I think, and very clear about things. I don't think Mr. Carlson will be visiting. She even changed the phone number to keep his mother from calling. They asked me to inquire whether you would consider treating Cindy?"

"No," I said. "Conflict of interest. I've already been involved in the case in a different way."

"I thought not," he said, and silence fell.

"Have you heard anything from Reggie Larsen?" Marv said.

"Yes, I saw him a few days ago. He's all right. He's out of clinical medicine, which is all to the good.

"If I'd only known the right question to ask Zania, Marv. It was Mrs. Larsen who had called and arranged to have coffee with her at the hospital the day I was poisoned. All I had to do was ask if Zania was meeting anyone." He looked confused. "The ketamine was for Zania, remember, not for me. I was just spur of the moment." I shook my head.

"Do you think Mrs. Larsen really wanted to die?"

"No, I think she really wanted Reggie to run to her side and—since the sun rose and set on him—she thought he could fix anything. I hate to say this but it was probably a good thing. The DA's office would have *had* to prosecute. The woman did try to murder two people. But, Jesus, imagine trying to put a seventy-two-year-old woman in jail, and imagine Mrs. Larsen actually going. I think she saved herself a lot."

Silence fell again, an unusually awkward silence for Marv and me. I had the feeling he was putting something off. Surely, he hadn't asked me to stay to talk about things he could have talked about in front of Carlotta. "Where's Robin?" Marv said.

"Adam has her. He's staying on a few days, to help out, until Zania's able to arrange a nanny."

The funny silence came back.

"So, how is Adam doing with Robin?" Marv asked.

"He likes her. Surprised both of us. I never saw Adam as a kid kind of guy. We've had to make some changes. No more guns in the house. And," I added sheepishly, "you can't really keep to 250 things with a kid around. You know, diapers, toys, it all adds up.

"Marv, I can't stand it anymore. You've got this look. What's up?"

Marv sighed and got up. I got up and followed him. He walked over to the pictures at the other end of the room. They were still sitting on the floor in a line just as I had left them.

"You left them," I said.

"Well, it took a while. I just couldn't see it. But somehow I couldn't put them away either. One day, I got up, walked in, and oh my goodness, it was so clear."

I looked at the pictures in amazement. It was a "duh" kind of thing once you put them in a line. The pictures got smaller, darker and harsher the more recent they were. By the end Marv had been buying tiny, dark, grotesque pieces of art. How had Marv not been able to see that?

"I've been thinking," he said, clearing his throat, "of what you said. I do need something in my life."

"You and everybody else," I said. "A pet? What are you thinking of? A dog? A cat?"

"Not exactly," Marv said. "But really, I suppose it's the same idea." He led me into the kitchen. I don't know what I expected to find but there on the table was an old cardboard chess set with plastic chessmen.

"Chess?" I asked.

"Yes," he said, "I played quite a bit as a child. Actually, I was rather good at it."

"Was this the set?"

"How'd you know? It was, indeed. The same set. I found it in the attic. Wonderful, isn't it?"

I smiled. "You don't want a dog?"

"Goodness, no, why would I want a dog?"

"Marv, let me see if I understand this. How will chess connect you with people?"

"People? I don't want to be connected with people. I want to find a way to get away from them."

"Well, you have to have people to play chess, that is, unless you're playing a computer."

"Surely, but, well, I'm playing against someone in Singapore right now. By mail. I have three weeks to make a move."

I just looked at him. "How long does it take to play a game?" I asked.

"Several years," he said cheerfully.

EPILOGUE

The message light was blinking when I got home. The caller didn't bother to identify herself. "Fixed his butt," was all she said. "Call me, that is, if you're not too busy." The sarcasm set my teeth on edge.

Nonetheless, with more curiosity than I wanted to admit, I called. "Mama?" I said. "So what'd you do?"

"Cost me a hundred dollars," she said, "that's all." Mama never did like to part with her money. "And I got Wilbur every dime of his money with interest. I tacked that on. I told him to make the guy pay interest and by God, he did."

"Mama, don't drag this out. I'm all ears. What'd you do?"

"Well, I suppose I can tell you, if you're not too busy to listen, that is. Somebody had to do something about Wilbur, you know."

"Mama—"

"All right. Now if you're on the inland waterway, there's only two ways you can go, north or south, that is, unless you're ready to take off for France or something, but the boat wasn't set up for France."

"Right."

"It's going into fall and I didn't think he'd be heading north. Only a fool would live in the north in the winter."

I made no comment on that. "Okay . . ."

"But I checked north too, only not as many."

"Not as many what?"

"Bridge tenders. Inland waterway has got a lot of bridges and most of them still have people running them. Bridge tending is a lonely business. Nothing much to do all day, don't you know."

"Jesus."

"Well, it makes sense, don't it. You gotta go through them, that is, unless you're going to stay out to sea and I didn't think he was that type. Kind of man who liked to be at harbor at night, liked his comforts.

"It didn't take much. I just called in the description to every bridge tender within a hundred miles south and fifty miles north. Offered a hundred dollars to the first one who spotted her. And I got lucky. Bridge tender saw him right before the South Carolina border. Then we just called marinas and, by God, he was staying in one right on the North Carolina side of the border. Might have been a little harder if he'd crossed over the state line but we'd have got him served one way or another. Sheriff impounded his boat when he pulled in that night. Couldn't get his boat back until he handed over the cash. Plus the interest, of course."

"Hats off to you, Mama," I said, honestly.

Mama was full of herself and went on for a while. But when the gloating was over, there wasn't much to talk about. Mama had just never been that interested in what was happening in my life so conversations with her were more of a monologue. Mama didn't ask questions.

I hung up and thought about it. Mama and Mrs. Larsen. Mama had always left me to fight my own battles. Had she once come to my defense? Had she once intervened with the school or anybody else in the known universe for me?

But then again, I wondered for the first time if she had ever really needed to. Wilbur had finally needed her and in a big way. He had almost lost his business and his means of supporting his family and his self-respect in one fell swoop and it was Mama, not her Harvard Ph.D. daughter, who had called the bridge tenders.

What would Reginald Larsen's life have been like in Mama's family? Well, he'd have been in big trouble by third grade for one thing. Big trouble. Hard to know what impact it would have had but, for sure, there would have been no one blocking for him and making it easy to keep going the way he was.

Life with Mama hadn't been easy. You could lose an arm and a leg while she sat around and lectured you about your own stupidity for getting in the situation in the first place. I had broken bones only to hear Mama said, "What'd you do that for?" as if falling out of a tree was something I got up that morning and decided to go out and do.

But there were limits, it now seemed to me, on how far Mama would leave you out on that limb. Not that she'd be warm about hauling your ass off it.

All my childhood I'd wanted someone to go to bat for me, someone to rock me and read to me like I saw other mothers doing. Mama was doing her crossword puzzles and flying off to the Grand Ole Opry in her sequined sweaters. Nevertheless, I thought. Nevertheless. I had never seen even a glimpse of that funny light in Mama's eyes. Mama didn't eat her children. She didn't live her life through them and in the end she was somewhere back there—maybe way back there—to back you up if you needed it.

All right, so Mama didn't do warm. Ask Wilbur what meant more to him: all the sympathy he got from other people or the fact that Mama called the bridge tenders. I got something, I realized, when it came to parenting and a whole lot of people in this world got nothing at all. I didn't drink so there was no glass to raise but in my mind, I raised one anyway to the little old lady in the sequined sweaters.

Adam lay on the living room floor fast asleep. Robin had succumbed finally, too, although it was pretty clear Adam had probably conked out first since otherwise he'd have put her into bed and gone to bed himself. I shook my head in amazement and remembered the old *Life* magazine study where they had an Olympic athlete follow a toddler around all day and do everything the toddler did.

The athlete had collapsed partway through the day.

Biology had it all wrong. It shouldn't take two people to make a child. *Two* people didn't have a chance against the average toddler. Biologically, it should take at least *six* people to make a child. Of course, getting everybody's schedules together to arrange to have sex would mean a lot fewer people in the world but look at the pay-off when it came down to toddler time.

Gently, I picked Robin up and carried her to bed. I tucked her in, the age-old habit of mothers to make sure the covers are just so. I went back and looked at Adam. I couldn't lift him so I tried to wake him but he was having none of it. He swatted me off like a gnat bothering him so I let him be.

I walked into the bathroom for a shower and opened the drawer and took out my birth control pills. For some reason I hesitated. Well, what was a woman over forty doing with birth control pills anyway? There wasn't a hell's bells chance I'd get pregnant. And besides, I'd been on pills quite a while and those things probably weren't too good for you, if you took them forever and ever. They probably caused some kind of Major Health Problem. I was almost sure I'd read it somewhere. I tossed them casually into the trash and headed for the shower.